ANTIPODES

MARIA-ANTÒNIA OLIVER

Translated by KATHLEEN McNERNEY

Published by arrangement with Edicions de la Magrana, Barcelona.
Originally published in Catalan as *Antipodes.*

Publication of the book was made possible in part by support from the Department of Culture of the Generalitat of Catalonia.

Cover illustration by Jana Rekosh.

Library of Congress Cataloging-in-Publication Data

Oliver, Maria-Antònia.
[Antipodes. English]
Antipodes / by Maria-Antònia Oliver : translated by Kathleen McNerney.
p. cm.
ISBN 0-931188-82-2
I. Title.
PC3942.25.L53A5813 1989
949'.9354—dc20 89-10199
CIP

Printed in the United States of America
First printing, October 1989
10 9 8 7 6 5 4 3 2 1

Seal Press
P.O. Box 13
Seattle, WA 98111

ANTIPODES

Acknowledgments

The translator would like to thank Enric Bou, Anna Sánchez-Rué, Montserrat Vilarrubla, and Maria-Antònia Oliver, who helped me more than they know.

Prologue

I've always been fascinated by sails.

Those sheets filled up with wind set off my imagination. The yacht entered the harbor majestically. My friends and I were sailing close to the beach in a little nutshell of a boat and we watched the ship with envious eyes. It rocked solemnly, the sails deflated slowly, and someone I couldn't see folded them.

On other days, from the lighthouse, we saw other sails on the horizon; would they drop anchor at the port? We were full of guesses, speculations, imaginings. Where did those yachts come from? What seas had they ploughed? Where were those unfamiliar flags from, with colors we didn't recognize? How many feet long would they have to be to support those sails?

I liked the little sailboats, too. How could you help it?

...

"Holy shit! Lòòòniaaaa! Jesus Christ! Is it really you? For real? Lònia! Jem, look who the hell's here! Jeeeem! Come on out here for Christ's sake! Jeeeem!"

I was standing on the moorings right in front of the *Mallorquina,* and it was all I could do to keep from falling over with laughter at Lida's gyrations when she saw me.

I'd taken a risk; they could have been away from Melbourne, that couple, but even so I'd given their names and address for my visa. Once I got to the city, it hadn't been easy to find them. But there was the *Mallorquina,* Lida on deck with eyes like saucers yelling for Jem.

"Jesus's balls! Holy shit! Judas priest, it's Miss Polonieta! Holy mother of God, Lònia!

Dear Lida, who had bawled us out so many times when we lived in the apartment full of Majorcans in Barcelona: You swear like sailors—I could hear her now. It seemed like she had collected all our favorite curses and let them loose all at once without taking a breath.

"Lònia! What on earth are you doing here?"

Jem stuck his head out, jumped up on to the deck, and over the rail—I was afraid he was going to fall on his face, because the *Mallorquina* wasn't exactly a small boat—and he bounded up to me. His hug was reassuring.

"Come on, don't just stand there like a dolt!" Lida yelled from above.

It was twelve noon. There. Because after more than twenty hours of travelling, I didn't know whether it was yesterday, today, or tomorrow. I used to get completely out of whack just from setting the clocks ahead in the spring and back in the fall in Barcelona; crossing meridians at that speed had made it about a quarter tomatos for me. Lucky it was a splendid spring day: I'd have to get used to the change in seasons.

"Why did you come? Is there something wrong? Why didn't you let us know you were coming? Do you have a tourist visa or a working one? You look tired. Sit down, sit down . . . or maybe you'd like to take a shower? Oh, I'm so happy to see you! Will you stay for a long time? No, don't be silly, it doesn't make sense for you to rent an apartment, when you can stay here. As long as you want, and if we have to make a cruise, we'll find you a place with one of our friends from the radio station . . . or you can come with us . . . "

"Let her talk, Lida!" Jem cut in.

"Okay, okay, I'll shut up. Come on, explain."

"It's a long story. To make it short, I came to liberate myself."

"Liberate yourself? Don't embroider, Lònia." Lida cut me off.

"A change of scenery, then. Some things happened to me in Barcelona that I'd like to forget . . . "

"No shit, Christ, you got so used to Barcelona once you stopped being homesick for Majorca. It must have been something tremendous for you to take off... I bet the years haven't gotten you over the goddamn tendency to feel guilty about everything... "

"Why don't you let her talk, Lida?"

I really didn't want to talk about it.

"Well, when a fifteen-year-old kid kills herself at your house because she's pregnant from being raped and she can't figure out what to do, and you don't know how to help her... and when a lady who, for the same reason, decides to put into effect what they say about castration being the best punishment for rape, and you don't turn her in for it... the best thing to do is jump ship for a while, don't you think?"

"Wow, that's pretty heavy," Lida agreed. "Who were the two women?"

"Clients of mine."

When I explained Gaudí's case, Jem said, "Don't you think that form of vengeance is a bit fierce? Qualitatively, you can get over three rapes better than three castrations... "

"You don't need to protect yourself, Jem, it wasn't me who wielded the scalpel." He had instinctively put his hands over his crotch.

"But you didn't do anything to stop it," he insisted.

"Shit, Jem," Lida jumped in. "It's incredible you're so stubborn. Can't you see she feels guilty? All she needs is for you to make her feel worse.... "

Lida was the one with the most money, in that apartment of Majorcans, the one who got the most packages from the island, the one who had the most dresses, and she always ended up paying the share of the rent of whoever was the most broke that month... that is, when she didn't pay the whole thing herself. And she still remembered my character.

"No I don't feel at all guilty about that," I said sincerely. "But Sebastiana's suicide... She was Majorcan too," I began hesitantly to explain.

Lida listened to me in silence. Jem, also without talking and trying not to make noise, made me some tea.

The *Mallorquina* rocked us, the water splashing its flanks. I spoke with the rhythm of that monotonous, insistent motion, and with the same insistence I raved on about my feelings of failure and guilt. The ray of sun that swayed on the table captivated and hypnotized me. I could see Sebastiana in the bathtub. I could hear myself speaking, but it wasn't really my voice. It was some sleepy droning that came out of some part of my body, but it wasn't really mine. At some point it seemed like I was the only one who could hear that voice. But Jem put a cup of tea in my hands and said,

"That's enough sad stories," and he began a flood of questions: The situation in general, the country, the city, our friends in common, politics . . .

"That imbecile, in Parliament? It can't be! In college . . . " Lida was amazed.

"Yes it can. For the very reason that in college he was such an asshole. . . . " Jem's opinion.

"But he never even wiped his own ass!" according to Lida.

Or:

"Director, you say? Well, it doesn't surprise me. He had no idea about journalism, but he was an expert mountain climber." That was Jem.

Or:

"But in the Neighborhood Association he shouted himself hoarse saying that that was not negotiable!" Lida was outraged.

The ray of sun was now oscillating on the dining room screen door. Had four hours gone by since I boarded the *Mallorquina?* It could be centuries, or only a moment. In fact, talking about all those things, it was as if I hadn't left Barcelona. Just that the space-time coordinates were on the other side of the mirror. And my body and my brain hadn't been able to deal with such a radical change yet.

"Christ, it's six o'clock!" Lida said.

They had to go flying off to the radio station.

"I'm so happy, Lònia!" Lida said from the moorings, through the porthole.

•••

The idea of living on a boat tickled delightfully that bit of my brain where I stored my illusions. It was an extravagance I never thought I would have allowed myself.

The maritime home of Jem and Lida wasn't exactly a palace. Barely even a little nest, with every corner put to use without exception. There wasn't a hole not being used or a crease without its function: behind the back cushions, bookshelves; under the seats, canned food and boxes of spare parts.

Life on a boat is not all a dream, though. First, the humidity, even though I expected that. Then, the constant swaying, it wore me out the first few days; on a boat, even if it's anchored, you never stop moving even when you sleep; the rocking is gentle but treacherous. And until your muscles get used to the idea. . . . Then, too, the tininess: the first few days I moved around cringing, pulling in my shoulders, my arms stuck to my body.

"You look like a hunchback," Jem teased.

Because the two of them could even dance in the living room, and Lida shut herself up in her cabin to write the radio scripts: she would sit cross-legged on the bed with the typewriter on the shelf they used as a headboard, and there she went clink clink clank, to the rhythm of the soft rocking of *Mallorquina.*

...

". . . We would have had to hire a maid, otherwise . . . " Lida told me.

"Don't think we offered you a place out of the kindness of our hearts. We can save a salary with you around," Jem said.

"But I don't know anything about sailing, even the names of things . . . "

"But I bet you know how to fix a gin and tonic or a salmon snack," Lida said.

"And if you want, I'll put on an apron and a little cap."

...

Now as silly as it sounds, you could say I'd started a new life.

If anyone had told me, when I used to watch the sailboats that arrived at our port with so much fascination, that some day I'd be sailing a boat like that, if I'd known that those brilliant, unattainable ships would be more than a dream, I wouldn't have believed it. Maybe they even would have stopped fascinating me.

But now as Jem and Lida slackened sails with that maritime skill I so envied—as if they hadn't even had to learn it—now, as the *Mallorquina* weaved its way among the other boats that entered and left Phillip Bay, I looked at the sails that started to inflate and I felt exactly the same fascination as I had twenty years ago.

A new life. The sails stretched; we were at the mouth of the port. The clients, a middle-aged couple with a spoiled twenty-year old son, had installed themselves on deck; the man got his fishing gear ready, I served refreshments, the son was obviously bored, the woman struggled uselessly with a too-wide-brimmed hat; Jem watched the instruments and Lida held the helm, all the while speaking the mysterious language of mast ropes, shrouds, and hawse-holes.

It seemed like centuries ago since I had traded Arquer the file of my investigations for a trip to Australia. Elena Gaudí seemed like someone out of a novel. Sebastiana was a faded pain, pushed way to the back of my brain. At the moment my whole world was filled with flaming sails. There was no past, no future. Just sails. And a sea so different from mine that it almost seemed like it wasn't me ploughing its waters, but some other person who happened to also be called Lònia Guiu.

Off to Tasmania. I was disappointed with the Strait of Bass. I thought it would be just that, a narrow strait, and that there would just be a stone's throw from one coast to the other. Not at all; it was really the open sea, as if we were going from Barcelona to Majorca. But our path was more like going from Majorca to Cabrera, skirting little islands and islets. Except that instead of being called sa Plana, s'Illa de ses Rates, sa Conillera, they were Devil Towers, Prime Seal, Chapell, Clarke, and finally the Flinders. And of course everything was much bigger. Everything is bigger and fatter Down Under, even the waves that surround the island.

•••

Dear Quim,

I bet you don't know what a "southerly change" is, right? Look, dummy, it's what sometimes happens in Melbourne: It's a horribly hot, tropical day, and suddenly a gust of wind comes up from the bottom of the earth, and since the city is at the low point of our world, the gust arrives directly without anything to break it, and the temperature plummets suddenly and freezes you. Too much, isn't it? You go wrap yourself up and start thinking it's worse than a real December is supposed to be, and then it gets toasty again. Literally.

I've had a hard time getting used to the idea that since I got here (almost three months ago—Jesus how time flies!) instead of getting colder as it should in October, November and December, it's getting hotter and hotter. It's a complete turnaround, as if the days were going backwards instead of forward. Once in a while I have to recycle my time-space coordinates. Christmas at over eighty-five degrees was pretty weird, too. But it was the "southerly change" that was really far out, as we used to say.

Lida and I went to Prahan to do some Christmas shopping: besides the food, presents for some friends, because Jem wanted a traditional Catalan Christmas. We also found "grape juice" from Penedès, but on Toorak Road, the most European area, that is, the most high-rent, and of course it cost us a king's ransom. Suddenly I noticed people looking around, like dogs sniffing the air. Then, whap! First a cool little breeze, which I liked. Then Lida says, This is the southerly change, and I didn't have time to ask what it was. Well, maybe I'm exaggerating a little, but wow!

We spent Christmas here, moored at the Elwood docks, even though we had a good chartered cruise to do. But Lida just felt like taking a break and being with friends. They're a great gang, mostly friends from the radio station: residents, like Telly, Deborah and Tom, all English; and Kathleen, who's Irish; legal immigrants, like Borg the Swede and Brig the Teuton; some with valid tourist visas, like Pete, another German; some with expired tourist visas, and therefore illegal, like Donna from Denmark and Nataly, who will soon be legal because she's going to marry Phil. . . . What a bunch of shit, don't you think? And it's because even though they have plenty of space, the diggers (that's a not very nice way to refer to Australians) make it very complicated to stay in Oz. Naturally there are some natives in the group, too, like Andrea, Alan, Peggy and Maurice (who's not French, though he looks like it, and he's charming—too bad he's a little young for me!) etc. But of the outsiders, we're the only "Latins"; we're just about the only ones of that "race" who get along with the "Britainoids" (my term). Because here everything has been very compartmentalized, kid. The city people vs. the bushmen; those from one city vs. those from another; the Aussies (another way to say Australian, but nicer) and "others," and among the "others," it all depends—where you come from, what language you speak, what kind of visa you have, and above all, your acquisitive powers. Naturally, there's a lot of talk about how Australian culture is a productive mixture, blah blah blah, but in reality. . . . And in the midst of all that, the aborigines are left out completely, as if they didn't exist. Of course, they do exist: there are lots of galleries of dreams that offer you the latest in Aboriginal Arts and Crafts. There are also plenty of shops where you can buy opals of all sizes, and others where you can buy a kangaroo coat.

All in all, it's a good land. I've been on the move a lot, both by land and by sea. I liked Sydney, but it's out of reach. The fact is that the idea of a city here is very different from ours, but it wasn't too hard to get used to. But cars driving on the wrong side of the road still freak me out.

In the interior there are some spots that seem absolutely unreal and impossible. No, I won't describe them to you, it wouldn't come out right. And I assume you've been getting the postcards I've been sending you from each new place. I say I assume, asshole, since I still haven't heard a single syllable from you. Are you still alive?

I want to learn how to handle a boat. That is, I'd like to get the license. But January and February we're tied up with cruises and contracts for excursions, so maybe it won't be worth the trouble, since it'll be time to come back by then. If

I decide to come back, that is.

I could look into working at the radio station where Jem and Lida work. It's kind of a hodgepodge station, ethnic you might say, with programs for all the different outside cultures on the island. Paid for by the government, naturally. Jem and Lida do a Catalan program. I could get into telling Majorcan folk tales.

How's everything with you? Come on, write! Tell me all kinds of things. Do it, it's not that hard. See? I was just going to wish you a happy new year, and look at the epistle you're getting.

A great big hug and kiss. I love you a lot, Quim. Really. I wish you were here. But I don't miss you a bit.

Lònia

I

Getting ready for a cruise to New Zealand for five people, besides the crew, was a tremendous organizational job. Fortunately, some friends from the radio station helped us in their spare time. They checked out the sails and replaced some of them, and a new transmitter too. We checked all the tools and bought provisions for an army . . . as if we were going to a desert island to start the population of the earth all over again.

It wasn't the *Mallorquina's* longest cruise. In fact, the boat had come from Barcelona to Melbourne, taking all kinds of twists and turns, stops and routes, depending on their pleasure and the situation at each moment. That's why Jem and Lida insisted on having everything reviewed, controlled, chronometered, much more than on other trips. Not a single SOS flare or bottle of gin could be missing; there had to be lots of spare parts and plenty of cigarettes, too. The travel agency that sent us these clients had also given us a list of their tastes and caprices, even including a particular brand of condoms.

"I suppose they'll bring their own, uh, oregano," I said.

"Oregano?"

"Of course . . . grass . . . and powder that gets you high, and junk . . ."

The awaited day came. Everything was set for the big voyage. I was more excited than a dog with a tasty bone. I had great expectations about this cruise: marvelous encounters, terrifying storms, maybe even heroic rescues. I was enthusiastic about obstinate calms on high seas, provoking the passengers to their limits. I was delirious thinking about profound discoveries of the human soul, secrets confessed on a night of the full moon, or when the *Mallorquina* was just about to capsize. Passionate declarations, and Halley's comet revealing all kinds of madness.

It was also my farewell to the Antipodes. The last peeling of the skin of my soul. The only thing I was sorry about was having to be a maid again.

But when I undid the last cable, I felt a shiver. Was it a premonition? I didn't have time to think about it; there was work to do.

While Jem, Lida and the sailor started the maneuvers, I set some chairs on the deck for the clients.

There were three men and two women; I hadn't been able to check them out at all, but it did seem that the oldest one, about sixty, was looking too insistently at Lida's majestically taut ass during the operation of rolling up the capstan chain. But maybe my overexcited imagination was just playing pranks on me.

When the *Mallorquina* began to vibrate, and the sails were whistling, the two women came out on deck to get some sun. The outfits left round bottoms, tight thighs and firm breasts out in the open. It seemed like they weren't wearing anything but sunglasses.

Lida was at the helm, Jem and the sailor watched the canvas sails and I approached the girls to offer them their first drink.

Then, at only two paces, I recognized her.

II

"Is this the line to Australia?"

It's strange enough to hear someone you don't know speaking to you in Spanish in the London airport, but the way she spoke it was even stranger.

"You're from Majorca, huh?"

She looked at me, surprised. She was a girl from a well-off family, longish blond hair—dyed—and a pasty face, eye makeup applied discreetly so the eyes seemed blue even though they were brown, expensively dressed, with well-chosen accessories, impeccable manicure with pink fingernails of exactly the right length. What Aunt Antònia would call a fine young lady. I guessed she was about eighteen.

"Why do you ask?" she said, still in Spanish.

"Because us Majorcans speak awful Spanish."

Completely taken aback, she went on in Majorcan Catalan. "You're going to Australia too, Ma'am?"

"Yes, and don't call me ma'am. I'm not that old."

"It's just that at my house we were always taught to say ma'am to people we didn't know."

What a baby.

She came on like a ton of bricks, poor kid. She was the prototypical spoiled brat, simple-minded and pretentious, vain and satisfied with herself and with her social status, someone for whom things had gone well so far, and she thought it was due to her own merits rather than to chance.

We looked at each other with a certain condescension, except that she didn't realize that I felt the same way about her as she felt about me. But in any case, since she was younger, she was also less secure in the world, and she latched onto me like a barnacle. We waited together until they called our flight, we sat next to each other, and she only stopped talking during the stopovers—she spent them buying perfume and candy in the duty-free shops—or to sleep. And when she woke up, the chattering began again.

It's true that she treated me to everything the airlines didn't give us for free, and the natural orange juice aboard British Airways costs a fortune, a luxury my budget wouldn't allow. On the other hand, I had to put up with all her delusions of grandeur, about herself and her family too:

"... Daddy didn't want to let me come, but between Mom and Uncle Macià they convinced him... Mom is much more modern than Daddy, she's a woman with a lot of personality and she has a lot of experience, and she says a girl should know something about the world before she can run a business... I already know English, I graduated and I've travelled a lot, but Mom says I need the finishing touches of a foreign school, I went to a good high school in Palma, the best of them all, but that's not enough, and I wanted so much to come to Australia, imagine, none of our friends has ever sent their kid to a girls' boarding school in Australia, our family is very well known, and not only for the chain of hotels, but also for the class of the family itself, my grandfather was a nobleman... "

It had been centuries since I'd heard language like that... nobleman yet! I thought the expression had disappeared. In my home town, Tineta was the only one who said it, Tineta, the most antiquated. Cristina paused. Maybe she expected me to marvel at travelling next to nobility, but since I didn't show any special satisfaction, she continued:

"... but since he was a Red during the war, they shot him. Lucky for Daddy and Uncle Macià, he arranged everything so they wouldn't lose their possessions and businesses... Our family was the first one to build a big hotel."

For the love of God!

"... and now we have five... six, I mean, oh, I'm not interested in business, but when Daddy married Mom they say two of the greatest fortunes in Majorca were united... after Mr. March, of course... and since I don't have any brothers or sisters, it'll all be mine, but Uncle Macià, who's a lot younger than Daddy... Mom's a lot younger than Daddy too... anyway they say that first I have to get out and have a good time, and also to learn some culture, since I'll have plenty of headaches when I have to run everything by myself. But Daddy didn't want to go along with it, being separated for such a long time from me, it would only be half a year, but he adores me and he wouldn't go along at all, but Uncle Macià told him, 'I did what you wanted with Cala Mura beach, and now it's your turn to do what I want, after all, it's all for Cristina's good... because Cala Mura is mine, in fact all of Morgana Island is mine, and Uncle Macià wanted to develop it, and Mom thought it was a good idea too, but I didn't want them to, and since I'm still underage, Daddy's my guardian... are you asleep?"

"Eh?"

"I thought you were asleep. So I convinced Daddy, well, the ecologists helped me too, but I don't trust those people at all, so I convinced Daddy not to let them develop, and when Uncle Macià said he had gotten a place for me at the Rutherford Residence in Melbourne, and he had had to use his pull because there they only accept the cream of the crop from the whole world, Daddy said it was too far away, but Mom and Uncle Macià argued and pressured, and here I am."

Yes indeed, here she was, what a cross to bear.

When we were about to arrive, she turned the record over: "What about you? What are you doing in Australia?"

"I have friends here."

"In Melbourne? Oh, you'll have to come and visit me in the residence. You'll have to give me your address. I want to have a party and I'll invite you, and your friends can come too."

I ignored that. I had come to the Antipodes precisely to unchain myself from everything, and I didn't intend to link myself back up with my country through that little fart. I answered evasively, and she didn't even notice. I don't know why she had become such a friend of mine with so little encouragement.

"I like you a lot, even though you're not in the same... " She didn't dare say it.

"Class? No, sweetie, fortunately."

Even though I'd put up with all her bullshit, she didn't do a thing to help me when the customs officials asked me impertinent questions, the dummy. As if she didn't know me. And outside, she didn't introduce me to that beautiful, elegant lady who had come to pick her up, with a uniformed servant, tall and well-groomed, looking like a giant, with a big moustache that covered half his face and a very showy tattoo on the back of his left hand.

"Well, Cristina, I hope all goes well for you," I said, thinking she could save me the taxi fare to the city.

It seemed that the beautiful and elegant lady didn't much take to me. She must not have thought I was high class enough for them either. Out of good manners, or because I had other things on my mind, I refrained from tearing up the paper Cristina had given me with the address of the residence. I really didn't ever plan to make use of it.

Naturally, it didn't occur to either one of them to take me to the city in their big, fancy car.

When my taxi started off, I had forgotten about Cristina Segura.

...

"Hi, Cristina!"

She took her sunglasses off instinctively, but she had to squint into the sun. She put them back on.

"Are you speaking to me?" she said in English.

I hesitated a few seconds. Her face was no longer pasty. Nor was she so refined. And her hair was obviously dyed a coppery color.

"Cristina, don't you recognize me? You've changed a lot, all right, but I haven't. Don't you remember me?"

"I'm sorry, I don't understand you. Don't you speak English?"

"What do you mean, you don't understand? Oh, yes, of course. In the London airport you were ashamed of your Majorcan accent, and now you're pretending not to understand me."

"What does she want?" the other girl asked her.

Cristina shrugged her shoulders.

"I don't know. She speaks something I don't understand."

"Can it be possible?" I said, angrily.

But the truth is that I was beginning to doubt. And with those great big sunglasses she was wearing, it could well be that I was mistaken. I felt ridiculous: I don't know why I was glad to find her again; still, and I don't know why either, it bothered me that she was ignoring me.

Lida had left the helm and approached us. She had heard my raised voice, and she must have been surprised to hear me speaking Catalan.

"Is something wrong?" she said in English.

"This lady," Cristina said, also in English, "I don't know what she wants because she's speaking some language I don't understand."

"You sure do understand me, dumbshit! You yakked your head off in the same language during the whole trip. The Segura family, so important! And the nobility, and the hotels... and that virgin island, what's it called? Morgana. Be sure to come and see me at the residence... I'll have a party and I'll invite you and your friends... And now you don't understand me!"

"Lònia... what the fuck is wrong with you?" Lida intervened.

One of the three men had approached us cautiously and now he was giving the girls an extremely dirty look. I saw him close-up for the first time: at first I didn't know whether he looked like a butler or a thug, but in any case I didn't take to him at all.

"Is there something wrong here?" he said.

"No, no," Lida said, "we only wanted to know if they wanted some refreshments," and with an imperial look she made me move away from them.

"I'm positive, Lida," I said, but it wasn't true. "I made the entire trip next to that girl."

"You hadn't said anything about her."

"Because I completely forgot. She didn't interest me at all. She's one of those holier-than-thous you can't stand, whose pompous ass is so inflated you can't cover it with a sheet. But it's strange, she told me she was going to a girls' boarding school. She must have been pulling my leg."

"Are you sure you're not mistaken?"

"Well, I guess I could be... Who are these people?"

"At the travel agency, they told us it was two couples and a secretary to one of the men. We didn't ask anything else. The guy who came up on the deck must be the secretary, because he's in a cabin by himself."

"And the other two... those girls are real young, and one of the men is pretty old."

"Both of them are. Have you turned into a Puritan?" she laughed.

The single fellow approached us; he wasn't old, in fact he had a magnificent torso mounted on a pair of legs that made you want him to braid them around your body. But he had a most disagreeable conceited expression on his face. He looked like anything but a secretary.

"What a hunk, my god! And he looks like such a bad guy!" I said.

Lida tried to make her laugh over what I'd said seem like a smile directed at the secretary, and she pulled it off.

"The little dears would like something to drink," he said, also with a smile that was meant to be charming.

It didn't seem the most appropriate thing for a secretary to call them, and he realized it; he looked at me seductively, which in another situation would have knocked me out, I swear. I like bad guys, it's my weakness—and he must have thought that with that smile he didn't need any excuses.

I went to prepare the refreshments, determined to follow Lida's advice; we had to spend several days with those people, and they didn't seem at all up for familiarities with the crew. I'd just keep my nose clean and hope for smooth sailing.

...

Well, we'd hoped for a good wind, but we got more than we bargained for and it wasn't that good. It was right at the beginning of the cruise; on the third day of navigation, when Jem asked for a weather forecast, they advised us to turn back.

"But didn't you ask for a forecast before we started out?"

the secretary said, looking grumpy.

He wasn't wearing shorts any more because the Antarctic wind, which insisted on blowing more than it should, had frozen the hairs on his magnificent legs. So magnificent that, among ourselves, we called him "Legs."

"Of course I did," Jem said, "But now they're communicating to us that that forecast has changed. Instead of a pleasure trip, we'll be letting ourselves in for an experiment in how to resist freezing. We could even become the first humans to hibernate."

"I don't think that's funny," said Legs, even grouchier.

But he had to back off. Him and the two couples. And us too—with that setback, we ran the risk of watching our whole budget go down the tubes.

"They could refuse to pay the rest," Lida said. "And with the investment we made . . . "

"You'll have enough to eat for a year," I said.

The two young women seemed more than pleased with the change in plans, though. In fact, the poor kids hadn't had a single occasion to enjoy the voyage since they came on board. Partly because the bad weather had come up just a few hours after we'd started, but even more because the old timers made them spend most of their time in their respective cabins, from which they only came to eat.

I hadn't tried to talk to Cristina again, but I noticed that the few times when Legs wasn't in view, she was looking at me from behind those dark glasses.

"I don't know whether she's your Cristina from Majorca or not," said Lida, "but that kid is trying to hide something; she won't take her glasses off for anything in the world."

"She's not wearing pink fingernail polish like when I met her, either."

Or of any color. She had them so bitten down they were raw, poor thing. She chewed on them insistently, desperately, in silence. Then Legs would give her an imperceptible signal with his head, and she would follow him docilely into the individual cabin. When they came out, after a couple of minutes, it was to wind up in the double cabin, where her mate was waiting for her. The return trip was the same.

Unfortunate creature. All her vanity was gone.

The day we changed our route, I caught Legs about to throw a plastic bag overboard.

"No, listen, not that... we only throw biological trash, biodegradable stuff overboard. Never plastic. We keep it and we throw it in the trash when we get to port."

I said it so nicely it was ridiculous: that man disarmed me, he was so attractive. I reached out to take the bag and he hit my arm. I didn't stop being fascinated, but not even the handsomest he-man in the world hits me.

"What the hell are you doing, idiot!" I yelled in Catalan.

The man was in a bad mood. And he was a rotten braggart. He didn't understand me, but it wasn't necessary: my tone of voice was explicit enough.

"Don't get mixed up in this, sweetie," he said in chewed up English, while he clawed at me with his paws. "You get the idea, so shut up, know what I mean?"

And he kept the bag. I ended up with a bruised arm.

I mentioned it to Jem and Lida.

"Lònia, sometimes seasickness comes as excessive imagination rather than dizziness and nausea."

"Is this bruise my imagination too? Do you have your eyes in your pocket? Don't believe me if you don't want to. Don't believe that they're watching Cristina, and don't believe that it is Cristina, if you don't want to. If you don't want to believe that something is happening to that girl, just don't believe it!"

"Don't get excited, Lònia," Lida tried to smooth things over.

"But don't you see that those poor girls... "

"I'll do this, Lònia: while he's on deck, I'll go look for the plastic bag in his cabin," Jem offered.

"It's not necessary. I know what you'll find."

"You know?"

"Needles. The two girls have tracks on their arms. But that's not what bothers me."

"What then?" Lida asked.

"The situation those girls are in."

"They're high-rent whores, and that's it," was Jem's opinion.

"I know that, too. But by choice or obligation?"

"Are you crazy or what, Lònia? Are there any whores who do it for pleasure?"

"I mean . . . "

"What do you want us to do? Go to the police when we get back to Melbourne?"

Naturally, that wouldn't have done any good. But I was determined to talk to Cristina, to make her talk, at any cost. If only to know whether all the blabbing I'd had to put up with on the plane was a pack of lies. My professional pride was at stake.

"If you keep on pestering me, I'll tell my friend's secretary," the bitch threatened me, the next day, in nearly perfect English. "I'll complain to the travel agency that sent us to you, and they won't send you any more customers."

"But what are you afraid of?" I insisted.

Nothing, she wasn't afraid of anything.

...

With the transmitter, we were able to advise the travel agency and the radio station about our failed trip.

In Elwood, a limo with a chauffeur had come to pick up the customers, and Maurice and Deborah were waiting to help us clean and straighten up. In the evening, we had a de-frustration party at Maurice's place; we had to cheer ourselves up.

Deborah was bundling up the sheets to launder them; she came up on deck with an envelope in her hand.

"Lònia . . . "

It was one of our envelopes, with my name written on it. Inside, there was a handwritten paper and another envelope, sealed.

"Lònia, you're right, I'm Cristina Segura. Please, mail this letter. Thanks."

On the sealed envelope, a name and address: Bernat Segura, Llucmajor, Majorca.

"Well?" I said, defiantly handing over the envelope to Lida.

"Holy shit!"

Should I open it? Lida said yes, Jem said no. Deborah and Maurice didn't know what we were talking about. In the end I didn't open it. I put stamps on it and mailed it.

That evening at the party, I got drunk. Since I don't drink much, it's usually enough for me to smell alcohol. But that time I didn't limit myself to the smell, not by a long shot.

The next day I woke up in Maurice's bed. My brain was a stone and my ears were ringing. Maurice gave me a beverage of gin and cream and who knows what else. After a while the stones had become cork and the ringing a dove's cooing.

"What am I doing here?"

"What do women usually do in men's beds?"

Men? Maurice was a twenty-four-year-old kid! It was flattering, that's for sure, that a young guy like him would pay so much attention to me. But he made me feel old. At that moment, besides feeling old, I also felt ugly, covered with marks and blemishes.

"How was it?" I asked, afraid of the diagnosis.

"That's for you to say."

"I don't remember a thing!"

"Too bad. 'Cause you're sensational."

He was only wearing a towel tied around the waist. All along his spine, a floral tattoo. What a mania the Australians have for tattoos! I remember a tattooed hand, but when I tried to remember whose, Maurice sat down on the edge of the bed and the knot holding the towel on came undone. Suddenly, I was dying to be sensational again, and especially, to be aware of it. That kid with the angel face had a body that turned the cork in my head into a pleasant, soft cotton.

We were both sensational.

I got off at the end of line 19. I wanted to observe the neighborhood rather carefully, because I had only seen that side of the city from the bus, on the way to Sydney. Fakers Road was right there, on the corner of the Hume.

It was a short street, but very spacious, with little traffic compared to the steady stream on the Hume leading to Sydney. It was surprisingly quiet. Alongside the sidewalks were great magnolia trees. English gardens had replaced the original flora of the zone, giving the neighborhood an elegance that had nothing to do with what I had imagined as Antipodean.

The European quality of Melbourne, of which the inhabitants were so proud, was quintessential here. In a way, the hilly sections of the "queen city" reminded me, with all the differences in the world, of the anarchist but modish hillsides of Barcelona, pretentious and who knows what else. But what the Sydneysiders say about Melbourne isn't true either—that Melbourne is a Puritan and boring city. No.

Sprinkled among the gardens were grand houses with maids wearing little caps cleaning square panes of glass and butlers with striped vests watering the flowers on the terraces. Well, in reality there weren't maids or butlers, but they would have fit right in and filled out the picture and the climate you breathed there: calm, comfort, gentry.

Rutherford Residence, with brass letters on marble.

"I'm here to see Miss Cristina Segura."

A butler, in fact, had opened the door, and he was wearing a striped vest.

"Do you have an appointment with Mrs. Joil?"

"I'm not here to see Mrs. Joil, I want to see Miss Cristina Segura. Who is Mrs. Joil?"

"Who are you?"

"A friend of Cristina Segura."

He turned his back on me without saying a word and disappeared through a door to the right of the vestibule. A round vestibule, with a domed skylight that diffused a relaxing milky brightness. At the left, a stairway curved up toward an interior hallway, from where some laughter and muffled techno-music could be heard. In front of me there were some huge windows showing an interior garden with a covered pool. Some young women were lazing around, some of them nude. Seen from the window, they seemed like photographs from an artistic-porno magazine. Two other girls, visibly less favored, stumpy, with heavy legs, wearing T-shirts and shorts—served drinks and massaged the pretty ones. A tall, well-built man, sporting a three-piece ivory-colored suit complete with a Majorcan straw hat, wandered among them, touching an ass here, a nipple there—and the pinched girl jumped up, hurt and annoyed, but she didn't dare let the three-piece man have it.

It didn't seem possible, but it was true: he was different, but the same. The only things that hadn't changed were his mustache and the tattooed flower on his left hand. So, Mrs. Joil must be . . .

"Mrs. Joil will see you now." The striped vest gestured for me to follow him.

And in fact, Mrs. Joil was the beautiful and elegant lady who had come to the airport to pick up Cristina, and the mustachioed chauffeur was the man with the tattooed hand, who I had just seen dressed up as a pimp.

"I'm very sorry to waste your time, Mrs. Joil, but it seems the butler didn't understand me. I just came to visit Cristina Segura . . . It wasn't necessary to bother you, she just had to be called."

Mrs. Joil listened to me with deference.

"We usually like to meet the people who come to visit the

girls." She paused. "Their families place their trust in us, and it's our responsibility to watch out for them. Our reputation demands it. Surely you understand."

Where would all this end, harpy?

"Who are you?"

When I identified myself, with half truths and half lies, she wanted to check it out with my passport.

"Listen, what is this, a residence for well-off girls, or a police station? Have Cristina come and she'll explain herself who I am, where she knows me from, and everything you want to know about me."

"Well, the truth is that there's no person by that name here. There never has been. In fact, I don't know of anyone by that name." Magnificently imperturbable, the lady—as if she were telling God's truth.

"For Heaven's sake, why didn't you tell me that in the first place? Why are you so interested in my documentation? Listen, lady, don't tell me your lies, because you and that thug you have out there at the pool took her away from right under my nose at the Tullamarine airport. It might be true that Cristina's not here now, but not that you don't know her. Come on, lady, you know me too!"

"Miss, allow me to point out that I am not accustomed to that tone of voice in this house. Will you kindly. . . "

"And I'm not used to getting the third degree in such an unrefined manner. Please be kind enough to tell me where Christina is. Where did you take her from the airport?"

"I'm telling you, you're mistaken."

What a stubborn goddamn dame!

"Come on, that's enough bullshit. Where is Cristina Segura?" I was even more stubborn.

"I am not willing to continue putting up with your impertinences."

The striped vest was already there, grabbing my arm not so gently and leading me to the door, which he shut in my face.

I walked along Fakers Road away from the Hume, turned the first corner, and walked around the neighborhood for a good while; I was sure that sooner or later I would find out who was following me. But I got tired. Nobody, either in a car or on foot. And I was so distracted watching the few people on the sidewalks and the few cars that passed by, that on traversing one of the cross streets, I instinctively looked to my left instead of to my right.

My six-month visa for Australia would run out before I got used to cars driving on the left. On more than one occasion I'd had to bolt back to the curb after starting off feeling less than totally secure. So that even though there were lights that gave pedestrians the right-of-way, the survival instinct made me make sure no cars were coming. Except that I made sure on the wrong side.

So that when I looked to the left and took a step into the walkway, suddenly a flash came from the right that almost shaved me. I don't know how I managed to jump back on the sidewalk without even yelling at the car or getting the necessary charge of adrenalin. The car, white, with exaggerated rounded forms and hugging the ground, rushed off without even realizing that it had just about reduced me to jelly. I leaned on the stoplight pole with my blood frozen in my veins.

"Are you all right?"

A lady in her sixties, chubby and placid, with a basket in her hands, was looking at me with pity. She's the one, I thought. She stood out a bit, a lady like her, in that neighborhood. If they wanted to follow me, they could have done it a little more intelligently. And when the lady offered me a handkerchief soaked in cologne, I rejected it without hesitation and started to run toward the streetcars.

"Poor lady," said Lida, "surely she did it with all the good will in the world."

"Maybe so. The problem is that good-willed people pay for bad-willed ones," I said philosophically.

I was irritated: neither of my two tasks had turned anything up. At the travel agency, Jem and Lida hadn't had any luck, either.

" . . . they only act as intermediaries between the clients and us."

"And you believed that, of course," I said with impertinent scorn.

"Well it's not strange at all, kid. This is a free country, no identity cards. And even if they'd paid with a credit card, they wouldn't have given us that information at the agency. It is strange, though, that they would pay with cash... this is the land of credit cards."

"If they'd left something on board, how could we have returned it?"

"What excuse did you think we used to get in touch with the clients? That they'd left a ring," Lida explained. "And they told us to bring it to the agency or to keep it, the clients could go to the trouble of looking for it."

"Lònia," Jem said, "I think it would be better if you would let this be. If Cristina needed us, she had plenty of occasion to say so, no matter how much Legs was watching her."

"Then why didn't she mail the letter to her father?"

"How should I know?"

"You shouldn't feel responsible, I know how you are," Lida said. "If you want to get involved in a bunch of shit, wait till you get back to Barcelona. You don't have much time left."

Lida was right. I didn't need to go to the Antipodes to do stuff like this. But I had just decided that I would forfeit the return ticket Arquer had bought for me and stay at the world's bottom until I had found Cristina.

...

I'm not sure to what point it was not wanting to involve Jem and Lida in what I was planning to do, or if it was just that I didn't want to have to explain to them what I was up to. In any case, Maurice didn't have to insist too much that I go live with him in his little house with a garden in Heltham.

"He's crazy about you," Lida said, not too happy about my decision.

"So you're not thinking of going back, for the moment?" Jem piped in. "You know what you're letting yourself in for, right?"

"It's exciting to be illegal," I lied. "And so is this thing with Maurice," I lied again. "As long as it lasts, of course."

"Don't act so frivolous, dammit!" Lida was really angry. Then cynical: "I thought you didn't like the young ones."

It was true, I preferred the riper ones, not the young ones. But way down, the truth is that I like the older ones because I think they're the only ones who'll like me. I'd started my mid-life crisis at thirty-five, to be different... and I still was in it.

What I didn't tell them was why I decided to go live with Maurice: the day before, when they were at the radio station, I had gone up on deck and I had seen a man standing at the very end of the mooring. He was dressed like a person who wasn't accustomed to sea-going. White pants, blue and white striped T-shirt, blue visored cap, rubber-soled moccasins so he wouldn't scratch the wood of the yacht. Impeccable. A giant, and a chameleon: the same immense mustache as the chauffeur and the pimp; and the same flower on his hand.

He had come looking for the ring, of course.

"Are you a secretary as well?" I asked.

But I must have said it in an incomprehensible English, because he didn't understand me. He looked at me like I was his worst enemy, but I couldn't help playing the hardass. In my own way, of course.

"A ring? I don't know, the owners of the boat didn't say anything to me. Where did you get the idea?"

"The travel agency told us."

"Oh, they told you. So they had to tell you. You didn't realize it?" I paused, and he was silently furious. "What kind of ring was it? A digger ring with an opal? Gold or tin? It's just that we have so many rings that people have left on board and then not claimed."

"Do you want to play guessing games, doll?"

"Not doll, and not anything, to you! But yes, I'd like to play. I bet you don't know, smartass, one of the dolls on the cruise? Cristina. Segura. And I bet you don't know either that she's the same one you picked up at the airport with Mrs. Joil half a year ago?"

He was running out of patience: until then I'd been on the *Mallorquina* and he'd been on the dock, but he suddenly jumped on deck and grabbed my wrist, not very nicely. His tattooed hand had sprouted a threateningly brilliant knife.

I did two things at once. I kneed him in the private parts—

my speciality—and started to yell at the top of my lungs like a damsel in great distress.

People started coming out of neighboring yachts. Sailors in service at the Maritime Club, and at the very end of the mooring, a police car appeared with suspiciously good timing.

The two cops took him away without handcuffs, because the poor fellow was still doubled over with his hands on his balls. But I had the impression that they weren't arresting him, but saving him from my clutches, and that instead of taking him down to the station, they'd leave him, safe and sound, at the Rutherford Residence. Because they not only hadn't asked me any questions, they hadn't even bothered to listen to my explanations.

...

Since Maurice paid all the expenses—I was his kept woman and proud of it—I decided to buy a secondhand car to get around in.

I returned to Fakers Road. I parked near the Rutherford Residence and wiped off the sweat. It's really rather cool in Melbourne in April: people have already started wearing their winter clothes. But driving in a city where you don't know the way around and on top of everything on the left side of the road is enough to make the most experienced driver sweat, even at those latitudes.

I saw people going in and out of the residence. Mostly girls, but always accompanied by one or two tall and well-built heavies, enough to dissipate anyone's intention of approaching. I wasn't going to get anywhere that way. Only on one occasion during the whole day did two girls come out alone. But I didn't have a chance to approach them; a car was waiting for them with the doors open, right in front of where the path led to the sidewalk lined with magnolia trees.

That evening, Maurice bought vegetarian pies. He was spoiling me, that guy. He told me about his childhood on the farm, in the outback, when they still didn't have school by radio, and his grandfather taught him how to read. I spoke to him about when I was a girl in Majorca, and the nun who tried to make us learn the alphabet with the rod.

Afterwards, he performed an amorous demonstration with great imagination and variety.

The next day, after a profound and relaxing sleep, I woke up fresh as a rose. Instead of going to the language school—which I had invented to cover up my activities—I returned to the Toorak neighborhood and planted myself again on Fakers Road.

There were fewer comings and goings than the previous day. When I saw two girls leave the house alone through a side door, I jumped from the car so that when they arrived at the first magnolia I was already at their side with a city map in hand, acting like a lost tourist. But I didn't need to hurry so much; no car was waiting for those two: they were the ugly ones. They weren't dressed up or made up like the others, only as discreetly as was appropriate for their physical attributes, not very favored by nature. They had Asian features and spoke a completely incomprehensible language.

"Please," I stopped them politely.

They looked at me, surprised. Scared, maybe? One of them looked furtively toward the house. That attitude was really weird in a city where nobody has to ask for directions because as soon as anyone sees you with a map in your hand they offer to help.

"What is that house you're coming out of?" I asked. "Don't tell me it's a residence for young women, because I know it's not that. Look, I want to find a friend of mine, I know Mrs. Joil. . . "

"No understand," said the more frightened one, in worse English than mine, and she grabbed the other one by the arm and pulled on her.

I grabbed both of them by the arm and kept them.

"Yes, you understand! Don't you see that if you're afraid you'll be locked up here all your lives? Let's go somewhere and talk. I have my car here, come on!"

The braver one seemed to have understood me and was ready to follow me. She said something to the other one, who shook her head no, terrified, and afterwards she said to me, in very rudimentary English, "You no tricky?"

"No, of course I'm not going to trick you. I want to know where my friend is. And I want to know what the hell is going on in this house. I want to help you, don't you understand?"

"Very dangerous. Very trouble."

I figured that. Nothing ventured, nothing gained, though.

The girls started walking, with me behind them. It seemed they were more interested in getting away from the house than in getting rid of me. But it was too late; at that moment I saw the striped vest coming down the path with great strides. They stopped by the magnolia, and looked at the approaching man as if they had been hypnotized.

I made a discreet but rapid departure, and by the time the butler had grabbed both of them by the arms and was leading them to the house, I had disappeared behind the bushes of another garden.

I went back to the car in a flash. I cursed my own bones. If I hadn't been in such a hurry, if I'd waited until they were out of the house's field of vision. . .

You're losing your skills, Lònia. You can't be so impulsive in this job. You have to play with reflection and intuition, and you, Lònia, have both of them pretty fucked up.

I didn't have time for too much self-recrimination. Now the Tatooed Chameleon was coming out of the house with two other thugs. They were walking up and down the street, watching. Not too hard, though, because they didn't see me. Of course I curled up under the steering wheel, but if they'd looked a little, they'd have nabbed me.

Just when they'd gone back in, a car approached from the Hume—the white car, with scandalously rounded corners, hugging the ground! It arrived without the stridency it had the day it nearly ran over me. Whoever was driving was going at the rapid but orderly rhythm of Melbourne traffic, which was like one of those animated conversations in which no one says a word louder than anyone else, nor interrupts what others are saying.

You should have realized, Lònia Guiu, that it wasn't logical that in such a polite city a car would give you a close shave like that unless they intended to take you out of circulation.

Now Joil was coming out of the house and getting into the

car. The car took off; I was behind it without a second thought.

For an expert at following cars like me, that chase was a pain in the ass. Traffic was more fluid than in Barcelona. More reasonable, calmer. And it seems that when you're used to complicated things, simple ones become more difficult. Especially when the simple things are the opposite of the complicated ones.

There was no problem while we stayed on the Hume: the white car in one lane, me in the other. But when the streetcar stopped and I didn't, I nearly ran into a passenger who was getting off. I heard them yelling at me, but I was in time to see the turn signal the white car was making and I got in that lane. Naturally, the street where we turned was two ways, and I got in the wrong lane. I braked just in time. But the car facing me delayed a few seconds and I heard the clatter of broken glass. I backed up causing the car behind me to swerve noisily. A scandal broke loose. Those things don't seem to happen much in Melbourne, and when they do, people explode easily. But I couldn't afford the luxury of trying to calm people down. Besides, I still wasn't handling the dimensions of the car well because the wheel on the right side was still throwing me off. So I closed my eyes and charged. The white car was disappearing down the road. I accelerated, passing all the other cars and getting myself—only my guardian angel knows how—going against the traffic, to the end of the road. I rushed into the street where the white car had disappeared. It became a highway and then a bridge. The river underneath couldn't be the Yarra, because even my disoriented sense of direction told me we were on the other side of the city, toward the west. But I wasn't too sure, even when I noticed that the planes were flying low and I imagined that we must be close to Tullamarine.

After a few more turns, I saw the white car.

The following became easy for a while. Not much traffic. I soon realized that driving on the left wasn't so traumatic. Well-spaced houses, an area like Maurice's but more urban, closer to the center. Somehow, I would situate all this when I got home. At the moment I couldn't permit myself to figure it out if I didn't want to lose Joil. I didn't have the slightest idea where we were going. Nor how long I'd been following the white car.

Then, in the distance, above the green, I recognized Jem and Lida's radio station building, which stood out. So we were relatively close to the Yarra.

The white car stopped on a street with low buildings, without trees. Joil came out with another woman, elegant like her but older. Whore! Looking like a young grandmother dedicated to charitable committees, she'd tried to run over me with her car!

The street had a strange atmosphere. The houses seemed like homes, but most of them had signs on their facades: a design company, a chess club, an architect's studio, a seamstress shop, an esoteric religious club, a doctors' professional association. It was all modern architecture, with clean lines that reminded me of the architect Sert. Aseptic but welcoming. A good mixture. Monash Street. The two women entered number 12. Osseto, the sign said. It could have been a macrame club, or anything else. For sure it was anything else.

The two ladies didn't give me time to come to any conclusions. The race continued. Toward the city.

I was driving mechanically, paying attention to nothing but the white car, concentrating on not losing it and not letting them know I was following. But traffic was increasing, and I was bothered by the wheel on the right and the cars coming toward me, dammit! And that fucking streetcar, blocking my way.

Now I had lost it. I had all of Bourke Street in front of me, two ways, with the parliament building at the end and a bevy of cross streets. And cars all over the place; calm and disciplined, but all over the place. I'd have liked to go more slowly, especially at all the intersections; I hoped to find those rounded forms just by looking one way and the other. But the other cars got nervous. Someone even honked, an unheard-of music there.

I don't even know how, but I found myself again immersed in a big brouhaha.

Hassles like that in Barcelona were nothing new for me. But I was the one who caused them, when I wanted to, for my benefit. To stop a car that was following me or that I was following, to distract a passerby who was in the way, to take attention away from an action that I didn't want noticed. But in Melbourne, all my driving skill became worthless, and without wanting to, I found myself in the middle of a traffic jam that had come about on its own.

I swear I don't know how I got out of it. I can still hear the screaming of that crowd of maniacs. If they hadn't been yelling so much, I would have understood that they really didn't give a fuck. I didn't know at that moment, either, which cross street I'd gotten myself into. I couldn't see a thing and I was about to stop in my tracks and do what I really felt like doing: start crying.

I stopped, but I didn't cry. I looked up and down, to the left and to the right. My guardian angel had abandoned me. I drove through several city streets, more calmly and carefully. Nothing. As if the car had gone up in smoke. It could have gone to any number of underground parking lots in the area, it could have taken one of the streets parallel to Bourke, it even could have sprouted wings and started flying.

IV

The pub seemed transplanted from Greenwich where I'd once eaten a shepherd's pie. Except that, since the meridian didn't pass through here and there wasn't a time ball that lowered at twelve sharp, it wasn't full of tourists.

That strange mania of the Aussies to imitate the Brits.

They mirrored and were enchanted with the metropolis. Even though some voices could be heard in favor of taking the Union Jack out of the flag. They also boasted of a certain way of life, autonomous and therefore different. But the differences came from influences of the rich and powerful relative, North America. In the case of that pub, the influences were a television set and a pinball machine.

The bar was of dark wood in the form of an L, lined with taps of draft beer. Behind the bar, a pale-faced bartender watched television distractedly, accompanied in contemplation by a client putting away a huge mug of beer.

In front of the wallet-cleaning machine a granny was making every effort, with great faith and little fortune, to make it sing the good luck song. At her side, two blond, well-built young fellows were dedicated obstinately to landing darts in the round cork target hanging on the wall. Their beer cans, with protectors to keep them cold, trembled on top of the pinball machine. But they had forgotten about the drinks and were having an inflamed argument about a millimeter of dartboard.

"A beer," I requested.

"What kind?" the waiter mocked.

Because of course it was absurd not to ask for a certain kind and quantity in the first place. But it would have been more absurd to ask for orange juice or a glass of milk.

"It doesn't matter. I probably won't drink it. And a telephone book."

Yes, it was there: OSSETO, Monash Street, number 12, in Sunshine.

"May I use the phone?"

The bartender pointed to a phone in the interior. When I headed for it. I heard him call the attention of the customers to something they were announcing on television.

I dialed a number. A woman answered.

"Mrs. Joil, please," I said, very decidedly.

"She's not here. She already left. Who is this?" the voice clearly betrayed a non-Anglo-Saxon accent.

"I'm calling from the Rutherford Residence. We need to find Mrs. Joil urgently. Didn't she say where she was going?"

"Don't you know, over there? Who's speaking?"

"Who are you?"

A few seconds of hesitation from the other end of the line.

"Alexia."

"I'm Prostie." I raised the stakes. "Listen, Alexia. . . "

"Prostie? I don't know you."

"But I know you. Listen, it's urgent. There's a dangerous visitor at the residence, and I have to let Mrs. Joil know without fail. I know she had some errands to do in the city, but they depended on the visit here on Monash Street. She didn't say where she was going, first of all? I could spend all morning trying to find her at different telephones, but I'm sure she wouldn't like me to have to do that. . . you know how she is."

"Yes, I know her too well." Pause. "She spoke on the phone with Mr. Mec and then she went to the agency with Mrs. Gardener."

"Which agency?"

"Gardener Agency, of course!" with some suspicion in her voice.

"I know that!" I had to stop her, and take a risk. "I mean, which branch?"

"The main one."

We weren't getting anywhere, I thought.

"Why are you calling instead of Toby?" Alexia said.

"Because Toby is taking care of the visitor I told you about. The central agency, you say. Are you sure?"

"Yes, of course."

"How are you so sure?"

"Because she said to Mrs. Gardener that Mr. Mec was waiting for them on Bourke Street. The central agency's on Bourke, isn't it?"

Finally. That's exactly where the white car had disappeared. And now I found myself on one of the narrow streets of the chess board of the city. It wouldn't be hard to find Gardener Agency.

"Good kid," I said. "Okay, bye . . . "

"Listen, you say you know me? From where? I haven't been at Rutherford for a long time. Are you new?"

"Practically. And I know you because Mrs. Joil has spoken to me about you."

Until then I had used a cutting, authoritative tone. Alexia, on the other hand, seemed half mistrusting and half afraid. Now she only seemed afraid.

"What did she tell you about me?"

"Listen, I can't waste any more time right now. I have to call Gardener."

"But what did she say about me?"

"If you like, we can see each other one day and I'll explain."

"Was she mad?"

"No, not really mad. . . . " I hesitated for a second. "But not very happy, either."

"Oh!" I thought I heard a sob. "What shall I do now?"

"Do you want to see me, one of these days?" I offered.

"How? Do they let you go out?"

"What? . . . Oh, of course. It's different with me, of course I can go out." My own special instinct made me add, "Mrs. Joil is very fond of me."

On the other end, the sobs were unmistakable.

When I returned to the bar, the bartender and customers looked terrified. The granny wasn't playing with the robber machine any more, and the two dart-throwers no longer considered the round of cork the center of their world.

"They have no right at all!" one of the guys was yelling. "And it's very well to say that that can't happen here," he said to the bartender. "With those things, it doesn't matter whether it happens in Russia or in Peru—we'll all get it! Sons of bitches!"

I grabbed the mug of beer that was waiting for me and took a big swig without realizing it. I was trying to figure out what had them so bent out of shape. But I hate beer, and I'm sure I made a face.

"It's gotten warmed up, honey," the old lady smiled at me, with a great mug of Guinness in her hand. "You have to drink beer real cold, and then it cures what ails you."

"It won't matter whether it's hot or cold, Granny, when we're all blown away!" one of the dart experts retorted.

"Don't exaggerate," the bartender said. "So far it's just a rumor."

"Yeah, and by the time they confirm it, no one will be around to listen to the confirmation."

I finally was able to figure out what it was all about: they'd announced on television that one of the nuclear centers in the Soviet Union had exploded. Unconfirmed story, contradictory information, official denials, etc., etc., etc. Now the dartsman was manipulating the television to find a channel that would give more information. In some kind of a strange defense mechanism, I grabbed the thing I had closest at hand, and drank the rest of my beer in one big swallow. Then, with the same mechanism working, I asked, "What street is this?" while I unfolded my map of the city.

Granny got real interested. Australians adore tourists, just as the Majorcans had adored them but for different reasons. Here they're grateful that it occurred to you to visit the bottom of the world, and they treat you like a king. There we stare at them and figure out what we can get from them.

Granny pointed out Hardware Street to me. I traced the itinerary to Bourke Street with my finger. Then I looked for the number of the Gardener Agency in the telephone book.

Granny was crazy about helping me.

"No, I can find it by myself," I said.

I wouldn't get lost in the city. I just had to take the principal streets of the quadrangle.

"But you probably won't know the shortcuts," she said. "Do you have a car?"

"Yes."

"I'll go with you, if you like."

"I wouldn't want to bother you."

"Look," the bartender winked at me. "If you pay for the beer she's had today, you'll be doing her a favor. And if you take her, you'll be doing me one."

I don't know why, but sometimes I surprise myself with how easy I am to convince.

On the street, the old lady commented as she got into my car, "I myself would rather kick off from too much Guinness than from some radioactive cloud. But today I had no luck with the machine."

I told her not to worry, that I'd be glad to treat her to whatever death she chose.

...

You could tell that what Granny really wanted was to go for a ride in the car.

Off we went, with her telling me which way to go, where to turn, very self-assured and satisfied with her role as copilot. She waved to other drivers from time to time, like a queen in her carriage.

On the other hand, the beer hadn't gone down well with me: the first consequence of the radioactivity.

The Gardener Agency had a big sign in the windows of the third floor of a very ordinary building—one of those with offices, steel, glass and advertising. The sign, with flashing lights, announced a matrimonial agency. Next door was a locked up church for sale. To kill time—I didn't want to run into Joil—I chatted with the old lady.

"Times are changing, honey, and people don't go to church any more. They'll make a restaurant out of it, or some shops, or a bank. It won't be the first church to have such luck and it's fine with me!"

Pretty progressive, the old gal.

"What are we waiting for on this street?" she asked then.

"I have to go to that matrimonial agency."

Sometimes sincerity is neither a virtue nor a defect, it's just silly.

"You want to get married!?"

"Well, yeah... " What was I supposed to say?

First she launched into a sermon about the advantages of remaining single. Then she confessed she'd had five husbands, three of them legal, and that she'd never been so well off as when she'd been on her own.

"It's easy to find a husband here, honey. There are more men than women. So when you want one, you just stick your hand out, as if you were calling for a taxi. I don't see why you need to tie yourself down to one. . . . " she paused. "Maybe you're looking for one so you can stay in Australia? I see, your visa has run out and you want to stay, right? But there must be other ways, sweetie, for sure... Maybe I could adopt you and... "

She was a sweetheart. Thin as a rail, with colorful clothes and eyes reddened by beer. Maybe that would be a solution, to be adopted. Better than marrying Maurice, who had proposed it, too.

Finally, a car stopped in front of the door. A few moments later I saw Joil get out. When I got out of the car, the old lady insisted on coming with me.

"I know how men are: I can tell by looking at them once what type they are, even in a photograph. Men here want a maid and a whore all in one, and for free. Since you won't follow my advice not to marry, at least let me help you choose."

I had the impression that the old lady was a hundred years old and was telling me stories about the gold fever era. The truth is that I felt a lot more like listening to her yak than paying the visit, but obligations before devotions, as Aunt Antònia would say.

"Wouldn't you rather go have a beer? I'll keep my promise to treat you to as many mugs as you can drink, so you can die the way you'd most like to."

"Afterwards. When we've done the job at the agency, you

can treat me. Duty first, then debauchery," just like Aunt Antònia.

The truth is that I let her come with me out of pure convenience.

With her company, my intentions would go more unnoticed.

I wasn't at all an expert in matrimonial agencies, but to me this place seemed like anything but that.

"Mrs. Gardener?" I asked the receptionist.

She was what Quim would call—rather snidely—a flag lady. I wondered why the hell she had to show so much of her bosom. When we were installed in the waiting room I could see that all the girls who were hanging around—and there sure were lots of them—were equally well-endowed. Maybe they were advertising some brand of silicone. But after seeing such a display, it would be hard to get the clients to be satisfied with inferior quality merchandise. I couldn't believe that all the women clients of the company had the same exuberance as those who were working to find them husbands.

Well, working is one way to put it. It didn't seem like they were doing anything except walking around going back and forth. They swayed ostentatiously through the vestibule and the waiting rooms—everything was separated by glass, except for a big door in the back and a little door alongside the entry—through the halls and through the work section, so to speak, where there were some tables whose only function seemed to be as a sitting place for the girls so they could show off their hips and legs right up to the crotch.

If Mercè could hear me thinking that way—so contemptuous, so unsupportive—she would for sure launch into one of her usual feminist sermons. And she'd be right, as always. And as always, she'd make me feel ashamed for not having figured out such obvious and evident things. But how could I feel pity for those women, so well endowed by nature? What they made me feel was envy.

There were a few clients in the other waiting rooms, some alone, some who seemed to be together. And the truth is that they didn't seem like they were looking for a maid and whore for free; just one of the two things, and willing to pay the going rate. Because after all, the only two women clients were the granny and myself.

The door in the back opened, and two very satisfied-looking fellows came out, accompanied by a girl who looked like a giant. Then another huge woman had two other clients go in.

"Listen," Granny told me, "why don't we go to the other waiting rooms? We could save the agency's commission."

"You want a husband too?" I laughed at her use of the plural.

"No, I'm just looking out for your interests." She got up and gave the men the once-over without any discretion at all. "There's more than one that might do for you . . . they're none too young, but they seem to be of good position."

But I was more interested in the girls. They seemed awfully satisfied with the life. Maybe they were only office workers in a marriage agency. Or maybe Lida was wrong in asserting that no woman is a whore out of pleasure. Or maybe those satisfied expressions were part of the job, whatever it was. After all, a job well done.

The waiting rooms were emptying. No one had come in after us. Suddenly I was hungry. I looked at my watch: four o'clock. I hadn't eaten anything all day, except a little toast before I left Maurice's. When our turn finally came, my stomach was churning. Maybe it was fear; I was about to put myself into the beast's lair: Gardener had already nearly flattened me like a fly the other day. Or maybe it was the beer that hadn't gone down well.

Mrs. Gardener politely asked us to sit down and the sexy miss who'd shown us into the office disappeared through the door in back of the director's monumental table. The table went nearly from wall to wall, like a fence that protected the woman from visitors as if defending her from attack.

She hadn't recognized me. That wasn't really too strange; it was out of the question that I would be there, right in front of her nose. But there I was, and since I was there I had to make the best of the occasion. Except that I hadn't quite figured out how to do that.

"Look, it's not that I'm crazy about getting married, but my granny insisted that I come. She says she doesn't want me to be an old maid all my life, and since I'm no spring chicken any more... But the truth is that I wouldn't like to commit myself to anything at the moment. I just want to look, and be able to think about it before I make a definite decision. And if I decide not to, then. . . . " I began, vacillating.

I tried to seem as stupid as I could. I must have accomplished it, because the lady treated me with a maternal condescension which, on any other occasion, I would have made her swallow by force.

"Don't worry, no client here is obligated to anything, and you always have, at any moment, the opportunity to back out. You must understand, Miss, that we are only intermediaries, we only help people find each other, and of course we try to get couples together with the greatest chances of getting along." Pause, cigarette, bell.

A girl came in to see if we wanted something to drink. I asked for water, and Granny, a beer. Gardener had a whiskey.

"Very well, let's start at the beginning," she had taken out a printed piece of paper and started to fill it out. "First we'll make a file out on you, then we'll study your personality, we'll do some psychotechnic tests, and we'll also have to do a medical checkup."

"What for?" I pretended alarm. "I'm a virgin!"

Granny looked at me with infinite pity.

"Virginity is of no importance to us whatsoever, Miss." She didn't have to swear to that, the pig. "Though we have clients who care a lot. No, I meant a general medical checkup. But that won't be until later, if you're interested in contributing as our client."

"Oh, okay."

She asked me my name, age, birthplace—"Your English accent is a little strange"—studies, jobs, hobbies, manias, religion, even political ideas—"even though all this doesn't matter to us, Miss, but there are clients. . . . "

I invented a wild story. I was born in Darwin twenty-nine years ago—if she didn't believe me, I didn't give a fuck—to an Australian mother and a French father. My father was a mining engineer who had come to work in the Northern Territory, where he met and married my mother. When I was five, we went to France.

"Oh, Paris?"

"No, not to Paris, to Montpellier. That's where I went to school. I also went to Italy with my parents, and to Dublin, that's why my accent is kind of a mixture, you know? No, I didn't go to college, the truth is I don't have much of a head for school. And why should I work? My father was working and he earned more than enough. But when I was twenty-five my parents died in a car accident, and since all my father's family was dead, I came back to Darwin with my grandmother.

"But I'm bored in Darwin. And now my inheritance has run out, and Granny thinks I should get married. I myself would prefer to work, but I don't know what I'd do. If I could find an easy job, even if it didn't pay too much, just to keep me busy and to treat myself to a few whims, because with what Granny gets from retirement and I get for being an orphan, we can live decently, but without any luxuries." I surprised even myself with my rambling.

"Well, we've had more than one client like you, Miss Frairet, and we've come to the conclusion that we're doing them a favor by finding them a job instead of a husband. Yes." Pause. "Do you know a lot of people in Darwin? I mean, do you have a lot of friends?"

"Why?"

"Simply because it might be better to start looking for a job in that circle."

Liar. But I could see exactly where she was headed.

"I don't want to go back to Darwin," I said like a spoiled kid. "It's boring."

"But how about your friends?" she insisted.

"No, I don't have any friends."

"And your grandmother?"

So interested in finding out who would miss me, the bitch. I decided to make things easy for her.

"Her either. We only know a few neighbors, and I'm sure they wouldn't miss us, she can tell you herself," I gestured toward the old lady, who shook her head no, very convinced.

"All right, perfect."

She couldn't hide her satisfaction, the sow. But what was I getting out of all that? I could see I'd have to keep playing the game and risking my skin. I'd have to become one of her protégées to disassemble that whole setup of residences for girls and matrimonial agencies, in order to find Cristina. I didn't like it a bit. In Barcelona or Majorca, it wouldn't have rattled me at all. I'd gotten myself into dirtier ponds, and I'd always gotten out. But Australia was a horse of a different color.

"Did someone recommend this agency to you? I mean, whether it's to find you a husband or a job, we'll need some references from you, I'm sure you understand."

She wouldn't let up, the swine. I thought of giving her an invented name.

"No, no one recommended me, if you want the truth," I said looking regretful. "We took a long time deciding, but Granny thought this agency had the most elegant sign of all we had seen, and . . . "

Mrs. Gardener smiled amply, a benevolent and tranquilizing smile.

"Well, it's against the rules of the house, but maybe in your case we'll make an exception," she said, generously. "Wait a moment and I'll have a secretary come to take information."

She left through the door behind the table.

"Is all that stuff you said true?" the old lady marvelled.

"Are you from Darwin, perchance? Are you my grandmother?"

"No, but . . . well, I was starting to believe it. It's such a nice story."

Suddenly a bitter wave of beer came up to my mouth, like a bad signal.

"Granny, I don't like this," I got up. "Get ready to leave here in a hurry."

"Why? We can't run out on such a nice lady."

I had already taken two steps toward the exit door. The old lady was just getting up, not understanding anything. But when I reached for the handle, the door opened by itself and I found myself face to face with Legs. Who, naturally, recognized me instantly. In fact, it seemed he already knew who he would find in Gardener's office, because he didn't act surprised at all.

The door behind the table opened too, to let in two more thugs.

But before they came around the wooden table, just as my ex-travelling companion from the New Zealand cruise grabbed my arm, I put Quim's teachings into practice, specifically my favorite move. Legs let me go with a hoot. He had doubled over, and I took advantage of the fact that his neck was at the level of my fists and I landed him a rabbit punch, which made him roll on the ground.

"Mr. Mec!" I heard one of the other thugs yell.

"Come on, Granny, get your legs in gear!" I cried without looking back. And I started to run.

V

"Lida, they tell me Maurice can't come to the phone."

"No, he's in the recording studio... "

"Just tell him that this evening I'll be late, not to wait for me, not to worry."

"Is something the matter? Your voice sounds funny."

"Really? No, well, it's just that... "

I needed to tell someone, but I couldn't tell Lida because she didn't know anything about my investigations.

"You've heard the news," Lida went on; it was an affirmation, not a question. "People are very upset around here, but the information is contradictory. I think they're going to organize a demonstration one of these days."

What the hell was she talking about?

"Lònia, are you there?"

"Yes, yes. A demonstration? For what?"

"Against nuclear plants, of course!"

Oh, that was it! But I had a more immediate task than to protest against nuclear plants: first I had to rescue my Australian grandmother.

"Don't worry too much... it could be a false alarm," Lida continued her tirade. "Can you hear me? Lònia, you seem really affected."

It's terrible how we're so much more moved by little private problems than by general faraway catastrophes. Removed from their real importance, from the number of people involved. The sickness of a friend affects us more than the massacre of a thousand Peruvian peasants: what your eyes don't see doesn't hurt your heart. It has to be a defense mechanism inherent to life itself: if not, all of humanity would have killed itself by now. And the fact is that with psychic defenses or without them, we'll end up killing ourselves. Suicide by force had already started, so what difference did it make whether the old lady had remained trapped inside the matrimonial agency?

"Yea, I wouldn't like to die of a dose of radiation... I'd prefer an overdose of beer," I said as a way of asking the old lady's pardon. "Well, tell Maurice not to wait for me... I might not make it back tonight."

"You found another one? My god, Lònia. Fuck, fuck, the world is coming to an end!"

What more could I ask for?

And I went back to the car, to wait.

...

I hadn't stopped until I got to the street. Then I turned around and Granny wasn't behind me. I crossed the street and turned around again. She didn't come out. I got in the car and waited a few seconds. Granny hadn't come out, but two new thugs had, running like me. One went up the street, the other down, looking to the right and to the left. I kept my eyes fixed on the entrance to the building. The old lady didn't come.

The two thugs had gone back in, and still the old lady hadn't come out. It was five. Punctually, the stores and offices were closing and the people and traffic increased. I'd gotten out of the car and gone to a telephone booth. I called the police: There's a woman in danger on Bourke Street, such and such a number, such and such a floor. When they asked me who was speaking, I'd hung up and returned to the car, running. With beer not only in my throat, but also at my ass. I didn't know if my sphincter could hold on.

When the police car arrived, Granny still hadn't come out. A cop got out of the car. Slowpoke. He went into the building and left five minutes later. He didn't have the old lady with him, but one of the girls instead. She didn't look like she'd been arrested, either.

The patrol car started up without the cop and the woman,

who, for their part, had gotten in a taxi looking very happy.

I was still waiting, I didn't know for what, like that dog I had when I was twelve, who would sit in front of a closed door and keep watching the doorknob, as if he expected the door to open all by itself.

I knew it wouldn't do any good to go back up to the agency, if I did the only thing I would accomplish would be for them to keep me too. And who would rescue us then, if no one knew where we were?

I felt guilty and idiotic. Guilty: first for not taking the risk of making the noble but useless gesture; and then for having escaped alone, without dragging the old lady with me. Idiotic: for having let the woman come with me. And for not having gotten anything out of all that rigmarole.

I didn't know yet that the mistake was to provoke not only feelings of stupidity and shame, but a real sense of guilt and impotence that would prove irreparable. And this time, not only because I had a tendency in that direction but for undeniably objective reasons.

So I waited. With my belly in a jumble. But I couldn't leave my watching place, neither to eat nor to relieve myself.

I wished I'd liked to smoke: my smoker friends had told me that time wasn't so heavy if it was mixed with tobacco smoke. Besides, now it didn't matter whether you poisoned your lungs with tobacco smoke. Having them clean was no antidote to radiation.

...

Little by little the street had become calm. Now it was practically deserted. The curbside parking spaces were empty. Stores were closed; the awnings didn't protect anyone now. At one end of the street the spires of St. Paul stood out above the columns of the Parliament; at the other, the red hues of the sunset made an extremely slow moving streetcar reverberate with color.

And I waited. I had abandoned the car to hide in Union Lane. I saw the Tatooed Chameleon arrive, again disguised as a chauffeur; I saw Legs come out, walking as if he'd been scalded—my knee number—with a guy who held him up by the armpit. I didn't think I'd hit that hard, but I wasn't up for feeling glad about it at the moment. After all, I was still the loser. Or rather, the old lady, who wasn't to blame for anything.

Afterwards the women came out, and they all got into a van that was waiting for them. Then Gardener, escorted by the other thug who had come running down to grab me.

How about Granny? How come Granny wasn't coming out?

A slow-moving porter, with his uniform jacket on his arm and cap in his hand, locked the door of an office building.

I shivered; if they did the same with the building the agency was in, I wouldn't be able to enter for sure: I was able to open any door, but I needed tranquillity and safety. Manipulating a street door didn't offer either of these two indispensable conditions.

I came out of my hiding place and passed cautiously in front of the building; there was a light on in the vestibule. I crossed the street: there was light in some of the windows. But the ones that corresponded to the Gardener Agency were dark, only the luminous sign kept sparkling. I made my decision.

I arrived at the third floor without any problem. But when I was in front of the door I realized I wasn't in Barcelona, where, when I left the office with some suspicion that during my work I might find a locked door, I went prepared. No, now I was in Melbourne, in front of a lock type I'd never seen, with my purse empty of all possible appropriate tools, and with my stomach more and more tormented.

A housekeeper was lazily operating a vacuum cleaner at the end of the hall. I approached her.

"The Gardener Agency has already closed?"

"Yes, can't you see?"

"I left some documents here this afternoon, and Mrs. Gardener told me on the phone that I could come and pick them up now. Do you need to go in to clean up?"

The woman looked at me suspiciously.

"Today I cleaned up before they closed."

"But don't you have the key?"

"Don't think I'm going to let you in."

"I need that file this evening," I begged. "Couldn't you go in and get it for me?"

"How do I know you're telling the truth? How do I know you aren't going in there to pilfer the files and blackmail the clients?"

What a woman! She was acting out a whole scenario she'd made up. Either she could read people's intentions on their faces, or perhaps it wasn't the first time someone had tried to sneak in and have a look at the files.

"I'm telling you I won't go in. Just go in yourself. I'll wait by the door."

"Why the hell should I do that for you, if I might ask? What obligation do I have to do that for you? I don't know you from Adam. What do I get out of it?"

A good part of my savings, she would get. Money is for when you need it, they say, and for lack of better tools, sometimes you need it to open doors.

She opened it.

I went in after her and closed the door.

When she heard the door, she turned around and gave me a sour look. You're not too nice, I thought. The worse for you.

"Didn't you say you wouldn't come in?" she said, very annoyed.

"Surely you don't want me to stand in the hall with the door open. Anyone passing by would wonder."

"It's all the same to me. I'm not doing anything illegal." She sounded like something out of a TV serial, this lady.

"I am," I said.

Before she could go on I landed my fist in her chops, as unexpectedly for me as it was for her. And it was such an accurate punch that while her eyes whited out she fell like a sack of sand. I had time to keep her from landing on the floor. I held her by the armpits and—she was dead weight, poor thing—I looked around. I dragged her to the only wooden door in the reception room besides the entry. It must be the toilet.

When I had her inside—a complete bathroom as luxurious as an Oriental spa—I set her gently on the floor. And I took the occasion to clear out my intestines, because I couldn't stand it any more. My God, what a relief! All my abdominal muscles were sore from holding in.

Then I went back to her and took back my savings. I left her one bill, for the work of having to reclean the toilet.

When I got up, I saw it. A dark shadow. The plastic curtain was translucent. If there hadn't been light inside the round tub, as immense as a pool, or if the curtain had been opaque, I never would have realized it.

I moved toward it with my heart in a knot. I knew what I would find there, I was positive. I pulled the curtain back. I didn't want it to be true.

But it was true, all right.

I undid the package deposited in the bathtub; it was Granny. Her face was purple, I didn't know whether because of the blows or because of asphyxiation. Or both.

Like Sebastiana.

Everything was swimming around me, turning white, luminous and blinding.

A wave of fire burned my whole body, but my feet were pure jelly. A sharp whistle pierced my ears. In a fraction of a second I thought I couldn't go on—you can't do it Lònia, you can't. My body reacted. My senses came back; I was kneeling on the floor, grasping the edge of the bathtub, my eyes fixed on the face of the cadaver.

An uncontainable force made me vomit everything I'd eaten for a week all over the clothing and plastic that Granny was wrapped up in.

I don't know how much time passed. I'd hardly breathed, and I wasn't conscious of where I was until the cleaning woman moved, groaning.

I jumped up and, before she regained consciousness, I left her in the same state again. It didn't matter any more.

I had to make a superhuman effort to go look for the files. If nothing else, so that the death of that woman would serve to liberate some others. Gardener's office, the door behind the table.

There was more than I expected. Lots of European women. Curiously, Portuguese, Greeks and Italians, especially from the south; some Turks, Irish and Asians. And in every file that said

Spain, the place of departure was the same: Majorca, Munditourist, even when the names weren't Majorcan. Except for Cristina.

In the files of all the women, there were photographs and complete documentation. Some had resident, work or tourist visas, some expired and others still good: it meant that they had entered the island legally. Others didn't; did that mean they had entered secretly? In any case, it didn't make sense that the visas were there. Australians don't have an identity card per se—they use credit cards or driver's licenses. But a foreigner would be required to show her identity and legality at any time. That hadn't happened to me, but I had always carried it with me, while it was still legal. If those girls had theirs in the file, it meant that they didn't need them, that they'd been taken away from them, or that they'd been given new documents.

In Cristina's file—and in some others—the name Rossenhill appeared alongside Gardener and Rutherford.

Suddenly I realized I'd taken too much time sniffing through the files. My hair stood on end when I heard a door opening. It hadn't occurred to me that sooner or later they'd be by to pick up the body.

Voices, quick steps in the reception room. I grabbed a few papers, documents from Cristina's file and from Alexia's and I went cautiously toward the exit. From one of the little waiting rooms I saw the bathroom door opened. The two heavies who had followed me were arguing in low voices, right in front of the cleaning lady, who was still under the effect of my convincing pounding. I understood that they were cursing the nosiness of cleaning women and that they thought she'd been knocked out by the impression caused by her discovery of the old lady's body.

Then everything went so fast.

I saw with my own eyes—and I was so disturbed that I wasn't even aware of what I was seeing—that one of the men was putting a silencer on his pistol and shooting, all in one gesture, right at the temple of the cleaning lady. My God! My God!

I recoiled, paralyzed—from horror, from panic, from desperation; it was the second time in my professional life that I would have liked to have had a gun in my hand. But what would have happened if I'd had a pistol too? Surely I would have shot at that animal, surely the other one would have shot me and maybe before that I'd have had a chance to shoot at him too.

Now, my hands were only good for covering up my mouth so I wouldn't yell out; but it wasn't necessary, I would have been incapable of articulating a sound, my vocal chords were rigid, I felt like I had a lead pipe for a trachea and a sounding board instead of a heart. My God! My God!

They wrapped up the old lady again in plastic and the cleaning lady in the shower curtain. Each one took a body and they left without looking around any more.

I was able to leave the office with no impediment. The vacuum cleaner was still in the hallway, leaning against the door.

...

I got to City Square without being aware of it. It wasn't me who was looking at the plants, that flash of light, the waterfalls in the interior plaza. It wasn't me sitting on a sofa in the center of the hallway; it wasn't me who heard without listening a young man, somewhat drunk, trying to convince me to go to bed with him. But it was me who realized that this mouth smelled like beer. Like Granny's.

And it was me, too, who got up and went to the bar on one side and asked for a mug of beer. The bartender took a mug out of the freezer and the glass was foggy, like the shower curtain. He filled up the mug and the cold of the liquid burned my soul.

I wanted to die from an overdose of beer, now that Granny couldn't do it.

Until the bartender said he wouldn't serve me any more. I left City Square, as the waterfalls kept on splashing, happy, indifferent.

If I went to the police to report the assassinations, they'd ask for my visa. And put me on a plane back home. And even if they arrested Joil and her whole gang, that wouldn't bring back the old lady or the cleaning lady. That is, if they arrested them. Because it was clear that my anonymous call hadn't done any good.

How about Cristina? Would they kill her too?

It was very late when I returned to the car. The thirty or so kilometers to Eltham seemed like the end of the world. It must have been some survival instinct that got me there, more or less safe and sound.

"I'm sure you've broken more than one law," Maurice said as he helped me undress. "Don't you realize that now you can't take the risk of that kind of foolishness? If they catch you, you won't get away with a fine. They'll send you out of the country."

He was right. Lònia, you're irresponsible. You don't report murders because you're illegal and then you drive drunk as a skunk.

"Lida gave me that rap once in Barcelona," I said with a cork tongue.

"I thought you were a teetotaler."

"No, that wasn't because of getting drunk. I stole a T-shirt from the Corte Inglés, a big department store. And when I showed it to my roommates, Lida said I was irresponsible to expose myself to the possibility that they would search the apartment, which was full of clandestine literature. And I'd even had a job at the store: catching shoplifters, as a matter of fact. And my roommates were pretty mad at me about that, too. It all means I don't even know what's good and what's bad, so I always do everything wrong... Ooooh, I'm really sick, this is worse than being on the *Mallorquina*."

"You're really loaded. Try to sleep. Don't talk so much, I can't understand you anyway."

"Why can't you understand me?"

"Because I can't understand Catalan," Maurice laughed.

"But you were understanding it!"

"Not even Lida would understand the Catalan you've been speaking. Come on, go to sleep."

"I don't want to sleep, shit! I want to talk. No, I don't want to talk either. I want to cry."

All the rest of that night I cried and vomited bitter dark beer, mixed with bile and desperation. Maurice's house smelled like fermented hops for a week. Maurice took care of me, but he didn't look too pleased. I wasn't capable of standing up straight.

"I'm going to get a doctor," Maurice said.

"No!!"

"Do you want Lida to come over? She's worried."

"What did you tell her? I don't know why you have to go around telling things that are none of her business."

"Lònia, what's the matter with you? Isn't Lida your friend?"

"Nothing's the matter with me! Nothing!"

"You're impossible!"

"If I bother you so much, I'll leave."

"No, sweetie, no."

Poor Maurice. He put up with me like that for a week. But by the day of the demonstration I felt better.

...

At the anti-nuclear demonstration I yelled until I wore myself out. I cried out all my own individual desperation, my rage, my guilt. I yelled at my inability to unite my yells with the others, I hissed at the impossibility of my solidarity with a communal drama, because I had my own special cause with which no one in the world was able to offer solidarity.

"You're really carried away, Lònia," Jem looked at me a little surprised.

The other demonstrators were shouting calmly, with equal rhythmic shouts. I was out of tune. Just like when I sang in the parish choir. I did it with all my heart, like now. But I couldn't get into rhythm with the others. Like now, too. Because then we weren't singing the same tune, the other kids and me, and now we weren't shouting for the same reason, the other people and me.

"You're acting very weird," Lida said, as she rested her throat for a moment.

"I wish this demonstration was like the February '76 ones, in Barcelona."

"With police like that, too? Maybe you miss them?" Jem's tone seemed too paternal.

"You weren't there." I felt like hurting him, I didn't know why.

"I wasn't with you, but I was there."

"Why would you want it to be like them?" Lida asked.

I couldn't explain to them that I needed something physical, palpable, to cry out against. An invisible guilty conscience and a radioactive cloud weren't enough for me.

"Weird, really weird, Lònia," Lida said, while Jem again added his voice to those of the others. "Is it Maurice?"

"Maurice?" I barely remembered him now. "Oh, no, I don't . . . "

I stopped myself in time. I didn't want to confess my whole drama to her. Maybe I should. But aside from the shame, I didn't feel I had the right to burden her with my problems. If I told her everything, I'd be making her share a load that was mine alone to carry.

"So, things aren't going well with Maurice?"

"Yes, yes, they're going well . . . but it's not a lasting thing. He's a terrific person, but he's too young for me."

"Listen, Lònia . . . He's crazy about you. He's really in love, he adores you. I mean maybe it would be better to disillusion him in time."

No, please; not problems of that kind. Not right now. Who told him to fall in love with me, shit!? I wanted a temporary relationship, an agreeable, superficial relationship without difficulties, especially no sentimental implications beyond mutual sympathy—and the first complication that showed up, that would be it. Maybe it would be better to break now, before the first conflict appeared.

All around us there were waves of shouts and signals. Maurice, at my side, looked at us but he didn't understand what we were saying.

"Did you come to the demonstration to tell secrets or to protest nuclear plants?" he asked.

"Don't be jealous of me, Maurice," Lida answered laughing, and she started to shout the slogan that was now in the air around us.

At the end of the march, Lida said to me, "We've got a trip planned. One week. It would be good for you to come with us. And good for him too."

"When?"

"We leave the day after tomorrow."

No way. I had to find Cristina before she ended up like the granny and the cleaning lady. My hungover week may have been fatal for her. And it was me who had put her in danger. Me who had drawn attention to her. Going to Rutherford, then to the Gardener Agency, stealing from the files. Over and over again, I had taken a visible shot and missed. And now, only finding her could save her and uncover the whole rotten mess.

That is, if by that time we hadn't all been blown up together, Joil, Legs, Gardener, the Chameleon, the people from Majorca who sent the girls, the police here and there who were all involved in the case . . . as well as all of us who were demonstrating.

And to think I'd gone to the Antipodes for a change of air.

"I can't, this week we have the tests," I said.

"And then you'll have the title?"

"If I pass."

A ship-captain's title. I'd wanted that all my life, and now I might not ever have the chance to get it again. The hours I'd spent on the *Mallorquina* at sea would have been very useful to advance me in the course. If I'd kept going to the classes, and if I could go with Lida and Jem now, I could have the title in hand, as it were. But I was on board a different kind of ship—sailing in a sea of shit!—that I couldn't get off. So, another illusion down the drain.

VI

The days following the demonstration were long and boring.

I pored over every inch of the telephone books: last names, offices, businesses, streets. Nothing. I looked at city maps, maybe it was a neighborhood, a hill... Nothing. Maurice had a fairly good encyclopedia, but I couldn't find an entry in it. I spent hours watching television: maybe it was a brand; it could even be a religion: we Anabaptists organize benefits and talks, we Presbyterians have a terrific library in Balacrava, we Catholics offer psychic testing, we whatevers from Hartwell have just put new easy chairs in our center... every neighborhood, every belief, had its ads on TV just like the ads for pasta or for deodorant. Even the Chinese from Footscray and Little Bourke tried to sell Buddha. But Rossenhill wasn't a religion or sect. Rossenhill didn't exist. Without a clue, I went to the Melbourne Tourism Authority, in spite of the terror I felt at getting so close to Bourke Street.

"Rossenhill?" the receptionist said. "Is it in this state?"

"I don't know," I replied.

I was aware how illogical my question was; she assumed it was a place name and I didn't want to tell her I wasn't so sure. She consulted the screen, she typed... "maybe a park," I heard her saying to herself. But there was nothing, no park, no inn, no cliff, no hamlet. She checked with the terminals of other states, and found nothing. Finally she went to get a dictionary—maybe the old-fashioned method would turn something up—but no.

"Couldn't you give me a clue?" she asked, disappointed.

"I'm sorry... maybe it's not a place... " I suggested.

"What do you mean? Don't you know?"

"Not for sure," I cringed.

"You mean you don't know what you're looking for?" The girl's friendliness went up in smoke, and rightly so. "Then why did you let me do all that work without telling me?"

"I'm sorry. They told me to come to Rossenhill as if it were a well-known place... I looked at the street map and couldn't find it... I thought it must be a neighborhood or park, too."

"Maybe it's a restaurant." She turned nice again. The girl had a lot of moxie, like most of the Aussies who serve the public.

"Maybe so... or a business, or a cinema... But I haven't been able to find it there, either."

"Maybe it's the house of someone named Rossenhill," she conjectured.

It could be anything. But after a whole day's work she hadn't found anything. She said I should give her my telephone number and she would keep looking tomorrow, and if she found it she would call me.

"I don't have a telephone. I'll come by." I didn't want to take any more risks.

...

Things had started to turn sour with my young man the very day of the demonstration. Suddenly his attentions turned me off; his innocent hung-dog look exasperated me when he thought he wasn't getting enough attention from me. And the truth is that with all the rigmarole I was going through, it wasn't at all easy for me to be nice, or calm. The more affectionate he was, the more I withdrew. If you can't bring your bad humor home, where can you bring it? If you can't let off steam in your own home, you're not in your own home.

"You don't love me anymore," he said, pouting.

I spent the whole day at the State Library. From ten a.m. to ten p.m. I consulted encyclopedias, history books, geography treatises, anthropology manuals.

Rossenhill must be a ghost.

"You were talking in your sleep last night," Maurice said, surly because I hadn't felt like making love that night either.

"Really? What did I say?"

"Rossenhill."

I'll be damned.

Neither Maurice nor his friends at the radio station had ever heard that name. The girl at the tourist office hadn't been able to find anything either.

I went to the patent office; maybe it was a brand of some kind. The consultation was a little expensive, but it could turn something up.

"It'll take twenty-four hours," the clerk said. "If the name's not registered, do you want me to register it in your name?"

"No, no . . . I'll have to talk to my partners about it. But before I make the proposal and try to convince them it's an attractive and commercial name, I want to make sure it's original."

"Yes, I understand."

But it wasn't a brand of talcum powder, or cigarettes or lawn mowers. It wasn't the name of a high school, or an editorial house or a chain of hamburger joints.

It wasn't the name of a boat, either. At least, not of any that had churned those waters for the last five years, or had moored at any Australian port. They were very nice at the maritime clubs at Port Phillip, and so efficient that they took my breath away; they didn't miss a single sailboat or launch, not the tiniest little boat. They even had the windsurfers under control. Everything computerized, all connected with the terminals of the other maritime clubs throughout the island, and by telephone with even the smallest, most insignificant ports. It was amazing, and it was diabolical. You couldn't put an oar in the water without them knowing about it. You couldn't put a sail up without them finding out.

But Rossenhill was still a mystery. Because, naturally, it wasn't a nightclub in Carlton, or the name of any of the Pussy Cat Escorts advertised in the papers and entertainment and restaurant guides. That was the first thing I'd looked at, of course.

So I went back to Eltham worn out from uselessly looking for the mirage. In the little over six months I'd been in Melbourne, I hadn't pounded the pavement as much as I did during those days. Going from one errand to another, from one end of the city to the other, I read business signs, brands on counters, inscriptions on statues in parks, the labels on each tree announcing its name and origin. What galled me was that I couldn't shake the idea that it was all a big waste of time, and that time was closing in on me. But I was incapable of doing anything else but look without stopping, stubbornly, stupidly, obsessively. It was as if with that kind of idiotic penance, I would be forgiven for my foolishness.

In the evenings, sometimes late at night, I would come home to Maurice's totally wrecked. But that business about the warrior's rest doesn't work for women, even if we're the warriors. I was physically tired and psychically undone. My soul was in pain, soul or whatever it was: it hurt. The guy oscillated between complaining and being sticky sweet. If I had to choose, I'd choose the complaining, because when he embraced me, poor kid, I could see the granny wrapped up in the bathtub. And when he tried to penetrate me, I could see the silencer of the gun that had killed the cleaning lady.

One morning, very offended, he left for the radio station without saying a word. He came back that night with company: I had to sleep on the sofa.

I had to make a decision. With respect to my boyfriend and with respect to Cristina.

For the investigations, I could hire a local detective, who maybe wouldn't waste as much damn time as I was doing. In Barcelona, I'd have discovered in one day—I'm sure of it—what the hell Rossenhill was, even if it was the name that the mayor, or the most anonymous person, used to call his sled when he was a kid. In Barcelona I had friends who moved in all kinds of circles, I had people I could trust all over the place. I didn't have anything in Melbourne: just a kid it wasn't fun to fuck with any more, a couple of friends who were off sailing in who knows what sea and two unreported cadavers. I was a professional in Barcelona. In Australia I was a disoriented dope looking for ways to put my foot in my mouth. I had to make a decision; maybe I should try to speak to Alexia, it suddenly occurred to me.

I was afraid to get back in contact with any of those people, even if it was a poor hopeless woman like myself. That's why I spent I don't know how many days visiting museums—me, Lònia, who gets hives and rashes from going to museums—looking through catalogues and archives for the title of a painting or sculpture. And stupidly asking guards and sellers of reproductions if the name Rossenhill sounded familiar to them, or telling them that I wanted a painting called Rossenhill. And even more days gaping at the banks at the Yarra, trying to read the names of sailboats and canoes.

And in all those days I only bought one sad lipstick in the Greek quarter.

One night, Maurice got to be a real pain.

"Sorry, kid, but I just don't feel like it."

"There's another man," he said, convinced. I broke out laughing. It was such a ridiculous thing to say.

"Why don't you take classes any more? What do you do all day long then?"

"Are you spying on me? We made it very clear that neither of us would interfere in the other's life." I was up for a few cliches that evening, too.

"Well, I'm simply not willing to put up with this situation any longer," he said, full of dignity.

I was on the brink of losing my temper. I had to do something about that kid. I decided to take Lida's advice:

"I don't want to hurt you. But I'm not willing to be your babysitter."

"If you don't love me I'll kill myself."

"Up to you."

"Get out, then."

"I had already made up my mind. But I'll have to wait until the *Mallorquina* comes back. Surely you're not going to throw me out on the street."

"You can go to a hotel."

"They'll ask me for my visa."

"That's your problem."

"You're a big baby, Maurice. A spoiled brat."

Naturally, I left. First thing in the morning. And I was glad to be leaving behind that thumb-sucking kid.

Kathleen let me use the sofa in her apartment.

And that very day, in the afternoon, we got the news that the *Mallorquina* had returned to port. It was odd, Kathleen had commented. They always gave a few days notice by radio. I thought a storm must have cut short their strip to the Barrier Reef.

...

Early in the morning that same day, I'd called Alexia.

"Hello?"

I hung up. It was a man's voice.

It was the third time I'd called, and I still hadn't recognized Alexia's voice. I'd hung up all three times. I assumed that it wasn't at all normal for her to get phone calls, and I figured I could get her in trouble if I asked for her. And she was the only hope I had.

Finally, around noontime, I lucked out.

"Hello?"

It was her.

"Alexia?"

"Yes. Who speaks?"

"Hi, I'm Prostie," I said in English. "Remember me?"

"Yes, you had called . . . "

"Listen, today I'm free . . . we can talk if you like."

"Why do you want to talk?"

"Listen, I thought you wanted to . . . I told you I'd call you, and I did as soon as I could."

Silence.

"Alexia? Can't you talk. Is someone there?"

"I'm alone. But I don't trust you. I don't know you. I don't know what you want. There's no Prostie in the Rutherford Residence." Short sentences, because of her limited English.

She stopped talking. And I went back to the authoritarian tactic that had worked well the last time. It was a pity, but that's the way it was.

"You're an idiot, kid. Imagine asking about me! I'm not surprised you have problems, you go out looking for them yourself."

"I don't have problems."

"It seemed you did the other day."

"I didn't say anything. And I don't know who you are. I don't wish to speak to you."

"Why don't you hang up, then?"

She didn't hang up. Hearing her silence on the other end of the receiver, I changed tactics again.

"Listen, Alexia, it's not strange that they tell you there's no Prostie at Rutherford." In reality, there were lots of them, but she couldn't understand that; I wonder how you said whore in Greek. "I escaped. Joil... I just couldn't stand her any more."

I heard her sobbing, just like last time when I mentioned Joil. I decided to test whether my intuition was right.

"You either, right, Alexia? She's a beast, when she takes a fancy to a girl... " Sobs. "Listen, I want to help you."

"Why? Why do you want to help me?"

"Let's say... because I want to get even with Joil... and also because I want you to help me."

"Why? That would make it worse, if you helped me. They have me really trapped." More sobs.

"Look, I don't intend to continue talking over the phone. If you're interested, tell me and we'll set a time. You need me more than I need you."

You've got a nerve, Lònia. Silence. I risked again:

"Listen, what's Rossenhill?"

Silence. Does she know, or not?

"Okay," I finally heard her say. "What do you want me to do?"

"Can we see each other? Where?"

"I can't go out."

"Can I go in? Safely, that is?"

"Yes, through the little back alley."

"No tricks?"

"Right."

It may have been a setup, but I took the risk. Monash Street had the same elite air it'd had a few days before, the same sybaritic calm, the muffled sounds in the streets of the area; it was like an oasis, a little too exaggerated for my taste in cities, but the fact is that it inspired calm.

I went to the alley in the back like Alexia told me and entered the house from the rear. Alexia opened the door for me;

she looked like the negative of the photo in her file. Joil was an elegant lady, she seemed to have good taste: with so many pretty girls at her beck and call, I didn't understand why she'd taken a fancy to this human leftover.

"I like women," she confessed, ashamed. "But I've never liked Mrs. Joil. She knows it and can't stand it . . . she can't forgive me for that . . . it's like she's punishing me, you know? And now she really has me hooked."

"If you want, you can come with me." I couldn't tell her anything else, I couldn't leave her there.

"No . . . what would I do, out there?"

"Go to a detoxification center, to start with."

But there was no way to convince her. Maybe I didn't really want to convince her, deep down. Because if she said yes, what would I do with her?

"You can't stay here much longer," she said. "They won't be gone long. It would be dangerous to try and hide you. You said you wanted me to help you."

I showed her the picture of Cristina.

"Yes they brought her here a few times . . . She started to shoot up here. Then I didn't see her any more."

"What's Rossenhill?"

"That . . . "

"Do you mean this house? Osseto?"

"No, no . . . Here or some other place . . . When they know you don't have anyone in the world to come looking for you, when they start to shoot you up . . . You can't get out of Rossenhill."

So it wasn't a place, it was a situation. I could have looked for the rest of my life without ever figuring that out.

"Where do they keep them, the Rossenhill girls?"

"Scattered around. Me here, others in other places, I guess. It's almost eleven. You have to go," she said, and she got up.

"You don't want to come with me?"

She didn't want to come.

...

"My god, what on earth happened?" I said when I saw the *Mallorquina*.

The *Mallorquina* was unmasted, warped, the sails shredded, the rudder broken and a piece of oar substituted, the hatch low in the water.

How could they have arrived with the hole in the timbers? What kind of storm had they run afoul of? What sea monster had attacked them? Were there giants in these waters too, like in Majorca? I'd told them it was crazy to sail in May, but they'd said that that was the best time in the Coral Sea. Yes, but what about the getting there? More than three thousand kilometers by land, so going along the coast was even further... But they'd wanted to profit from those clients, and now...

Lida was sitting on deck, her face messed up and an arm bandaged; Jem was on the pier, frayed, one lip fat and the other split.

"What happened?" I repeated.

"They were after you," Jem answered.

"They thought I was you," Lida added.

"They don't want snoops, Lònia."

Halfway to the Tropic of Capricorn, between Sydney and-Brisbane, far from any help, a launch had approached them. The two men who were their clients had first seen to destroying the radio and throwing the life rafts overboard. Of the three men on the launch two had come aboard the *Mallorquina*. With the help of the two clients they made a shipwreck of the boat and left my friends for dead. The ones who'd beaten Lida up had told her that she wouldn't come snooping around any more. For sure, now. And she wouldn't have any memory left to remember Cristina with.

And when the five pirates had returned to the launch, they damaged the side of the boat. And then they took off, sure the boat would sink without fail.

"I don't know how we got back. I just don't know."

"Why didn't you go to the closest port?"

"When we entered Port Macquarie we saw the launch anchored."

As I took them to the hospital, I explained everything to them. I don't know whether they refrained from insulting me because they were too destroyed, or because they were such good people. But a good dressing down would have made me feel some relief.

"Poor Lònia, your wounds are even worse than ours," Lida said, instead.

Sometimes people say things like that. In another situation I would have burst out laughing, but now I started to cry.

"What do you intend to do?" Jem asked when he helped her get out of the car.

When I took them back—Jem, with a broken rib and three stitches in the lip; Lida, with a dislocated jaw and a split eyebrow; both of them pounded from head to foot—we continued the conversation.

They would continue at the radio station, and I would be in charge of the repairs to the *Mallorquina.*

And when we found Cristina, we'd make the necessary decisions.

I felt weird; it was as if all three of us had suddenly gone back to childhood and we were planning a guessing game or street strategy.

After I'd left Jem and Lida at the radio station, I returned the car. I could no longer allow myself the luxury of renting it or maintaining it.

Then I went to the local sailing school. It wasn't at all difficult to convince the monitor to let a group of students come and help us rebuild the *Mallorquina.* As practice. Without paying a red cent.

Finally, I went to hire a detective. It didn't have to be one of the most important agencies. In fact, it was better not to be. One of our friends from the radio station recommended one. Henry Dhul.

"His name sounds like a dessert," Jem had said.

And he turned out to be just as delicious.

...

Crazy Lonia,

Have you lost your mind, kid? Imagine telling me on a postcard, that's nerve! It's not that I need you here, your eyes would fall out at how I get rid of the work. I like you, what can I do? But I think it's total idiocy that you've decided to stay at the ass of the earth, for all I know it's a fat-assed guy, he can't be that great. What made you decide to stay? You'd already hinted in a letter that you'd like to stay, which I don't understand at all, to tell the truth. But what I understand even less is why the fuck you didn't get your papers straightened out in time? I don't know what nonsense you're talking about with the non-renewable visa. If instead of sending me a few words you'd have written a letter *comme il faut* maybe I'd understand what this is all about. In any case, I'm sure you could have found a better solution than becoming illegal. It's not that I have a weakness for legalities, but frankly, it seems to me (and it surprises me) that you think it's funny to be illegal. And the truth is that I'm not too sure what it all means. But I think you're making a mistake, Lònia, and that it's about time you started acting like an adult, you're old enough. It's as if you were afraid to be an adult: which doesn't necessarily mean distinguished and boring.

Okay, I'm hitting you with a sermon and I don't like it. Don't they say on your island, "You made the bed, you'll have to sleep in it?" Well, that's it. I'd just like to know how long the Antipodes madness is going to last, and what you're going to do then? And don't tell me what your friends think about it. Will they be able to help you if something happens? Or is something already happening? You have a way of getting yourself into a hornet's nest. I suspect you're in a heap of trouble and don't want to tell me. That's fine—go ahead and get in trouble and don't tell me about it. That way I'll be pleased as can be here in Barcelona. On the other hand, maybe you've found a boyfriend and now you don't want to have anything to do with me. When's the wedding? For that occasion, I would be willing to go down there. Ms. Paloni married! Stranger things have happened. You know something? A really strange thing has happened here, but I'm not going to tell you. If you want to know, you'll have to come back.

Oh, well, the hell with you. Here's a big hug, anyway. And I hope that as soon as you receive this letter, you'll write me one with all the gory details, right, sweetie?

Quim

VII

Lida almost convinced me that it had all been an accumulation of adverse circumstances and that things would have happened just the same even if I hadn't gotten mixed up in it.

"Please, Lònia, don't get swallowed up in your guilt complex. Yes, yes, of course, I absolutely agree that you've been a perfect idiot, but you were right. You have a professional nose—you sniffed around for Cristina and you smelled something rotten and you were right. We thought you were imagining it all, but no, it was true. You weren't an idiot about that, it's just that you thought Melbourne is like Barcelona and . . . "

"Mushrooms sprout up wherever it rains," I proclaimed.

"Okay, Melbourne is like Barcelona, but . . . "

"But I'm not the same Lònia in Melbourne as I am in Barcelona, that's the problem."

"Anyway, it wasn't you who killed the old lady and the cleaning lady."

"If it hadn't been for me, they'd be alive."

"That's enough, Lònia. Now it's a question of finding Cristina, and the detective will find her. Then we'll go to the police, as if it were our thing, without involving you . . . "

"It won't do any good: those guys have their backsides covered, and it's the police who are covering them."

"How do you know that? Because you saw one who got paid off in kind? In that case, it won't do us any good to report anything when we find Cristina."

"We'll have a witness. And our embassy to put on pressure.

Besides, there's the business about Majorca."

"Okay, when it's time we'll decide what to do. But don't you get involved any more."

I let myself be convinced: I needed it. I needed to be the know-it-all and let them spoil me like when I was little and had a stomach ache. Really, Quim was right: I'd never be an adult, and to tell the truth, that was fine with me.

Jem, on the other hand, came up with a gentle gesture: he gave me a lipstick on his own initiative.

"You worry about the *Mallorquina* and let this detective take care of finding Cristina," he insisted.

...

He was pushing forty, he was two fingers shorter than me, he had blue eyes and his skull was starting to show around the crown. He wasn't what you'd call really handsome, but he sure was sexy. As soon as I entered his office, I was taken with him. I'd never had a favorite type of man, but as soon as I saw him, I knew he was my type.

He took to me, too, right from the beginning. I realized it from the way he was looking at me; he tried to hide his attraction to me behind a professional pose and a cynical twist to his lips. And with that current of charm, it wasn't hard for us to come to an agreement.

"Would you like something to drink?" he said. "I don't have any alcohol . . . "

"Are you a teetotaler?"

"Vegetarian."

Magnificent coincidence! And very difficult, if not impossible, to find in our profession. He made a fruit shake for both of us, and in an atmosphere of relaxation and confidence, I told him the story with every detail:

". . . so my friends convinced me to put it all in the hands of a professional from here, that is, someone who knows the ins and outs of Melbourne, I mean the world of prostitution . . . It's not that I . . . well, what's necessary is to begin to look among the girls in the business and . . . Well, if I were in Barcelona, I wouldn't mind at all . . . I'd do okay, because I know expedients in that city . . . In fact, it wouldn't be the first time. I mean . . . "

He was staring at me, and I could have slapped myself for jabbering away like that. As if I was afraid to say something out of line! What I wanted to say, and wasn't saying, was that I, Lònia Guiu, couldn't go around from bordello to bordello, I couldn't call up the girls who put ads in the paper, I couldn't go down to Carlton with a picture of Cristina.

"I understand, Miss Guiu," he smiled at me with complicity, and maybe a little teasingly, seeing me so disconcerted. "Don't worry. I accept the job."

"Then I'll pass on to you all the information I've been able to gather so far."

"Very good."

"As for the fees... "

"Do you know the Marlow?" he cut me off with a fascinating smile.

"Not unless it's the... "

"No, it's not what you think. It's my favorite restaurant in Melbourne." His teeth were very white, and when he laughed, he had dimples in his cheeks. "A vegetarian restaurant, naturally."

So we talked about the conditions of the job and the fees over dinner.

"... we may not be able to afford your fees, Mr. Dhul.... "

"Don't worry," he said. And after a pause, he added with an expression that was trying to appear cynical, "If the parents of the girl are as rich as she says, we might assume that they'll be generous when we return them their daughter safe and sound. And please don't call me Mr. Dhul... I'm Henry. Do you mind if I call you Lonnie?" with the sweetest voice.

"Of course not!" I bristled with vanity.

Wait till Quim finds out!

"What I find strange," Henry said, "is that the parents haven't shown any sign of life yet."

"They're surely just as deceived as she is," I said without much conviction. "Maybe they've done some asking and I haven't found out."

Over dessert, attacking a tropical preserve with delight, he said, "I'm sorry you're in this situation. If you like, let's get married, and then you won't have any problems about illegality. Well, at the beginning you would, because the immigration people won't believe at first, since you're illegal, that we married for love, but . . . "

"The immigration people wouldn't be too far off base."

"Maybe so . . . but I offer myself as your husband for other reasons than to do you a favor."

"For what else?"

"Do you think it's possible to fall in love immediately?" His eyes were moist. I didn't believe he'd fallen in love with me at first sight. But I had. But I didn't accept his offer of matrimony. On the other hand, I did accept his offer to go to his place that night.

And with him, I didn't see the dead granny or the silencer on the pistol. With him I saw colored stars.

...

As long as we couldn't go back to live on the *Mallorquina* Kathleen had also offered provisional shelter to Jem and Lida at her place.

When Henry got up early to go to the Frankston Yacht Club the next day, I went to the radio station to notify Jem and Lida that Henry Dhul had agreed to search for Cristina and that I, from then on, would be staying with him.

"That's good news," Jem said, still a little incredulous. "At least we'll have more space."

"But I suppose we can still count on you to direct the work on the *Mallorquina*, right?" Lida asked.

"Naturally. I don't have anything else to do, except . . . "

"You don't have to explain your intimate life to us, sweetie," Lida teased. "I'm glad for you, kid. From yesterday to today you've changed from black and white to color. This guy Dhul must be a real man, huh?"

"You bet!"

"I'll be damned, Lònia! For ten years you've been saying you didn't have any luck with men and now they're raining down like cats and dogs! One after the other, and then some!"

"This one's different, you can believe it."

"Don't tell me you've fallen in love!" She said it laughing, like a mom whose ten-year-old daughter is telling her about a marvelous classmate.

"Well, I think so. This time yes... And another thing," I said solemnly. "Henry has found us a maritime club to put the *Mallorquina* in dry dock. He says it's not a good idea to keep it in the usual place."

"I see he's a sensible person, this Henry of yours."

He really wasn't at all. And just because of that I'd fallen in love with him.

...

The Frankston Yacht Club was super hotshot and very guarded. We didn't need to worry about Joil's men showing up there.

After breakfast, Henry'd go to his office in Collinwood, general headquarters for his investigations, and I'd take the train to go to the Yacht Club.

It was cold and it rained a lot, but the shipyard of the club was covered and the heat was high enough to bother you.

After lunch, the sailing students came to work. It was lucky that the monitor himself directed the works, because I'm not that good with my hands, and hardware isn't exactly my forté; but he gave me some specific jobs and I made an effort to do them as well as I could. That way I kept myself entertained and distracted. The physical work anesthetized my thoughts, just as Henry anesthetized my heart.

When Jem and Lida finished at the radio station—now they were doing extra hours to recover economically—they came too, often with someone from the group. Jem had laid a whopper of a story about storms on them, and since they hadn't a clue about waves, winds or boats, they'd swallowed it hook, line and sinker.

Among all of us, we made progress fixing up the *Mallorquina*. As a matter of fact, we had determined to leave it better than it had been before: since we were working on the framework, we might as well make new curtains, rearrange the furniture, redecorate, change the rigging... It was like making a doll's house, and more than a job it seemed like we were playing. If it hadn't been for Henry—his investigations, I mean—I surely would have forgotten about Cristina's letter and the deaths of the two women.

...

He had started with the Gardener Agency.

"They asked me if I wanted normal service or something special. Naturally, I asked for special service, everything included. They showed me a series of photographs and I picked one of a girl who looked Latin. One of the girls from the office drove me in her car to a house far from the center of town. No, it wasn't a white car."

"Listen, Henry, I'd prefer not to hear all the details." I felt a disagreeable harshness, which at first I didn't recognize as jealousy.

"As you wish . . . as a matter of fact it's not my professional style. I only make out a report when there's something interesting to report, and naturally I don't explain every step I've taken . . . but with you I thought I'd make an exception."

"Don't make any professional exception, then. In any case," I became a little mischievous, "make other exceptions, I like that better. I want you to work according to your own style. I wouldn't interfere for anything."

I could tell by his satisfied face that he like my attitude. Better for both of us.

...

Henry was sort of Bohemian. His apartment was chaos, it took me a week to discover that the refrigerator was a good place to keep the iron and that the teapots looked nice on the shelf of the photo lab; and that in the medicine cabinet, naturally there were not only medicinal herbs, but also a stamp collection. He had no idea what shirts, socks and pants went together, but he knew a lot about painting. He was obsessed with body hygiene, but he hated to brush his teeth.

Every day, at some point, whether he picked me up at the Frankston Yacht Club or I went to get him at Collinwood, whether he was already at home when I finished working on the *Mallorquina* or I had to wait for him until late at night, he always brought me flowers.

But he diligently kept our agreement not to tell me details about his work. So much so that at times I was the one who tried to loosen his tongue. That way, I found out that he spent a lot of time going from bordello to bordello, trying to link up the threads of the Gardener-Rutherford network. I also found out that he had a surfer friend who worked at immigration, and that friend had found some suspicious material, not registered, in the office of a higher-up.

"What kind of material?" I asked.

"Didn't you say you wouldn't get involved in my work?"

He said it smiling, but I could see that my interference bothered him. I decided not to ask any more questions, no matter how much my curiosity was gnawing at me.

But, he told me anyway that it had to do with false documentation of visas, comings and goings of people, mostly of the female sex, curiously.

"We need to find out whether it's related to some prostitution ring." he said.

"Can't I help? I could watch the fat cat... "

He didn't want me to. I had my job and he had his. My mother never wanted anyone to come into her kitchen, he said. I didn't insist. He was proud of his work, and I didn't want him to think I didn't have full confidence in him.

But I had the impression that the task of finding Cristina had become secondary for him, and a kind of professional jealousy was added to my sentimental jealousy. I shook my head hard to get rid of disagreeable thoughts.

...

The *Mallorquina* only needed a few finishing touches. My romance with Henry was going along with wind in the sails. But I was starting to get nervous.

"Lonnie, what's wrong? Are you angry?"

"No, I'm not angry. And don't call me Lonnie, dammit! My name is Lònia, do you hear? They named me Apol.lònia when I was born and I don't like it. In my town they call me Polita, which I didn't like either. Quim insists on calling me Paloni, which drives me crazy. And you make me feel ridiculous with Lonnie. My name is Lònia, understand? Lònia!"

"Okay, sweetie, okay."

And then I really felt ridiculous. Love had made me lose my dignity.

"I'm sorry, Henry... it's just that when you come so late, or you don't come, I worry about you."

It wasn't true. I assumed he knew how to take care of himself. And Aunt Antònia had always said that you should never show a man your jealousy.

"But I've never let a single day go by without getting in contact with you, precisely so you wouldn't worry."

It was true: he always called me at the Frankston, when he was going to be late or not come. But now I'd gotten used to sleeping with him, and sleeping alone was painful.

"I'm not worried now," I said.

"It won't happen again, I swear it."

That night he more than made up for it.

It would have been easier to just tell him to let it go, that Cristina could go jump in a lake; that we should get married and work together on new cases where we wouldn't be so involved, so we could separate the job from love.

But I couldn't do it. Not only for Cristina, but also for the old lady and the cleaning lady.

...

To celebrate the launching of the *Mallorquina* we threw a top-notch party. Jem and Lida's group came, plus some others from the radio station I'd never even seen. The gang from the school had put so much confetti and so many streamers around that it was impossible to see how nice the boat looked, so different, painted blue and orange and with the letters even changed to a new style. A group from the Yacht Club came too, and the manager gave us a bottle of Coonawarra for the rechristening, which our friends refused to break against the side of the ship and insisted on making Jem, Lida and me drink.

Some of Henry's friends came, too. The ex-surfer, of course—us Aussies are all either surfers or ex-surfers, he said amid general laughter—two sometime collaborators of his, an old guy who looked like a gold prospector who everyone called uncle, and a girl as ugly as sin.

"It looks like he realized you're jealous," Lida teased me when I introduced her. "By the way, where is he?"

"He's been whoring around lately," I said, surly.

"Come on, Lònia, don't be an ass," Lida said.

"I can't take it any more, shit! I try to hide it, and I'm plenty embarrassed about being jealous. I never would have thought this would happen to me . . . And the silliest thing is that I'm sure he doesn't do anything with those girls. But when I think about him hanging around those places, and that he's doing it because of a job I asked him to do, I wish I'd never met Cristina . . . When I even think about him looking at another woman my hair stands on end. I've got it bad!"

"Then don't think about it, dumbshit!"

"What are you whispering about, looking like thunderclouds?" Jem came up to us sporting a gold paper hat and a party whistle. "Lònia, are you trying to spoil our party? Isn't Henry coming?"

"Sure, he'll come!" Lida said. "You sure have a way of saying the right thing, pal!"

"What's wrong?" We didn't answer. "You know what I think, Lònia? You ought to marry Henry. Now come on, come on!"

We rejoined the party. I tried to have a good time, but seeing people making fools of themselves depresses me. For distraction, I starting thinking that it was a pity Jem and Lida had fixed up the *Mallorquina* just now, when it was getting really cold, and it had been so cozy in the covered shipyard. I was lucky I had Henry's apartment, which was small but comfortable, with heat, and I wouldn't have to get used to the rocking of the *Mallorquina* again, swaying out there in the wind, though they'd put a heating system in it too and Jem and Lida were happy with it. Maybe I should marry Henry, like Jem said, but thinking about marriage makes me break out in hives, although, what difference does one more document make? After all I couldn't go on living with him my whole life without a visa or resident documents, they could catch me and throw me out of the country at any moment, and then what?

"What are you thinking about?" his voice made my ears tickle.

"Henry!"

"It looks like these people are having a good time. How come you're so sad?"

I realized there was a royal ruckus going on and I hadn't made any effort to join in.

"I'm not sad," I hugged him. "I missed you."

He gave me a great big hug, too.

"T'estimo." I'd taught him to say it in Catalan. "And I have good news," he went on in English. "I think I've found her."

"Who?"

He laughed. Who was he supposed to find? I laughed too. At that moment, the person least on my mind in the whole world was Cristina.

VIII

"Okay, so I can't infiltrate the cathouses unless it's as a whore, and that's why I hired you. But I can do other things. I can do tailing, for example. I could go to the travel agency they used to hire the *Mallorquina* and see what I could find out there. I could go to that fabulous newspaper library you have in Melbourne and research the news about... "

"No, Lonnie. I don't want you to. We agreed very clearly that you had your job and I had mine, and that there wouldn't be any interference."

"Listen, Henry, I don't want to interfere in your job, that was clear from the beginning. You're in charge of the case, I'm just offering to help... to do whatever you tell me... You have your job, but it happens that I've finished mine. The *Mallorquina* is finished and there's no trip planned until winter is over. Five days ago you said you thought you'd found... "

"It isn't very nice for you to throw that bit of bad luck in my face."

"I'm not saying it because of that! I'm saying it because for the last five days I've spent my time straightening up your house, ironing your shirts, shopping and cooking... and I'm sick to death of it! I don't like it, I'm bored, and I feel stupid... Besides, I don't want you to support me."

"If we got married I'd be supporting you."

"No, that's out of the question. If we get married, we'll run the business together. Now, the business belongs to you, and

I'm grateful that you're not charging anything until we return Cristina to her home, but if in addition to that you have to support me too... "

"It's a pleasure to support you, love."

"Not for me. It's... "

"Do something else."

"Who's going to give me a job, with an expired visa?"

"Study English."

"I know enough already. But why the devil don't you want me to help you? Would you mind telling me?"

"It's just that, look, darling, the truth is that I don't think it's a job for a woman."

Oh, fuck!

"What do you mean?" I said like an idiot.

"Just what I said. There are jobs for men and jobs for women. And private investigator is not a job for a woman. I wouldn't like for you to go back to it."

I froze, completely unable to react. If Mercè had heard that, she would have scratched his eyes out for sure. But I was in love with him and my only feeling was bewilderment. As much for his way of thinking—which I never would have suspected—as for his refusal of help that would have rushed the job along. We would have found Cristina and solved the whole murky riddle too.

"Well, I have to go now," Henry said, and he kissed me on the cheek.

Was it my imagination, or was it true that he seemed less passionate the last few days? Nice, and gentle, yes. But more distant, like distracted. Did he feel like a failure, maybe? He'd been so sure, the night of the *Mallorquina's* party, that he'd found Cristina. But the next day, when I was waiting at the house, sure he'd confirm the good news, he'd returned down and depressed. It had been a false hope. The contact who'd recognized her in the photograph had deceived him. And someone had laughed at him for confiding in that scoundrel, known in the underworld for tricking the gullible.

That was the time he did the most explaining. Maybe that was why he didn't want me to stick my nose in. Not to have a witness—professional and therefore critical—to his goofs.

That same evening, looking like he was pissed at the world, he presented me with a typewritten report.

"It's still provisional," he said dryly, and then sat in the armchair to read the paper.

The fat cat in immigration was a member of the administrative council of an international transport agency. It was a semipublic business based in Victoria, and therefore controlled and unstained. But it had commercial relations with a similar private business in Sydney which made irregular trips, mostly to Singapore and New Guinea. There had been complaints in the Parliament of New South Wales, discovered by Henry in that fabulous newspaper library, precisely because of the commercial connection. Turns out that the company in Sydney was being accused not only of fiscal fraud, but also of transporting very unusual merchandise—persons. After the scandal, more than a year ago, they closed down the administrative council altogether, and the president, Mrs. Gaynor, ended up in the clink.

Henry had enclosed a photograph of Mrs. Gaynor. If she wasn't the twin sister of Mrs. Gardener, she was the same person.

Mrs. Gaynor-Gardener had been exonerated half a year ago and had become the manager of a matrimonial agency, property of Joil's ex-husband, who was a close friend of the department head of public relations of a ministry in Victoria, who was a regular client of the Rutherford residence. The girls acted as hostesses at all the symposiums, conventions and meetings of that ministry.

I didn't say a word when I finished reading the report. Even though I'd dedicated most of my professional life to much simpler cases, I also had some experience with complications like that one: it wasn't new to me. From the day of my visit to the Rutherford residence, from the day I'd talked to Joil, I'd known the case was mired in a lot of shit. Underneath deals like that, there's always someone with power who protects them and benefits from them. If there weren't that someone, they couldn't exist. Pure logic, right?

But I wasn't used to being a detective's client, and it was driving me crazy to find out just the results. In fact, knowing the results without knowing the process that had brought them about seemed like a cheap trick. In a way, I didn't believe that story. I really felt left out. I didn't give a shit.

And I was sure that the charming man I was so in love with felt the same way about Cristina as I did about her fairy tale. Because he didn't even mention her in the report. He didn't give a shit about finding her, surely because he was more interested in what he'd discovered himself. That's why he hadn't found her.

I felt frustrated, cheated. I gave him back the report without saying a word.

Lònia, that's spite. You resent Henry for not wanting you to work with him and you're looking for self-justifications because of it: that he doesn't want you to see his failure, that he's not interested in the case. But in fact, the explanation is much simpler: Henry's a Neanderthal. He's a chauvinist, that's for sure. And I thought, how Mercè is going to make fun of me, when she finds out. But Mercè is never going to find out that I fell in love with a rotten patriarch, because I'm sure not going to tell her.

On the other hand, there could be another explanation: that he doesn't love me anymore. He hasn't brought me flowers for five days, and jealousy is eating at me. He must have found some gal who fucks better than I do, and he must think I'm a jellyfish.

"Do you want to eat?" I growled.

We ate in silence. Afterwards, he didn't even help me clear the table. When the little dining room was straightened up, I went to bed. If that night he'd even mentioned wanting to play around, I'd have sent him straight to hell. But when he came to bed, I was offended; he didn't even give me a chance to reject him. I squirmed.

"Aren't you asleep?"

"No."

"I think you're exaggerating, darling. The report is only provisional, I told you."

"To hell with your report, damnation! I didn't hire you to investigate some Australian scam, but to find a Majorcan girl. What have you found about Cristina? A false lead. How long have you been working on this case? I'd have had it finished in Barcelona ages ago! And then you say it's not women's work, what a nerve! Of course you don't want me to interfere... to find a few obvious things I suspected from the beginning, all that professionalism wasn't necessary, fuck!"

"Listen, I'm real tired, we'll talk about it tomorrow, okay?"

It takes two for a good fight.

...

I felt a strong blow inside my brain, like a noise heard in a dream, and I jumped. But everything was quiet and dark. Henry was sleeping deeply at my side. I closed my eyes.

But then I heard footsteps. And I felt a presence in the dark. I wasn't dreaming. Someone had come in.

I turned on the night table lamp. It wasn't one presence, it was two.

The blow I'd felt on the inside as a premonition became real, delivered right on the cranium.

When I came to, the body of a man thrown with force crushed me into the cushion. Henry had thrown that body toward me, and now he was fighting with another body, which had him by the arms and was holding him against the wall. I rolled the man who'd fallen on top of me on to the floor and then jumped on top of him, all stretched out like a sack of potatoes. I ran to Henry and delivered a rabbit punch to the assailant, who fell, spread out on the floor. But he'd already had time to leave Henry dazed, so I found myself with three men fallen at my feet, like three dainty damsels in a faint.

Henry had a lump on his forehead, but he revived right away.

"Thank you, honey," he said without looking at me, and he took the pistol out of the holster.

It drives me crazy to be called girl, and even more to be called honey. It was the first time Henry'd called me that, but I didn't complain. There were more important things to do, like wake up these scoundrels and get rid of them.

"Okay, now it all comes together. The truth is that I really didn't believe it," Henry said.

"What comes together?"

"The trafficking in women with the drug trade."

"That always goes together. It's a recipe for beginners," I said scornfully.

"Yes, but it's not so easy to put in exactly the right ingredients."

"If you explained it to me, maybe I'd know what you're talking about. Whether you like it or not, I'm a colleague, and it wouldn't be at all hard for me to understand. Besides, I think I recall that you're working for me . . . it wouldn't be out of place for you to let me know how things are going, instead of limiting yourself to a provisional report."

He flashed me his most charming smile. "Are you still mad?"

"Do you know them?" I asked instead of answering.

"No, but I guess I shouldn't have done it, it was a mistake on my part. . . . " What was he talking about? "Before I came home, I went to the morgue . . . they told me there was an unidentified girl, dead from an overdose. I don't think it was your friend, but it was Rossenhill for sure."

One of the thugs was starting to come around. With a gesture, Henry indicated that I should hide in the kitchen, and he helped them along with light kicks.

"It's better if they don't see you," he said, paternally.

From the kitchen I could hear Henry ordering them to get up and asking them what they wanted him for. They didn't want anything from him, they just wanted to warn him not to stick his nose in other people's business. Henry: "Where have I stuck my nose?" He knew well enough.

I thought I'd mastered the Australian variation of English. But the truth is that I lost the better part of that conversation.

"That means I'm on the right track," Henry said in the kitchen doorway, after he'd made them leave at the gunpoint. With one of his charming smiles, he said, "You're not mad any more?"

"I'm sorry, Henry . . . sometimes I act like a kid, I know."

"I love you," he said without moving from the door frame.

"Ets una monada," I said to him in Catalan.

"What?"

Suddenly I was overcome with a wild desire to hug him, but

I held back. I could tell from his face that if I did, we'd leave the house very late that day. So I started to make coffee.

"Have you figured out who they were?" I asked.

"Weren't you listening?"

"I was all ears, but I didn't pick much up. It sounded like they were talking with their asses."

"They told me to tell whoever I'm working for not to be so curious, that everybody would end up paying for it, and for us to stay in our own zone—they think I'm working for another clan... I already figured that there was some kind of internal warfare going on. The eternal rivalry between Sydney and Melbourne. I told them I didn't know what they were talking about, all I wanted was to get high with a little powder and a girl who was up for anything without making a fuss, at a good price. Naturally they didn't believe me. They said that a P.I. is never to be trusted because no matter how much of a son of a bitch he is, he always keeps a smattering of honesty. And when I told them I'd go to the cops, they laughed. They don't have any fear of that. They said that if I did, I'd end up in even worse shape."

"They all say that."

"And it's always true. Anyway, I told them I didn't like this kind of visit and I was getting tired of the conversation. To take off if they didn't want me to really start dishing it out. And that I'd keep looking until I found what I was looking for. And they left."

"Without asking any more questions?"

"It's not much fun to ask questions when someone's pointing a gun at you."

"What are you going to do now?"

"Well, for the moment, keep on the same track, more cautiously. They don't suspect that I'm looking for a specific girl, and that gives me some leeway of time and movement without putting Cristina in danger. She is in danger, though. Not only her, but all the Rossenhill girls. There's a batch of adulterated stuff in circulation. Legs is one of the clients, because it came from that dealer I told you about, remember?

"Yes," I said, not too convinced.

Because the fact was that it was the first time I'd heard anything about adulterated drugs of "that dealer."

"They already killed him, but the adulteration wasn't his doing, it was from Sydney."

"From that transport company?"

"I'm not quite sure yet."

"Why didn't you explain all that in the preliminary report?"

"Listen, Lonnie darling. . . I'm sorry, but it might be just as well, at least until things are cleared up, well, maybe you could go back and stay at the *Mallorquina* for a few days. They'll follow me everywhere and it would be best if they didn't see me accompanied, besides it could be dangerous for you."

...

It was even harder than the first time to get used to living on a boat. When a person's in the sorry frame of mind I was in—wishy-washy, that is—things that seem acceptable one day, maybe even marvellous, might seem a punishment another day. The constant splashing of the water drove me crazy. The scintillating streaks of sunlight on the table hypnotized me. The humidity set inside the marrow of my bones and all my muscles ached from trying to maintain balance against the incessant rocking of the hull. Luckily the heating system worked perfectly and I couldn't complain about the cold, but I couldn't stand the idea that at the beginning of June it was the middle of winter. I started to get homesick. I bet the sycamores in Barcelona were covered with leaves and those trees on Consell de Cent Street—what were they called?— must be giving off that mysterious and sensual odor. The pergolas on Rambla Catalunya must be full of people sipping *Orxata* in the evenings, and the shop windows would be stuffed with summer clothes. And in Majorca, the beaches would still be empty, with the water warm and the sand clean and white. And here I was, inside a boat anchored at the bottom of the world, short on space and economic possibilities, dying of revulsion and boredom. And I couldn't complain to Jem and Lida; I'd put them out plenty by coming back to stay with them.

I didn't tell them, either, that Henry wouldn't let me work with him. I was ashamed. Even though I tried to convince myself that it had been a subterfuge of his to keep me out of danger. But what if it was true that he didn't like women being detectives? What would happen then, when that case had been solved? Would I go back to living with him, would I get married to solve my problem, then watch him go back to work while I looked for some other kind of job? Even if we got married, they wouldn't give me resident status right away, so I still wouldn't be able to get a job. What was I going to do in the meantime? After all, I had a profession. More than once I'd cursed the moment I'd decided to dedicate myself to it. As a matter of fact I was in Australia right now because one day I'd wanted to leave it all behind; sometimes in Barcelona I rejected the whole business. But then, all alone on the *Mallorquina* with the rain drumming on deck and making little bubbles on the surface of the water, I concluded that leaving a job of your own free will was one thing, and leaving it for someone else's was quite another.

But when Henry came to see me, somehow I never found the right moment to bring up the question. In fact, I was afraid that he would confirm that he hadn't said it because of the circumstances, but that he really believed it. Because if he really did, I'd have to tell him to get lost. I was sure I'd regret it, but I was also sure that I wouldn't throw in my cards. Someone wanting me to do something was enough for me to not want to do it.

Besides, whenever he came, either Jem and Lida were there or else he got a phone call.

"Couldn't we see each other in another place, Henry, or couldn't you come at another time?"

"Lonnie, I feel as bad about it as you do, but I come when I can, and I never know whether I can come until I actually get away. I'm about to find her, this time for sure."

"I've been here for a week, disgusted with everything."

"There's no need for you to stay here all day long, darling."

"I don't feel like going out, with this weather, besides, you wouldn't find me here when you did come."

"If you want, I won't come for a few days, and then you'll feel freer."

He said it innocently, nicely, but my insides turned over.

"Okay, that's a good idea," I said, nicely, too. My resentment got the better of me. "Don't come until you've found Cristina."

...

"For Christ's sake, go see him, or call him," Lida told me.

"Me? No. When I'm working, I'm the one who goes to see my clients, they don't come to see me."

"But Henry's more than a professional whose services you've hired, dammit."

"We agreed that he'd contact me when he'd found Cristina. I can't make a move to see him because it might spoil everything."

"He didn't say that. What if something happened to him?"

"Like what? Maybe he got involved with one of those whores, maybe that's what's happened to him."

"Don't be such a fucking baby," Lida said. "Love has really deranged you, shit! If you won't call him, I will... "

"Don't you dare!"

"You'll see if I dare. We're his clients too, in a way. I'm worried about Cristina too, don't forget. What an asshole, Jesus Christ!"

I couldn't help laughing.

"You sure have a dirty mouth, Lida," I said.

But we didn't need to call. The next day, just before Lida and Jem left for the radio station, Henry showed up at the *Mallorquina.* I resisted the impulse to hug him and played the hard-ass. Nor did he make any effort to soften me up.

"I found her yesterday," he said. "I paid for her services tonight: a menage à trois, me, my wife and Lola."

"What are you talking about? Who's Lola? Your wife?" I answered, alarmed.

"Lola is Cristina. They've changed her name, of course. And you're my wife, naturally!"

"What the hell!"

"That's the only way you'll get to talk to her, Lonnie. It won't arouse any suspicions."

"Now I'm not so sure I want to talk to her."

"Dammit, Lònia, if you don't go, I will," Lida chimed in. "Don't be pigheaded."

"She's really hooked," Henry said. "If we don't get her out of there, it'll be too late."

"Then why haven't you saved her yourself?"

"She'll only talk to you. She's refused to say anything to me."

I gave in, against my will. And my self-esteem kept me from asking Henry for an explanation for the ten days I hadn't seen hide nor hair of him—why he hadn't called, why he'd abandoned me without showing a sign of life. I was dying to know how he'd finally found Cristina, my curiosity was both professional and morbid. But I didn't ask a single question. And he didn't make a move to give me any explanations.

"We'll meet at the Royal Park an hour before the time. Four o'clock," said Henry.

"What a time for a three-way toss in the hay!"

IX

It was raining cats and dogs, and the arbor at the Royal was dripping all over the place. We had a cup of tea and got a taxi. I didn't say a word the whole trip, no matter how nice Henry was trying to be. It wasn't just that I was mad at him. I was nervous, afraid, insecure. Maybe Henry was right in thinking that women weren't good detectives.

It was a darling cottage-type house, with porches all around and railings of carved wood. Next to the stairs to the porch, there was a willow without leaves that replaced my rage and fear with a soft and deep sadness. But Henry was already opening the door and I didn't have time to reflect on my sensations.

Henry headed straight for a room ahead of me, without anyone either welcoming or hindering us.

"Isn't there any reception in this house?" I asked, and it came out in an ironically bold tone.

"There never are in these places. You make the date ahead of time and they're waiting for you."

Cristina was waiting for us in the room with her head buried in a pillow. Her left arm was covered with tracks.

Henry stood in front of the bed, white as a sheet, with his fists clenched so tight his knuckles were about to burst.

The air conditioning was on full blast.

My God!

I was about to turn the body over to see the face, but Henry grabbed me and led me away from the bed. Then I realized that my legs were jelly and everything seemed to be flying around me. Henry, completely unglued, made me sit in an armchair at the other end of the room.

I couldn't hold back the tears. I didn't feel anything: not pain, fear, rage, or remorse. The crying was a physical release, a tension built up over a long time that finally came bursting forth on its own.

Henry returned to the bed and turned the body face-up. From the armchair I could see Cristina's disfigured face.

"Animals," his voice was a thread. "What a beating, poor girl."

"They beat her up?"

Henry looked at her arms.

"I'm not sure... I'd say that it's been hours since she shot up, or they shot her up... That's why the air conditioning is on."

"Is it the adulterated stuff?"

"Maybe. Lonnie," he was standing right in front of me, sweating, "We should get out of here right away, it could be a trap, or they might come any minute to take her away."

He wiped away the sweat. Poor Henry felt so guilty that I didn't dare tell him everything I was thinking. Because, of course, I thought he was to blame. If instead of trying to uncover the whole network of traffic in women and drugs, if he'd just concentrated on finding Cristina... But after all, wasn't that what he'd done? Things don't always turn out the way we want them to.

Yes, we had to get out of there; we couldn't do anything for her now. Once again, I'd gotten there too late. But this time it wasn't my fault. Or was it?

By the time I got up, the artificial cold had frozen my body. Or was it a natural cold, my own cold, that was freezing me? Henry covered Cristina's body and face with sheets: a useless gesture, the gesture of a good person which made me love him even more than before.

I leaned on the headboard of the bed, and the cold of the metal made me aware that my hands were boiling. The cold I was feeling was coming from inside.

Henry took me by the waist and pulled me out of the room. At the doorway, he turned toward the bed again and stopped suddenly. I turned around too and looked where he was pointing: there was a letter on the night table.

I rushed over; the envelope was just like the one she had left for me on the boat. The same handwriting, the same address in Majorca.

We went out the same way we came in. This time I did read the letter, during the taxi ride back.

...

"It doesn't seem like you, but I think you're doing the right thing," Lida told me.

Because according to Lida, my most natural reaction, after finding Cristina dead and reading the letter, would be to go to Majorca and snoop around. Instead, I had decided to abandon everything related to Cristina and Majorca, stay in Melbourne, marry Henry, and start what they call a new life.

This time it had been a final blow. If you can't prevent the death of a person who asks you for help, like Sebastiana, it's kind of a hatchet job on the soul that you get over by going to the Antipodes. But when the same thing happens in the Antipodes, with two other useless deaths besides, you don't get over it even with the help of an instinct for vengeance.

When Henry found Cristina and told her I'd go see her, she wrote me a letter: a sign that she trusted me. I was the only one she could trust, at the end of the earth, and I'd failed her, like I'd failed Sebastiana.

I'd gone to Australia to look for the opposite of what I had in Barcelona, and it turned out I'd found exactly the same things. A detective agency just as full of bravado as mine, a girl killed by others, but a death that was really my fault. And because of it, an unlimited desperation. But with one major difference: Henry. And now that I was seeing that he was just as overcome as I was myself, I loved him more than ever. All the jealousy of the previous days, all the mistrust, all the rage because he wouldn't tell me what he was doing, had all disappeared.

"What does Henry have to say?" Lida asked.

Henry had proposed that I go to Majorca, either alone or with him. This death can't go unpunished, he'd said, and it sounded to me like something a cheap detective would say. Besides, there could be other deaths, and his conscience dictated that he unravel the whole scheme he'd discovered between Melbourne and Sydney. In Majorca, I could find one of the major threads of the network, and as a Majorcan, I must be interested in exposing the part of the network anchored on my island.

He almost had me convinced. In fact, his friend who worked in Immigration falsified my expired visa so I wouldn't have any problems at customs when I left the country. But I felt tired, worn-out, beaten. So I used up my remaining strength to make the decision to stay.

"Don't you think it's better to turn them in from here?" I'd asked Henry. "I think that, with all the information we have, there's more than enough to untie the knots, here, there, or anywhere they might be."

He believed that there were still some questions that could only be answered from my island, and besides, he was convinced that if we made what we knew public in Australia, the threads of the network would be broken and the Majorcans involved wouldn't be touched. But:

"I don't want to insist," he finally said. "I don't want to interfere. You have to do what you think best . . . "

What I thought best was that I should move back in to his house, and that's what I did. He started to arrange for a legal marriage.

Jem was surprised at my decision, too, but he thought I was right. He asked me if he could be a witness at the wedding and I felt comforted.

...

"Miss Lònia Guiu?"

Henry'd told me not to open the door for anyone, but I wasn't willing to live in hiding.

I should have listened to him.

The man let me make one phone call, but Henry wasn't in his office in Collingwood. He let me make another call, but Henry's friend who worked at Immigration was on vacation. The man let me make a third call; they put me on hold at the radio station because Jem and Lida were on the air. We listened to the Catalan program until the end—he was getting a little antsy—and then I called again.

"Lida," I said, trying to sound unworried. "You can tell Jem he can't be the witness at my wedding, for the moment. I have a pal from Immigration here. Within half an hour they'll have me on board a plane."

"What the fuck? It can't be! What happened? What did you do? Where are you calling from? I'm coming right away!"

"There's no time. This clown I have in front of me has been pretty patient so far, but he's starting to fret. He's showing me the plane ticket paid for by the government of Victoria to throw me out of the country."

"Can't Henry do anything?" Lida's voice was desolate; for sure neither she nor Jem would be able to do anything.

"He's not in his office. I couldn't find him. Tell him this evening and he'll decide what's to be done."

"What do you mean, what's to be done?" Lida yelled from the other end of the telephone. "He'll have to go get you in Barcelona, and you'll have to have the papers ready to get married. That way you won't have any problems coming back."

"Yes, I suppose that's what we'll do."

"And above all, Lonieta, don't get involved in any shit in Barcelona while you're waiting for Henry, understand? Understand?" she repeated.

"Yes, yes. I won't go to Majorca, if that's what you mean."

"Just understand me. Forget about Cristina and the whole mess. Maybe you'll pay attention to me for once."

"Yes, yes, I will."

But I knew I was lying to her. Because if I'd been planning to pay attention to her, I wouldn't have tried to take the papers I'd robbed from the Gardener agency with me, or Henry's reports. But I couldn't, because there weren't any papers at the house. They were all at Henry's office. All I could take was Cristina's letter.

...

I read the news story from *The Age* a thousand times on the plane:

"Drug addict found dead. The autopsy has shown an overdose of heroin. The police still haven't been able to identify her."

Nor would they.

"She seems to have been Latin, about eighteen years old. She probably entered the country illegally."

What a sad obituary. She'd been so happy, so satisfied about her Australian adventure nine months ago. Poor crazy kid.

And other news:

"Fire on a yacht in Melbourne Bay." That headline made my heart leap with fear, but a quick glance at the story made it jump for joy: it wasn't the *Mallorquina*.

"A fire was started this morning on the yacht Rossenhill, bearing an Australian flag. All the occupants were saved. An unusual crew: a dozen girls, presumably Indonesians, with no documentation whatever. They confessed to having started the fire themselves, in order to escape. The police are investigating."

I thought it was odd that the yacht hadn't appeared on any of the computerized lists when I was looking for Rossenhill. I was sure the police investigation wouldn't turn anything up. I was sure, too, that Henry would investigate.

And once again I read Cristina's letter to her father:

> ". . . or have you already forgotten that you have a daughter? I don't understand at all, Papa. I came here to go to school: you didn't want me to, I know, but I can't believe that you're so angry that you could abandon me like this. What's going on? Papa, the place my uncle found for me is no school. It's a bordello, Papa, a terrible place. I can't understand why you haven't come to get me. I came here for six months. And if I'm counting right, it's been nine or ten months already. I don't know if I'll last another one. I'm very sick. They give me drugs, you know? I can't get by without it now, so they can make me do whatever they want. I can't understand what has happened. Don't you find it strange that I write so little? Didn't you get my letter? I gave it to a Majorcan girl to send to you. Maybe she didn't mail it. I'm going to see her again today and I'll give her this one. I can't send letters, or telephone. I'm a prisoner, Papa. They watch me day

and night. They took all my documents. They changed my name. Know what they call me now? Dolores. I'll ask that girl to call you, too. And I'll tell her that if anything happens to me, to go see you and explain everything to you. You'll pay for her trip. But if you don't remember that you have a daughter, or you don't want to hear anything about her, only the girl who's coming can save me. But I can't believe that. So why don't you come to get me?"

Then I dozed off. The words Rossenhill, Gardener, Henry, Rutherford, Joil, Cristina, Cala Mura all danced in front of my closed eyes. And especially Munditourist, the name that was on so many of the files, with an address in Majorca.

“It just isn’t done, Lònia.”

Quim was making such a face that I couldn’t help but laugh.

“Go ahead and laugh.”

He was frankly angry, and rightly so. I hadn’t told him I was back, I just showed up in the office unexpectedly. I went in without knocking: there was a sign on the door that said “come in” and I came in.

Quim was seated at my desk—rather, in the place where my desk had been: because what was there didn’t look like a desk, it was one of those pieces of junk that instead of having legs has inclined surfaces at angles every which way whose main function seems to be to defy the laws of gravity. Like the little tables in the trendiest shops, or the ones on the news shows on TV.

At another so-called desk there was a fellow of about twenty, a real angel face. Before the angel had time to ask me what I wanted, I planted myself right in front of Quim’s desk—he hadn’t raised his eyes—and I dropped Cristina’s letter on top of the papers he was reading. At the same time, I said, imperiously, “Find out everything there is to know about this family right away.”

Quim raised his eyes, blinked, got up, astonished. Me, I just laughed.

“It just isn’t done, Lònia,” he’d said.

Then I realized that it wasn’t just the office that had a new look: he didn’t seem like a seventies liberal any more either. He’d traded in his sneakers for Reeboks, his blue polo shirt and pseudo-jeans for a wrinkle-is-beautiful shirt and high-rent pants. He'd cut the woolly curls off the back of his neck (with everything those curls carried in image and significance), that had given him a benevolent aura; now he wore his hair close cropped, and instead of the beginning of early baldness he had a clear forehead. He'd plucked the hairs between his eyebrows, his nails had been manicured, he'd shaved off his Che beard and he was freshly showered.

"Hey, Quim, you look terrific!"

"It just isn't done, Lònia," he repeated, very serious.

I looked around; the new office, which he'd rented himself after the Gaudí case had been settled, was neat as a pin. The decor was surprising; more than an office, it looked like the latest bar, cold, supermodern—maybe I should say post-modern—with impossible lamps. Pretensions of simplicity and purity of lines, but pure decorativeness in reality. I'd have to get used to the signs of the times. If that style now invading the city and even my own office—something similar must have happened during the modernist period, I guess, to judge by the examples that still survived—had at least been comfortable, I'd have gotten used to it without too much effort, but it was uncomfortable, irrational, inhospitable. I was old-fashioned, Quim would say a few days later; modernism was uncomfortable and irrational too, and besides why would I reject something as being irrational, since I was the epitome of the irrational myself. He was right about that. And that I was old-fashioned, and proud of it.

"I see the business is prospering," I looked at the angel, who observed me with some impertinence. "Have you turned yuppie?"

"One surprise deserves another, Lònia. I'd like you to meet Joan, my boyfriend."

I felt like I'd turned into stone, and my brain into fluffy cotton.

Suddenly, I understood a lot of things about Quim: his first job at the gym, where I'd met him, the quarrels with the owner; his immediate acceptance when I offered him the job; his sudden and mysterious disappearances; the almost pathological discretion about his intimate life; the fact that he'd never introduced me to any friend of his, when I was constantly telling him about my amorous successes and failures; our capacity to understand each other tacitly, the complicity we'd established without even trying; his misogynist outbursts that came out even if he tried to suppress them; and above all that sort of indefinable sadness that dragged him down, which was now curiously absent from his face.

I started to cry without knowing why

"Now what?" he said, offended.

"It's from joy, Quim," I tried to clarify.

"Don't be an ass, Lònia! You're crying with joy because I'm a queer? Who the hell can understand you? I don't know why you'd be glad."

"Do you want me to be sad, dumbshit?"

"No. Neither sad nor happy. I don't give a shit. It's my business, nothing to do with you. You don't need to play a liberated mother for me."

"Go to hell."

I sat on the clients' armchair, such as it was, and the tears kept flowing freely. I made no effort to stop the flow at all. I was crying for Quim, for myself, for Cristina, for Henry, because I was happy to be back in Barcelona in my office, and because I didn't miss Australia one bit.

Quim and his friend let me cry as much as I wanted, without saying anything, without trying to comfort me. In fact, Joan had started to get up, but through the tears I saw Quim signal to him to stay where he was.

When I'd calmed down, I started to tell them the whole story. Lunchtime came and I was still talking. Since it was Saturday, we closed the office and they took me to their house to eat.

But first, I bought two postcards, one for Jem and Lida and one for Henry.

My car, which I'd been letting Quim use looked brand new: not a scratch, upholstered pearl gray, floor rugs immaculate and painted pink.

"It must have cost you a fortune. But don't you think this color is a little flashy? It's as if Mercè had her gynecological instruments painted lilac because she's a feminist."

Silence. I figured out that it had been the boyfriend's idea.

"Joan is an expert in cars," Quim finally said very proudly. "And now, if you just take care of it a little."

"Is that a criticism?"

Quim's apartment was just the same: with a mixture of styles, no borders or limits, an overwhelming fantasy that I liked. Rugs hanging on the walls like tapestries, tapestries on the floor like rugs, a lace tablecloth over a round table, embroidered bedspreads covering the windows, towels on the armchairs, photographs, dried flowers, candles, stuff gathered any which way and placed with a special grace on just the right place. The whole was welcoming, much more than my apartment, with a hodgepodge of plants bursting forth with erotic exuberance, with a special studied messiness. I could see it now: I should have realized it before, the other times—not many, that's for sure—that I'd been in that house. And now I felt betrayed because he hadn't had enough confidence in me, he'd been hiding the way he was from me, his essence, as if I were an outsider.

"Oh, how pretty," I said, looking around. "You can see the feminine touch."

Joan stood in front of me, furious. But Quim's laugh disarmed him.

"That's what women are like!" Quim announced.

It lightened my heart: there was still the same complicity between us. We still felt like friends, aside from our respective love affairs.

You're sentimental, Lònia.

Poor Joan was really taken aback when Quim, laughing, hugged me and covered my face with kisses.

"Welcome, sweetie," with a sincerity that made me tremble with satisfaction.

"Do you want me to start crying again?" I said.

"Never mind," he replied. "Come on, help us set the table."

Joan looked at us wide-eyed, without understanding anything, stiff as a board.

"Don't be scandalized, man," Quim told him. "You have to let Lònia say stuff like that—and even worse things." And he added, teasing, "She doesn't mean it the wrong way."

"He's not scandalized, he's jealous," I said, way off base.

The kid was going to complain, but I got ahead of him and hugged him too.

"Don't worry, Joan, Quim and I have known each other for a long time, and we like to play at flirting, but it means nothing at all. You can have him. The truth is that he's never interested me as a man... and now I know why. Shit." I started laughing. "Besides, I found my missing rib in Australia."

Quim had started to set the table, and he froze, staring at me with the plates in his hands.

"It's the other way around, Paloni: women are the ribs of men, don't you remember your Bible?"

"My Bible? What's that? A misogynist treatise?" I'd learned that from Mercè.

"Okay, okay," Quim said as if he was very offended. "Now that we're all happy and all friends, now that we've let everything out and cleared up all the misunderstandings, how about giving me a hand?"

"Can I take a shower? I'm sticky from all the sweetness in this place."

When I came out of the bathroom I found lunch on the table: a mixed salad, that is, a potpourri of everything green we could find in the kitchen.

"Now," Quim said, authoritatively, "tell me about this Australian rib. Is he an Aborigine?"

I picked up my story where I'd left off. They let me talk, without interruptions or questions. When I'd finished, Quim noisily gulped down some air and started to speak.

"First, just to keep in practice, you've bitten off more than you can chew. I think Lida's right, and if I were you I'd let it all go, but I'm sure you won't pay the slightest fucking bit of attention to me. So go ahead, but don't count on us. You won't get anywhere, and at the first wrong move they'll accuse you of murder, and furthermore, no one is going to pay you a cent. It's clear that Cristina's parents don't give a shit about their daughter... if what she told you was the truth. That's if everything goes well. Because if you get mixed up in prostitution and that whole scam, you might find yourself with cement boots on in Palma Bay."

"Listen . . . "

"Don't interrupt me. Second: your Australian adventure was a failure, and if you don't want to end up even worse off, you might as well admit it. You left here with your head in the clouds, dreaming about fantastic voyages in exotic waters, discoveries of new places and new ways of life, breaking with reality and trips to dreamland." He made gestures. "And what did you find? Everything exactly the same as here. You not only didn't liberate yourself from the problems you have here, you added fuel to the fire. Adventure, my dear friend, is either inside you or not. You're too grown-up to be doing such kidstuff."

"Look who's talking!"

"So, listen to me, go ahead, circle the world, and then come back where you started. And third: it's too much that you had to go to the Antipodes to find the love of your life, but what really sucks is that he's a detective. So little imagination, sweet Mother of God!"

"Now you're the one who's jealous," Joan said timidly.

"You've got it, kid!" I said. And to Quim, "Now that your ritual sermon is finished—and I must say that your coming out of the closet hasn't changed you at all, you're still the same harasser—I'm going home to unpack and call a few friends. I'll spend tomorrow walking around Barcelona, who must be pretty mad at me for having abandoned her for so long, and I'll be at the office first thing Monday morning to get to work."

"The boss has spoken," said Quim, standing up, "but like I told you, don't count on me."

Naturally, I knew I could count on him no matter how much he said I couldn't. To begin with, before I left, he gave me some money, without me even having to ask for it.

I called Henry that night at one o'clock. In Melbourne it was nine in the morning, more or less.

Henry had already found out about the fire, of course. And he knew that the yacht belonged to an Australian branch of a company based in London: Gordon Ltd. No, not a transport company, a travel agency, tourism and stuff like that. He still had more investigating to do.

"Do you love me?"

"Yes . . . "

"Do you miss me? I miss you a lot. I wish you were here."

"If you want, I'll come today," he said solicitously.

"No, no, just write to me."

...

I'd have liked to stay in Barcelona for a few days, breathing in the polluted air, listening to the deafening music of the traffic, sucking in the scent of bus fumes. It seems the spaciousness of Melbourne, its serene equilibrium between the old and the new, between urbanism and parks, had gotten to me.

I like cities on Sunday. Especially Barcelona. Closed stores, the silence of parked cars, the absurdities committed by Sunday drivers, people who seemed dressier even though they're wearing exactly the same clothes they always wear. Sundays are for walking around by yourself and feeling your thoughts. For believing that you really are the queen of creation.

But that Sunday was different; nothing seemed to make any sense to me. It was as if I'd suddenly discovered the Truth about things, and therefore the existence of the Absurd. People insist on living as if life were to last forever, whereas with luck and stretching it, it might last seventy or eighty years: How could it be worth it to build houses, plazas, factories, empires, political parties, monuments, scientific theories, atomic bombs or works of art? To pass over the earth like a puff of air, wasn't that absurd? I spent hours and hours wandering through the Eixample neighborhood, under the leafy sycamores, relishing the heat. And I got into nihilism. In a low moment, I realized I didn't have any desire to go to Majorca to investigate, or to return to Australia, or even to see Henry. Nor was I eager to take over the administration of my agency again, as Quim recommended. What did I feel like doing, then? Nothing, absolutely nothing. I didn't feel like going to the movies, or to the theater. Not even calling Mercè, because she might not be home.

That's the terrific frame of mind I was in when I got to the Sant Santoni market. The usual people pawing through old books. That special odor of paper and years of accumulated dust touched me. The boys on the curbs, cautiously selling pirated videos. Two musicians playing Beethoven with a violin and double bass seemed a whole orchestra. A group had formed around them, they did it so well.

I bought a lipstick at one of the stands—my welcome present to Barcelona. And a very old book, illustrated, for Henry.

A little more reconciled with the world, and with myself, I crashed from two on Sunday until ten in the morning on Monday.

...

By eleven o'clock, without moving his ass from the chair, Quim had found out that:

"There is a Segura family in Majorca, from Llucmajor, owner of hotels and apartment buildings in Magalluf, s'Arenal and Cala Millor. They also own land in the interior, in the Son Servera area, and a large farm near Lluc . . . "

"Jesus Christ! They own practically the whole island!"

"As well as the island Cristina told you about, Na Morgana."

"Looks like I'm condemned to jump from one island to another, smaller each time. I'll end up on a little rock, all alone. . . . "

"Get serious. Munditourist is, in fact, a travel agency on Passeig Majorca, in Palma, part of an English tour operator, called . . . "

"Gordon Ltd?"

"Yes . . . "

"See? I'll have to go to Majorca, sweetie," I said triumphantly. "What's the relationship between Munditourist and the Segura hotels?"

"That I don't know yet."

"See? Impossible to not go to Majorca."

"Do what you damn well please, but don't count on me. Who are you calling?"

"I have to get a reservation. I'm not going to swim there."

"It might be good for you. Hang up, I already got it for you." Quim smiled maliciously.

I was amazed.

"You're an angel, Quim."

"I'm just as crazy as you, Paloni."

"They call me Lonnie now."

"No shit! No doubt something your new flame came up with," and he burst out laughing.

•••

This one was a real island, not like Australia for Christ's sake! The sea mist softened the majestic, wild mountain, and converted the violence of the meeting of earth and sea into a dream. First I thought I never should have left Majorca, and then immediately I was glad I left in time. So much beauty is a trap, I thought. And as soon as I thought it it seemed like an idiotic thing to think.

The mountain descended toward the plain and was lost in the grayish blue. I still couldn't see any crack in the rock, any towns or any woods. Just a dark silhouette, softly standing out against sea and sky. I wondered where that friend of mine ended up—the one who used to say that Majorca didn't exist, that the Majorcans just made it up. And then I thought of another friend who said Majorca could be heaven if it weren't full of Majorcans.

We were getting close to the cliffs, and now you could clearly see the waves at the bottom of the precipices. It existed, all right. The Roqueta myth was God's truth: a sensation of homesickness was drumming in my brain, just like raindrops that drum first on the rooftops and then splash down and reverberate. The plane made its inevitable jerks due to the change in air temperature. The wild mountain, still preserved, moved me so. I felt a part of those cliffs, and that sentiment inflated my heart.

You're so sentimental, Lònia!

And right after that, the plain. Squared, with clearings and thicketed hills, colored, unchanging. We passed over my hilly town, almost touching it. The belfry and the mills. For me, the mountain was dream and the plain reality: my mom working in the farmyard always grumbling. The mountain always filled my heart with tenderness... and rage. I still hadn't decided whether I'd go see her or not. She drove me nuts, my mom.

Pushed me to the limit. But I'd have to go see her, her and the rest of the family. What else could I do?

...

I did get along with Aunt Antònia. She was waiting for me at her house in Palma, with Majorcan pastries and bushels of gossip. It was glorious.

"Eat, honey, eat, they don't make pastries like this in Barcelona."

"Aunt Antònia, do you know the Seguras?"

I gave her a few details, to orient her. Aunt Antònia was a fount of wisdom. She knew everything. At least she had her own version of most everything that went on on the island.

". . . they say she ran off to Australia, and she didn't even come back for the funeral."

"What funeral?"

"Her father's funeral! Don Bernat died three months ago. . . and they say it was because of grief, because the girl was the apple of his eye. She was a spoiled brat, they gave her everything, and look how she repays them."

"His daughter did something awful?"

"Yes, she went off to Australia, to study. Imagine, to study! You don't need to go that far to study. Like you, you upset your mother a lot. . . "

"Come on, Aunt Antònia, stop talking nonsense. You're the one who advised me to go to Barcelona."

Aunt Antònia looked at me with complicity, glad to have collaborated in upsetting her sister. And she went on.

"Now don Macià is running everything, and they say he's a real jerk. Just the opposite of poor don Bernat. No, and now he's a scammer in the government, he's in the paper a lot. . . but when somebody makes that much money, it can't all be clean, you can be sure."

"Don Bernat made quite a bit of money, and you say he was a good person."

"I didn't say that, honey, I said he wasn't a jerk, like his brother, which doesn't mean he was a good person, just that he seemed like one."

"What about his wife?"

"A pompous ass. Empty-headed."

For Aunt Antònia believed that a married woman who talked more to men than to women at a dinner party was at best an aspirant to whoredom.

"Don't you want any more pastries, honey?"

"Aunt Antònia, I've already gobbled down six! Now I'd like to take a little walk around town."

She gave me the keys to her place and asked me if I needed money. I just took the keys.

Before going out, I called Henry. It was eight at night in Melbourne. He wasn't at home or at the office. I left Aunt Antònia's number on his answering machine. On the street, I bought a postcard of the government palace and sent it to him.

XI

"Donya Carme Llofriu?"

"Yes, I'm Mrs. Llofriu . . . "

"I'm a friend of Cristina. I just got here from Australia and Cristina gave me your address and telephone number."

My intuition kept me from mentioning the letter. First I wanted to size her up.

"Oh, my God, Cristina! You say you're her friend? Why don't you come over and we'll chat a little."

Perfect. I was there in ten minutes. The Seu neighborhood, shady, quiet, not much traffic. The bells on the tourist carriages resounded against the ancient walls and tinkled, sacrilegiously, into the patios.

Alzamora Street. An ancestral house with an unusable brass bell and a chiming doorbell.

"What a coincidence," donya Carme said as she showed me in. "I just received a letter from Cristina yesterday and I was answering it when you called. Come in, come in."

I made a supreme effort not to turn white and I followed her.

She was dressed in mourning, but her step was agile, as if the widowhood hadn't slowed her down any.

The house, shadowy like the street, faced north. Dark and sober, its decor was even more sacrilegious than the tourist carts decked out in their Sunday best. Whoever heard of putting flowered wallpaper on those walls! That furniture, shiny as patent leather, imitating God knows what style, had probably taken the place of walnut trunks, imperial mahogany sofas, knotty pine buffets. The floor, which should have been red tile, shiny from age, was a scandalously bright striped marble. And I'm sure that the beds were covered with rose-colored tulle instead of lace bedspreads. But donya Carme went perfectly with that decor, covered, as she was, with gold, down to the toenails. She let two little tears fall.

"I've been so lonely without her, all these months."

"Cristina complained that she wasn't getting any letters from Majorca."

"What are you saying? How can you say that? My God! I've been sending her two for every one she sent me. But she's okay, isn't she? Isn't she homesick?" Sigh. "I'll never understand why she didn't come to her father's funeral, as much as they loved each other. She told me, in a letter, but my God, a father is a father."

Segura's widow stopped talking when a maid came in.

"Would you like something to drink?" she asked me.

"Yes, some orange juice."

"With a little vodka?"

"No, I don't drink. No, thanks, I don't smoke either." She'd lit up a cigarette and offered me one.

The maid went out and donya Carme went to an ugly, pretentious secretary. She showed me some papers.

"Look, she writes me such short letters. And look at the one I was writing to her, I just started and it's already twice as long as hers."

Indeed, Cristina's letters were short and absolutely laconic. A square sheet, a few typewritten lines and a signature.

"I thought she didn't know how to type," I suggested.

"You're right, she never wanted to learn here, she said it broke her fingernails. But they must have taught her at the residence. Were you at the residence too? Oh, sorry, I haven't even asked you your name, or where you're from. Oh, honey, since Bernat's death I've lost my head." A little tear.

The maid came back in with whiskey for the lady and orange juice for me. Naturally, the orange juice was artificial.

"You see, Cristina could be so comfortable here in Majorca, and she says she'd rather stay at the other end of the earth. Until a little while back, I was sure Cristina would come back, but now I'm beginning to suspect she'll stay there forever."

You can be sure of that, donya Carme.

". . . I'd like to know what there is there that she can't have here. Maybe she found some boyfriend? She doesn't tell me anything in those letters, but if it was that, I'd understand. But when Bernat died," a little tear, "may he be in God's glory, almighty God! I sent her money to come back, I'm sure she didn't need it, because she has an account, but anyway . . . "

Either that lady was dumber than a turkey or smarter than a fox and she was sizing me up. Should I give her the letter or not? Should I start an under-the-table interrogation, or should I just let her talk and see where she'd go? I felt uncomfortable there, false, like in one of those plays the nuns used to put on. When the doorbell rang, I jumped, as if an intruder had come to expose my game. Donya Carme raised her head with surprise, too.

"Were you expecting someone? I don't want to bother you," I said.

The maid entered and announced a name, and donya Carme said, "Oh, yes, it slipped my mind."

Mechanically, I took advantage of the occasion to stick one of Cristina's letters in my pants pocket.

A few minutes later I was out in the shady street again. Segura's widow couldn't spend any more time with me, she had an unavoidable appointment she'd forgotten about, but you must come back, honey, and tell me more about Cristina, that kid, my God! especially now that she needed her more than ever, she was so lonely, etc., etc.

Once out on the street, I decided not to try to figure out whether donya Carme was superdumb or supersmart. At the moment I had more important things to do.

...

"Good morning. I'd like to talk to the person in charge of trips to Australia," I asked, slipping back into my Barcelona accent.

"I beg your pardon?" the woman asked me.

She looked like Sister Magdalena, but she didn't have that

dried up spirit. She seemed affable, calm.

"I want to speak with whoever is in charge of trips to Australia."

"Do you want to go to Australia? Do you want a ticket for Australia?"

"No, I know this agency organizes trips to Australia . . . "

"I'm afraid you're mistaken. If you want to go, we can sell you the ticket and arrange for hotels . . . just like if you wanted to go anywhere else in the world. We also organize group trips, charters, but there's no one here who specializes in trips to Australia."

"How can that be? I've been sent here by Mrs. Joil, from Melbourne, because she wants me to be in charge of the next charter."

"I'm afraid you've been misinformed, dear." Very nice, she was. "We don't have any charters to Australia planned. And we haven't done any since I've been working here."

She didn't seem to be lying, even though she did look like Sister Magdalena.

I hesitated a few seconds. Lònia, you're getting yourself into another bramble, like at the Gardener agency. That's not the way to do things, sticking your nose in like that. Well, how are you supposed to do them, then, for Christ's sake?

The woman was looking at me with that stereotypical friendliness that people get when they work with the public; but at least it was friendliness, which meant she was for real. So, confident that she was for real, I pushed a little more.

"Are you sure?" I changed from my self-assured tone to a meek one.

"Of course I'm sure! Do you think I don't know how to do my job?" Now she did look like Sister Magdalena.

She was waiting for me to go, but I stayed put in front of her desk, really sorry. Not pretending this time. I was just wondering whether to let some other name from Melbourne drop as bait. But finally, she got up and went inside to talk to someone in the agency. When she returned she really had a sour look.

"What's your name? What business did you say sent you? May I see your ID?"

"What is this, a travel agency or a police station?" I showed great dignity.

I was out of there as if shot out of a slingshot. I wouldn't find out anything there.

I left Munditourist in a rage. Passeig Majorca, which I liked so much when I lived in Palma, seemed ugly and provincial. And I was such an idiot, as usual. Because if the agency had had a "correspondent" from the Gardener Agency, what the hell would I have said? I was lucky I'd dealt with that mule guarding the corral. But the fact that they wanted to know so much about me proved that they had something to hide with respect to Australia. From now on I'd have to leave the main drag behind and proceed on the cart trails. More holes and rocks, but less traffic going the other way.

...

When I showed Henry la Roqueta, I wouldn't take him to s'Arenal, or Cala Millor. Not because we wouldn't find out anything there, but because that atmosphere drove me nuts. I wouldn't take him to Magalluf resort either, even though we would find an open door there.

But it was depressing; there wasn't the slightest bit of countryside left. The tourists were fat and ugly, and what's worse, they didn't know it. They didn't know where they were, and they didn't need to. As long as there was sun, they toasted themselves; then they'd drag themselves along, bored, into the souvenir shops, all clustered together, where there was never a single object in good taste to buy; and they were enraptured by the "hand made" embroidery, done on electric sewing machines.

I'd never found them quite as stupid as now, all those tourists. And just think when I was little, I believed they were superior people.

There was a waitress at the bar of the Playa Dorada Hotel. I ordered a natural orange juice in Majorcan and she asked me in German whether I wanted it carbonated or not.

I asked her in Spanish where she was from, and she was amazed I could speak her language. I hadn't said I was German, but it wasn't necessary; on the side of the bar I was on, there could only be Germans or Swedes, and she'd figured I was German. I didn't set her straight. We became friends right away. And I started to ask questions.

Was I from the police?

"No!" I laughed.

I was a journalist. We agreed to meet that very evening at the Tasmania Bar—what paradoxes—after ten, which was when she got off work. She'd bring some girlfriends, and that way I could do the article for the magazine—German, of course—I worked for.

"Will they take pictures of us?"

I hadn't thought about photos. She seemed disappointed. I cheered her up—we'd do the pictures another day.

...

Paloma: No, it's a lot of fun.

Remedios: Not really . . . sometimes it's pretty boring, cleaning up other people's shit.

Paloma: We're not the ones who clean up the shit, Reme, don't exaggerate.

Lolín: I do. I clean the bathrooms and wash the dishes. You guys are luckier . . . But I can't complain . . . it's better than the olives.

Paloma: Yeah, better than picking grapes, too. When I found out there was a guy around looking for people, I didn't give it a second thought. A cousin of mine went to the Costa Brava, and she never came back.

Remedios: But we won't stick around, this time

Lolín: But it would have been worth it, and maybe we'll have a job we can count on for next year.

Remedios: Not me. I'm not coming back next year. Not even if they offered me the moon.

Paloma: Come on, Reme, you'll find another one. There won't be any shortage of men around here.

Remedios: Maybe you guys, but not me.

Lolín: You get too sentimental, you can't go around falling in love with the first guy who winks at you. Things are different here, everybody wants to have a good time, why shouldn't we have a good time too?

Remedios: I'm so tired all I feel like doing is sleeping.

Lolín: I have the hardest job, and you know what I do? I don't think about the job while I'm doing it. I think about what I'm going to do when I'm finished with it. That makes the job a lot easier.

Paloma: It's the way they do it. Just a small amount every week, and the whole salary at the end of the season. Since we have room and board, we don't need anything else, and that way we're forced to save.

Lolín: I wish they'd give us a little more every week. There's so much atmosphere here, and things are so expensive. You always have to find someone to treat you to everything.

Remedios: But nobody treats you to something for nothing.

Lolín: So what? Does anybody treat you to anything, in your town? There's more to choose from here, and besides, no one wags their tongue afterwards.

They were talkers, those girls. Their Spanish was picturesque, very dialectical; it didn't have anything to do either with the Language of the Empire I'd been forced to learn in school, or with the Spanish you hear in the mass media. Sometimes I couldn't even understand what they were saying, and they reminded me of muddles my godmother used to get into with that old lady who'd just arrived from the country. The old lady would ask for something and my godmother was incapable of figuring out what she meant; the granny would end up furious because she couldn't understand how the godmother could be such a blockhead that she couldn't understand her; godmother would freeze up—why can't this woman speak right? And the old lady would say, why don't they speak like Christians around here? The truth is that things hadn't changed much with respect to that from my godmother's times to mine; but that didn't matter at all at that Tower of Babel called Magalluf.

The tape recorder taped and taped, and I tried to guide the conversation where I wanted it to go. Because it wasn't my intention to do a socio-psychological study in social realism about the seasonal girls who worked in hotels on the island, nor a special report with generic pretensions on the life of one of them.

But they yakked and yakked, hopeful, funny, astonished or

embittered by that cheap cosmopolitanism they found themselves in the middle of.

"But a long work day like the ones you put in has to be exhausting, doesn't it?" I said.

Paloma: It's worse harvesting, in two days your back is broken.

Lolín: And the boredom, when there's nothing to do. I really think we're lucky. But it was hard for me to decide. But now, when I think about my girlfriends who didn't come because they were afraid, or because their parents wouldn't let them . . . mine didn't want me to come either, but I didn't want to miss the adventure.

Paloma: I was homesick the first few days, but since I couldn't go back . . .

"Because of the contract you signed?"

Paloma: Contract? We haven't signed any contract. No, they don't pay for our tickets until the end of the season, and we don't have money to buy them. But I don't want to leave, I'm not homesick any more. I'm satisfied.

I thought of the girls around the pool at the Rutherford Residence and the old gals at the Gardener Agency. They seemed satisfied too. And it seemed to me that the only difference between the two groups was the ones in Melbourne hadn't been able to choose, and these ones had—a pretty bold decision, but the alternative was to stay in the town and become one of the drudges of the island, which after all, was only paradise for some.

Do you think there are whores who do it for pleasure? Lida had said to me. I myself would prefer to rent my cunt like the whores than my hands like these girls. In the end, how come the cunt is always considered more sacred than any other part of the body? If a woman wanted to rent her body to a man for fucking, didn't she have as much right to do that as she had to rent herself to him to write his letters or do his typing? Or for washing his dishes and underwear and not even get paid for it? The problem is that it's always women who have to rent something, her box, her hands, her back or her head . . . I'd have to talk about all this with Mercè, she'd help me straighten it out.

Paloma: . . . in Australia.

Lolín: That's really lucky!

"What? What?" I suddenly broke away from my musings to listen to the girls.

Paloma: A friend of ours is going to Australia in September.

Remedios: "Many are called and few are chosen."

Lolín: You could have said yes, and me too. So don't be a hypocrite.

"To Australia?" It had taken me nearly three hours to get to that, and now I couldn't believe it. Even though I suspected it, even though that's exactly what I wanted to talk to these girls about, now that I had evidence I couldn't believe it. "What's she going to do in Australia?"

Paloma: Work.

"But why Australia? How did she find the job? What kind of a job is it?" my voice was wavering.

Remedios: Do you want to go, too? They want younger ones. Pretty and young. That's why they're only taking her.

Paloma: I don't know why you have to get nasty, Reme. What's the harm in it? It's not her fault that they didn't take you.

Remedios: Did they say anything to you?

Paloma: Well, they asked me if I was interested.

Lolín: How lucky!

"Who proposed it?" I asked, trying to hide the curiosity that was gnawing at me.

Paloma: A friend of the hotel owner. But we aren't supposed to talk about it. He said I should be discreet.

I pretended to turn off the tape recorder to indicate discretion.

"A friend of don Macià Segura?" I asked.

"No, the hotel owner is don Leopoldo."

"Don Leopoldo? Don Leopoldo who?"

"Cabrer, I think."

"What kind of a job did he offer you?"

"Waitress, maybe, like here, but easier and better paid; or maybe receptionist, or taking care of rich people's kids. What's for sure is that there are jobs, for two or three years at the least."

"Under the same conditions as here? Not paying you until

the end of two or three years?"

"We... hadn't talked about that, yet..."

"What about this friend of yours?"

"She has a job, all right—waitress in a young women's residence."

God help me!

"Do you already have your passport?" I asked.

"No, not yet. But Ampara has hers. That friend of don Leopoldo takes care of everything, she hasn't had to worry about anything, her ticket or anything."

"Who is this guy?"

"I don't know. I still haven't seen him."

...

I wandered around the Playa Dorada all the next day, hoping that Paloma would be able to point out don Leopoldo to me. Milling around among the tourists, dressed like them so I wouldn't attract the attention of the personnel, the disgust nearly killed me. These scraps of Majorca weren't my Majorca. They were like kidneys transplanted by a not very skillful surgeon, that the rest of the body can't finally quite reject, but can't accept either.

I was under an umbrella by the pool when Paloma came to let me know. Don Leopoldo had arrived. I went to the bar, like any other customer, and a few minutes later I saw two men coming out from behind the reception desk. One of them was don Leopoldo.

"Who's the other one?"

"A customer. Since I came here at the beginning of the season, he's been living in a suite on the third floor. But he doesn't act like a tourist. I think he's Majorcan."

Paloma was delighted to help me. She felt like a star in a film. I suppose she suspected that I was more than a German journalist, but for the moment she seemed willing to be discreet. And I was most unwilling for her or any of her friends to go to Australia.

The two men separated in the parking lot. Each one got into a car and I got ready to follow don Leopoldo Cabrer.

The unbroken stretch of hotels, apartments, stores, bars and dancing halls was depressing. I knew that beyond that there were the packed beaches of Palma Nova, Portals Nous, Illetes, and the open sea of the bay; on the other side was the hill of Na Burguesa. I'd like to have been able to take a glance at the past and see how all that must have been in other times, but don Leopoldo's car didn't leave much room for my imagination. How he whisked through those closed, twisted streets! If I lost him in that zone, I'd never find him; that chaotic conglomeration gave me claustrophobia, both physical and mental, and I wouldn't be capable of staying there a single second to look for him.

With relentless discontinuity, the highway became Joan Miró Avenue. Cas Català, Sant Agustí, Cala Major, everything just alike: hotels, apartments, bars . . . and slob tourists. I wasn't sure whether at that moment it was the job that made everything seem so ugly, or the ugliness all around me that made me hate the job. In any case, I felt more like an outsider there than in Melbourne. And that really sucks, I thought. The high walls of Marivent Palace—with the Saridakis Museum closed to the public because the king and queen were there for the summer—what a nerve!—Campsa's oil deposits . . . I almost lost don Leopoldo in a crazy convergence of streets and highways. The buildings on Joan Miró del Terreno were ramshackle, rundown, but full of tourists. Don Leopoldo turned left. Those little streets of the Terreno leading to the Bellver Woods seemed like another world. In spite of the shameless and hapless incursions of some completely uninteresting bars, they managed to keep the placid atmosphere of twenty years earlier, as if the sleazy old cosmopolitanism of Gomila Plaza and Joan Miró Avenue—poor Joan Miró, alas!—hadn't been able to invade them. Bellver Castle, golden and imperturbable, looked on it all with medieval indifference.

Don Leopoldo's car stopped in front of a little white turn of the century chalet on Dos de Maig Street, alongside the Bellver Woods. The high stone fence and the garden gate, of iron with sheets of zinc, hid everything except the highest windows, which had bars instead of blinds. When they opened the gate, I could see two guard dogs, shiny and black, heading for don Leopoldo. Before I could see whether they bit him or licked him, the door closed.

The street was silent, without a single person or a breath of air. For a moment it seemed like I was on Monash Street, and I shivered in spite of the heat. A presentiment? Or was I missing Henry? I realized I hadn't thought much about him since I'd gotten to Majorca. I also realized that I'd gotten more work done during those few days on the little island of Majorca than Henry'd accomplished in a month on the big island of Australia. I asked myself if I loved Henry as much in Majorca as in Australia. Was Lonnie the same person as Lònia? Troubled, I had to admit she wasn't.

But I had no more time for philosophizing. The two dogs were barking, the iron gate was opening, and out came don Leopoldo with two girls and another guy.

Following a car in Palma is completely different from following one in Melbourne or Barcelona. The traffic is crowded, like in Barcelona, but undisciplined. On the other hand, the advantage is that you can drive just as crazily as everyone else, and no one complains. We left Gomila Plaza and continued on Joan Miró. We took Marquès de la Sènia and turned right on the Passeig Marítim. We passed Es Jonquet, el Baluart de Sant Pere, the Interinsular Council, the Exchange. How I loved going down Passeig Sagrera, and what a long time it had been since I'd looked up to see the green fronds of the palm trees! We went around Blessed Ramon Llull and turned up toward the Born. Palma's so small, you always end up passing the same places. That's why I like it. And I like Barcelona for just the opposite reason, how about that? We took a right on Unió and I saw don Leopoldo's car park at Santa Catalina Thomàs Plaza. While I was mentally chanting Santa Catalina's song, *Sister Tomaseta where are you, you better hide, the devil's looking for you, he's going to throw you in a well,* I saw the two girls and the other guy get out of the car and go into a stairway. I couldn't see the facade of the building too well from where I was because of the sycamores, just some winter balconies and a few signs.

I didn't have much time for contemplation, because don Leopoldo started the car again, and I was after him.

Weyler Plaza—Theater Bakery, you still haven't gotten yourself a pastry, Lònia, and you're so crazy about them—the Theater, the parking lot at Major Plaza, and up the Rambla. We got off at Baró de Pinopar—what a ridiculous name—and we turned into the avenues; then left on General Riera. Don Leopoldo was going full speed ahead, and I had to remind myself that in Palma the yellow lights last long enough for you to run them with no problem. I ran a lot of them. Even so, don Leopoldo's car was getting away from me and I had to push that rented car to the limit, and it was already starting to complain.

Along Establiments Street, it became easier to follow and I relaxed. I shouldn't have. We went up to the coast of Son Berga practically together, but when we got to the town church, I didn't see his car. I kept on going, as far as the straight stretch of the Esporles highway. Not a sign of the car. I turned back and drove the car through every street of the town that I could, and I did the rest on foot. I finally had to admit that I'd lost don Leopoldo Cabrer's car.

XII

I went back to downtown Palma and left the car parked near the Institute. I stopped in for iced coffee at a bar where I used to do Latin homework with a friend when we were in high school. What should I do now? Should I go back to Magalluf and try to pick up don Leopoldo's track? Should I call that place on Terreno to see if they'd let me have a look around? Should I go to a graphologist to confirm that the signature on the letter I'd stolen wasn't by the same person who'd written the letter I got in Melbourne? Should I go back to see the Segura widow and tell her Cristina was dead, to see what would happen? I decided to go to the Santa Catalina Thomàs Plaza to see what I might find at the apartment where don Leopoldo had left the guy and the two girls. But I'd do it later. At the moment I didn't feel like doing anything.

The fact is, I don't like to lose. Losing don Leopoldo's car wasn't too serious maybe, maybe trailing it wouldn't have added anything crucial to my investigation. But just losing it, apart from whether it might have been important or not, put me in a foul mood. I left the bar and started walking around, aimlessly. I like to wander around, watch people, window-shop, daydream. And it had been a long time since I'd done that in Palma.

Without even realizing it, I went along the way that led from the Institute to the convent. From Roma Street, I went to Santa Magdalena Plaza—but I didn't go in to see the bejeweled mummy of who knows what saint, or nun or holy lady they had in the church, which had scared me to death one day. I took Sant Jaume Street, so lordly, the houses with overhanging eaves so that you can barely see a little strip of sky. It was still as shadowy as it was on the day I saw my first exhibitionist; he came out of one of those great portals brandishing his tool, he seemed so proud of it. He startled me so much that instead of bursting into tears or running away, I broke out in laughter. All the pride of that erect bird melted away, and the man, humiliated by an adolescent, tucked his little pecker away and zipped up his pants.

There weren't any tourists in the narrow streets of that area. Bisbe Street was still so white, Caputxins Street, asymmetrical like a train going around a curve, with its haughty palm tree, still guarding over the high wall of the Capuchin nuns' garden. I went into the perfume store on Jaquotot. It was exactly the same as before: two steps to go down, tiny display cases with blurry glass on each side of the door. I bought a lipstick with the same feeling I used to have when I would buy three ounces of perfume because I couldn't afford the whole bottle. It wasn't the same salesgirl, though. And when she asked, may I help you ma'am, I almost started to cry. They'd always said, what do you want kid, to me in that store. But twenty years had gone by and now it freaked me out when they called me ma'am.

But I had to accept it; time had gone by and I wasn't the same Lònia as before. Now I was Lonnie, who'd come back to my roots, unable to get an amorous patina I'd acquired in Melbourne off my skin. The mess I found myself in was incredible: a mother who was getting letters from her dead daughter; a dead daughter who thought she was going to study in Australia and ended up in a whorehouse full of heroin; a hotel owner who wasn't one; a travel agency that trafficked in women and some hotels that supplied it with the raw material.

Clutching the lipstick tightly, as if holding on to it would keep my youth, I went into Ca Street, a cul-de-sac with that little toy-sized apartment, where the guy from Eivissa used to sell contraband light tobacco. I went out on toward Pueyo where it meets Rosa Street and Weyler Plaza. There were tourists around again. From the corner of Weyler, I looked at

Santa Catalina Thomàs Plaza, where not even two hours ago don Leopoldo's car had stopped to let out the passengers he'd picked up at Terreno. From there I could clearly see the building where the guy and the two girls had gone in. The sign sent chills up my spine. To calm myself down, I turned on Rosa Street and in front of the convent of the Reparador nuns, I looked up; that window right below the rooftop used to be my room, when Aunt Antònia had pressured mom to let me go to school in Palma. Mom's condition was that I wasn't to live with Aunt Antònia, poor thing. She hadn't been mistaken, my mom; the nuns kept me under their thumbs much more than her sister would have.

Then I decided it wasn't the time to hide my head under the wing of old memories, and I went straight out into Santa Catalina Thomàs Plaza from Caputxins.

...

The sign wasn't luminous like the one at the Gardener Agency. The building didn't look like the one in Melbourne, either, nor did I see any opulent girls like the ones there working here. It was a bare office—more or less like the one I had before I moved to the Ronda—just one office with dirty windows and gray walls, full of dust and time. In fact, in appearance it was just the opposite of the Melbourne agency, but only in appearance—its function was exactly the same. My suspicions were confirmed five minutes after I started the conversation with the "manager" of Happy Life Marriage Agency.

"So you're all alone in Majorca . . . yes, we Majorcans are not very open, they say, but I'm sure we can find someone for you. Haven't you thought of going back to your country?" The man I'd seen leaving the chalet in Terreno with don Leopoldo was saying to me.

I was passing myself off as a Bulgarian—God help me! I'd escaped from a team of artistic skaters from there who were vying for a championship in Paris a few years back. I hadn't wanted to ask for political asylum in either France or later in Spain for fear of extradition. I'd gotten into Spain in a car, and no one had asked me for a passport or anything at the border. I'd been getting by for five years in Majorca, but I was sick of it.

Besides things were getting difficult with the new laws for foreigners. And on top of that, I was broke. All I wanted was a little company and a minimum of economic security for the time being.

"No, I can't go back. I fled, and if I went back, the best I could hope for would be prison."

"But you must have friends, you must be in touch with your family. . . " He was paternal.

"No, there's nobody there who'd be happy to see me again. That's why I left. I thought I'd find some friends here, but not really. Maybe it's my fault, but it's clear I don't have the capacity to make myself loved," I said bitterly.

"What about the years you've lived here?" He smiled. "You can't tell me you haven't made any friends in Majorca? You must have worked, you must know someone. . . . We have rules in this agency, we can't offer our clients... well, I mean, of course we can make a few exceptions, but this is a proper agency and we usually ask our clients for some kind of a recommendation at least, some kind of personal endorsement. For example, who told you about us, who suggested that you come to us for our services?"

I'd heard that song before. The extremes come together, the Antipodes reach out to each other.

"Nobody," I said. "That's exactly what I want your services for, because I don't have anybody to recommend me or to advise me."

The man had the satisfied smile of a shepherd who'd just caught a stray sheep.

"If it's so hard to find a man who'll marry me under my circumstances, I mean without documentation or anything, you could say that legally I don't exist. . . . Well, I mean if it's as difficult as all that," I was getting cynical, "I must tell you that I can't afford to be too picky, I know I can't demand legal papers. . . . Just a little company and so I won't have to run around all over the place trying to earn a few bucks to survive on, you know what I mean."

He sure did know what I meant. He looked me up and down, persistently. So much that I, who am not exactly a prude, ended up lowering my eyes uncomfortably. That man got you dirty just looking at you. But I kept on.

"And if there's some job attached, I wouldn't turn that down either, I just want some security, not so much moneywise, but, well, physical, too, you know. Someone who'd really protect me."

"What kind of a job? What have you done so far?"

"Oh, a little bit of everything. Clerk in a souvenir shop, rent-a-cop on the beach, assistant to an antique dealer, call girl with a friend. . . "

"So you do have friends. . . "

"I did have. . . . that friend found a guy and ran off and stuck me with all the bills."

"Where do you work now?"

"No place. I'm tired of running around." I filled the long pause with sighs. "Well, the truth is I wouldn't mind a change of scenery at all. I'd like that. But I can't get out of Spain without papers, and France is even worse. I mean if you find someone who wants a travelling companion, or needs someone who's not from here, I won't ask for anything but protection, you know what I mean."

"Yes, I see. Where do you live?"

I hadn't been counting on that. I always forget something, dammit! I had to improvise quick.

"I'm renting a room from a lady, but I can't pay the rent and one of these days she's going to throw me out."

"Here is Palma?" he insisted. "Where?"

I had to give him Aunt Antònia's address. I'd have to deal with that one later. But the jerk still played hard to get.

"Well, that's a horse of a different color, if I've gotten your message. This agency doesn't do that, I don't know what I can do for you, really. But maybe," he assessed me with the eyes of a pro, and I had to suppress the urge to make him a new face. "I do have some clients who are looking for steady company, with no legal strings attached, but as a general rule they want something a little fresher, greener."

Of course, I was an overripe fig, about to fall off the tree!

". . . but you have class, and that's a big plus. Naturally, we'll have to give you a physical, that's routine, and we guarantee absolute confidentiality."

I laughed. I had class, all right, but he sure didn't. The Gardener woman had much more. But that's why Gardener was more dangerous than this creep passing for a Mafia boss but looking more like an almond picker.

"The truth is, I don't care about confidentiality: nobody in the whole world is going to hassle me about what I do or how I do it."

"Okay, then, I think we can help you, but I'll need a few days. Come in tomorrow around closing time."

He gave me his hand, which was like a limp rag, and asked me what my name was.

"Lonnie... Lonnie Dhul," came out without me realizing it.

...

They showed up at Aunt Antònia's house at eleven at night. It took some doing to convince her to play the role, but when the time came, she really pulled it off.

"Yes, she lives here," she told them. "But not for long, because she doesn't pay, besides, she's a little weird, you know how foreigners are. I don't know why I've kept her as long as I have, I don't like her much at all, who knows what she is. . . . "

She explained all kinds of things to them for half an hour, without letting them ask any questions. She was really wound up. I think they left more tired than convinced. I didn't sleep a wink, myself. Even though that jerk seemed like a moron, I was afraid. Not of him, specifically, but of the whole mechanism behind him. Because I was sure I'd found the thread that linked Majorca to Melbourne, the thread that had hooked Cristina in. Now I would follow that same thread without arousing suspicions. Through the man at the agency at Santa Catalina Plaza I could get to Cabrer, and through Cabrer to Munditourist. I could find out how and why Cristina had ended up at Rutherford, and how she'd ended up Rossenhilled. For sure I could break that threat and use it to hang a whole gang of scumbags who trafficked in women.

On the other hand, Cristina's letters kept me awake, too. Obviously her signature was false, obviously someone didn't want it known, first that she'd been the victim of a brutal swindle, and then the victim of an overdose. But who? And why? How was it possible that her mother didn't suspect a thing? Could she really be that dumb? Or, up to what point was it true that donya Carme didn't suspect anything?

By dawn I was dozing off. Aunt Antònia had told me that Mom had found out I was around, in Majorca—she'd told her herself, of course—and that Mom was mad as hell that I hadn't gone to see her. Maybe I'd give her a buzz.

When Aunt Antònia woke me up, I was dreaming that Mom and the thug from the agency were harvesting beans in the corral at my house, in our town. When they saw me coming, their looks got ironic and they started whispering. Suddenly the bean plants grew and grew and the two of them were hidden behind the plants. Christ, you didn't need to be Freud to interpret that dream. While I was dipping my pastry into coffee and milk, I leafed through the newspaper. I'd go to Santa Eugènia to see Mom. I put the paper down, in a bad mood. I didn't like the idea, and even less when I thought that of course I'd also have to see my brother and sister-in-law.

"Did you see this?" Aunt Antònia said.

"What?"

"Weren't you asking me about the Seguras the other day? Well, they're in the paper now. Along with those guys that are giving them such a bad time."

"What do you mean?"

"Here, look for yourself."

It was about the Seguras, all right. Because the EGM was starting a campaign to save Na Morgana from the shovels and excavators. Pete Seeger's song crossed my mind, but I couldn't remember the name or how it went.

"What's EGM?" I asked.

"Oh, they make a lot of racket once in a while. And they're right," Aunt Antònia replied.

I read their ad. The address of the Ecologist Group of Majorca and a request for the collaboration of anyone interested in saving Cala Mura from destruction.

"Auntie, I won't be going to Santa Eugènia today either."

"Good God, your mother will kill me," she wailed histrionically. But underneath, she was glad.

...

I left the car at Sa Porta des Camp, at the end of the avenues, and went into the streets behind the walls: grand old houses that still maintained a certain dignity, at least on the outside, mixed with downright vertical slums. Closed convents with suspicious looking splotches of humidity on the walls, and silence of streets without traffic because they're too narrow for cars, the yelling of immigrant kids. And a splendid sun trying to get in through the eaves but only half succeeding.

It seemed like centuries since I'd been in that area of the old part of town. I'd gone to a friend's house once in Sa Calatrava: you could see the bay from the living room, looking like a mirror of the sky, and I thought how I'd like to live in a place like that. I wonder what ever happened to Maria? I'd seen her a few times in Barcelona in the early seventies, but she wasn't in our group. Afterwards, I lost touch with her completely. I thought how much I'd enjoy getting together in one place all the people I'd known until now, and loved or appreciated, to whatever degree. It would be a colossal potpourri.

The brightness of the bay blinded me. Those gardens above the wall were a little abandoned, but they still had their charm. Beneath the wall was the Parc del Mar—they'd soon finish it—and it was spectacular, grandiloquent, but so far without the charm of the humble, beaten-down land I was walking on at the moment.

Standing in front of the EGM address, on the same little street, I wondered if we are always the same toward everyone we deal with, or if we act differently, according to who we're with. But by now I was going up the dark stairway and I had to abandon my philosophical-sentimental reflections if I didn't want to take a tumble.

A little fellow who moved like a mouse opened the door.

"I read in the paper that you're asking for anyone who wants to save Cala Mura to get in touch with you. . . "

"Yes, come in, come in." He was resolute.

There was an entry with some chairs and a table full of propaganda flyers. The walls were covered with posters. A partly opened door led to a large, luminous room with windows that suggested the sea. The racket and the voices told me there was a good sized group. The guy breathed satisfaction.

"I heard about Cala Mura in Australia. I thought its virginity was assured," I said instead of introducing myself.

The satisfaction on his face turned to suspicion.

"In Australia? Who told you about it in Australia?"

"Cristina Segura."

"Who sent you here, Miss?"

What, again?!

He didn't try to hide his surprise, nor the fact that he didn't trust me. To begin with, he'd dropped the friendly greeting and called me Miss, for distance.

It didn't surprise me; they were probably used to getting hassled from all sides. On the other hand, young people who get together to protect things—the countryside, whales, clean air—strike a tender chord in my heart, I can't help it. So, though it would have been logical for me to at least answer him in his same tone, I decided to be nice and facilitate things.

"Nobody sent me. I simply met Cristina Segura in Australia and she mentioned Cala Mura to me."

"Oh, Cristina, huh? What were you doing in Australia?" He was impertinent.

"Listen, sweetie," in spite of my good will, I was losing patience, "I don't mind telling you my life story, but I don't think it's of any use to your cause. I'm a friend of Cristina and she told me she'd convinced her father not to develop Cala Mura and now I see it isn't true... "

"Yes, it is true. Well, sort of. She convinced him thanks to us." Pause. Reflection. "So you're a friend of Cristina. Of Cristina, or of don Macià?"

"Don Macià?"

"If don Macià sent you to spy on us, you can go tell him we don't have anything to hide... "

"Wait just a minute! Don't get on your high horse in such a hurry! I read about you in the paper, you gave this address, and since Cristina... "

"She's too much, that Cristina," he interrupted. "A real spoiled brat... she didn't give a shit about saving Cala Mura... "

"She told me she cared about it a lot."

"She cared about it so she could have a private beach for herself and her friends. She came looking for us so we would raise a stink, because her uncle and her mother wanted to develop Na Morgana, including Cala Mura, and they were about to convince her father."

"Yes, she told me don Bernat was her guardian, but now that she's legally of age . . . "

"Yes, but now she doesn't seem to give a shit. She used us last time, but she won't fool us again . . . we're going to mount a real campaign and if necessary. . . . " He stopped suddenly, as if he was afraid of having talked too much already. "If you're a friend of Cristina, you must know all this better than we do. And if you really want to collaborate with EGM, you ought to be giving us information instead of asking us for it."

"Listen, I haven't asked a single question so far! You're the one who started giving me explanations."

"It would be better if you talked to the president," he cut me off, as if he wanted to get rid of me.

"Okay, where can I find him?"

"If you tell me where I can get hold of you, I'll arrange an interview with him and let you know."

"Either he's extremely busy and important, or else your organization sure is secretive." I was sarcastic.

"No, it's not that," he seemed a little ashamed now. "We all have other jobs, and we have to find a time to get together."

"I was just kidding." I wrote Aunt Antònia's telephone number on a piece of paper. "I can see you don't trust me, but I'm here with good intentions."

"No, I, well . . . Are you from Majorca?"

"Yes, but I live in Barcelona. Set up the interview as soon as you can."

...

I waited until an attendant indicated that there was a parking space available. Then I went into the offices of Ultima Hora newspaper and asked for Miquel.

A few minutes later, the little vestibule's elevator door

opened and out came the same old Miquel, scornful but smiling.

"Lònia, is it really you? Shall we go downstairs or go out, what do you prefer?"

"It's up to you."

He had his arm around me, but it left me indifferent. You wouldn't know to look at him—a little flabby, half bald, no eyelashes, so unassuming—that he was such a good lay. But I'd had the experience and I considered him one of the best. At least, I had five years ago, the last time we'd tried it together. But now things were different for me, and I hadn't come to see him for that.

"Come on, Miquel, don't make me beg you, shit! I need them to trust me, and if I don't go with someone they know, they won't."

"But I don't give a shit about nature's equilibrium and all that baloney. And since I can't say no, they'll end up getting me involved, I can already see myself writing committed articles against hotshots on military maneuvers on Cabrera; those people are very persuasive."

"I can see they're more persuasive than I am, because you can sure say no to me."

"If you were to ask me for something else . . . "

"Come on, Miquel, don't be a nerd."

"How come you're suddenly so interested in those guys? What have you got up your sleeve? If I'm going to stick my neck out for you, I want to know what's at stake."

"Nothing's at stake, for you. Do you think I go around doing beastly things to people?"

"Yes, for sure! What more could I ask for than you doing a few beastly things to me, sweetie . . . "

"Don't be gross, Miquel. And don't tell them I'm a detective."

"Why not?"

"Just don't."

"Okay, you're the boss. But sooner or later I'll make you talk . . . I have a system of my own for that. When do you want to see them?"

"I don't know yet, they're supposed to call me at Aunt Antònia's house."

"Aunt Antònia, shit! What a harpie, don't tell me you're staying with her?"

"Well, I am. It saves hotel bills, and besides, I love her."

"You love that witch?"

I laughed when I remembered where the grudge had come from. Which was mutual, by the way. Whenever Aunt Antònia heard me mention Miquel, she'd say, "That shameless ne'er-do-well?"

"She's not a witch, Miquel."

"Why don't you stay with me? I have a great big bed."

"Yes, I know. But no thanks."

"At least you'll have dinner with me."

"Not today. Aunt Antònia's expecting me. I'll call you."

XIII

The Bosc Bar was still sort of the navel of the city. It was there that friends would meet to decide what they'd do that evening. It seemed the obligatory place to find people when I lived in Palma, and now too, almost twenty years later. You could always count on running into someone you knew there, if you knew anybody. It was an institution that kept itself solid and effective, right in the middle of such a changing world. Even if the secretary of the EGM hadn't asked me to meet him there, at some point during my stay in Majorca, I'd have asked someone else to meet me there. And if not, I'd have gone there for coffee, or a nightcap; it was a must, like seeing the Seu or Joan des'Aigo's place.

The president of the ecological organization hadn't come alone, either; the thin guy and a girl from the junta were with him.

Indeed, having Miquel along was like making a loan payment to a creditor.

"We've been burned a few times," the president apologized when I teased them about their wariness. "They've tried to stop us more than once, any way they can."

"Okay," Miquel said. "Now that they trust you, I'm not needed here. I'm going back to work."

"No, man, don't go. You can be very useful to us. You can give us a lot of publicity in the paper."

"Friends, you know a person can't do everything. I have my work and my worries. Besides, what can I say? I don't care whether they develop a beach or ruin a marsh. But this girl here can help you for sure, if she feels like it."

"That's right," I said, getting right to work: "For example, there's something I can't figure out. Cristina has reached majority now, and she can dispose of her godmother's inheritance. The last time I saw her in Australia she said she wanted to preserve Cala Mura. Who can decide that, if not her?"

"She's the one who decided," EGM's president said.

That gave me a chill.

"When?" I asked in dread.

"When what?" the president said.

"When did she decide not to preserve it?"

How long had it been since I'd seen Cristina dead?

"We don't know, but . . . "

"Have you seen her recently?" I asked.

"No, we haven't. She gave her uncle full powers to develop the beach."

"What do you mean, full powers?"

"Full powers: don Macià can do whatever he pleases with Cala Mura. Less than a year ago Cristina came to ask us for help to keep them from developing the beach, when her father was her guardian. We succeeded in stopping them, and now it's Cristina, from Australia, who changes her mind without saying a bloody word to us."

"What kind of a man is don Macià Segura?" I asked. "Doesn't he have enough with all his family's hotels? Does he need to build more?"

"That has nothing to do with it." My naivete made the president smile understandingly. "Some people never have enough, and Segura is one of them. But besides, it seems that all his hotel businesses aren't going as well as they should. He'd committed himself to a tour operator to build some deluxe bungalows and a big hotel at Cala Mura. The tour operator has already invested a fortune in it. And when we got them to stop, his other businesses took it through the nose."

"Why?"

"Don't you know how tourism works around here? You don't seem Majorcan."

"I live in Barcelona . . . "

"That's just an excuse. Anyway, it doesn't matter. The tour operator wanted to recover the money it had invested and the Segura family had to fall back on their other businesses."

"But, what was the investment? Had they already started construction on Cala Mura?"

"No, not at the beach. But what with surveys for the island, projects, maps... The tour operator recovered by paying less for each client sent this season to the Segura hotels... or to put it another way, they claim that in fact the hotels now belong to the tour operator."

"But if they develop the beach," the girl intervened, "the tour operator will get his investment back and don Macià can recover... well, not exactly recover, he can keep on doing what everyone involved in tourism does here. At least he can hold on like he did before, with pressure from the multinationals who have all the tourist businesses here mortgaged and who set whatever price they want. Do you think it makes sense that a roundtrip ticket on a regular airline from Barcelona to here costs as much as staying in a nice hotel for a week, with the trip included, to London or Yugoslavia? That way the companies keep getting ahead and the ecological system of the island gets worse and worse, with less and less chance of recovering."

It's not that I wasn't interested in what the girl was saying, but I hadn't come to Majorca to do a study of the unbridled capitalism of the tourist industry. I'd come to find out why, and because of whom, Cristina had died. Maybe that savage capitalism had killed her, but I was looking for more concrete culprits, with faces and legs. Not structural culprits who faded into sociological theories. So I reguided the conversation.

"That must be why Cristina finally gave in and let them develop the beach," I said.

"When we found out that the whole thing was starting to move again, we wrote to her. We wrote again when we found out about the full powers, but she hasn't given a sign of life."

Naturally, poor thing.

"We thought it was strange that she didn't come for her father's funeral, but that's family stuff," the girl, Queta, said. "Just the same we sent her a sympathy card, which she didn't answer."

"When did the development start up again?" I asked.

"Not even a month after don Bernat's death. It wasn't made public, but we found out about it and wrote to Cristina."

"How did you find out?"

"A request for a permit to begin work turned up at the city hall of Llucmajor. Some of the people who work there are in our organization. So we wrote to her right away, and never got an answer. Then we had an interview with don Macià and he told us he had that document."

"When was that? Did you see the document?"

"It was what, about two months ago, right?" the president asked the other two. "He said the notary had the document and we could see it any time we wanted. He said he and his lawyer had gone to Australia and Cristina had signed. He also said he wasn't like his brother and he wouldn't be impressed no matter what kind of hell we raised."

"What did he mean by that?"

"Don Bernat paid a lot of attention to social prestige. He didn't like being in the papers as a person who didn't love Roqueta, as someone who didn't care and would allow the ruin of Majorca to continue. He'd always presented himself as benevolent, as someone who loved the outdoors. He was furious that his name came up in the Balearic Parliament, where his brother defended their interests any way he could . . ."

"Is Macià Segura a congressman?"

"Yes, way to the right," the office guy said scornfully.

"Don't you know any shady deals he's been involved in?"

"What we consider shady deals might not be considered shady socially," the president of EGM said. "But he seems to have his ass covered, or maybe not so much, depends on how you look at it, but he's like everybody else, more or less."

"We've heard he whores around," Queta added. "But even if it were true, it would only be a scandal, and maybe not even that. In any case, it wouldn't help or hurt the cause of the beach. If it was don Bernat instead of don Macià, we could threaten to spill the beans, though we'd rather not use those methods, but don Macià wouldn't give a shit."

"Where does Macià Segura live?" I asked.

"In a suite at the Playa Dorada. Until last year he was the

director, but now he's a client."

"How are your relations with him?"

"A disaster. He's already tried to accuse us of who knows what. Drugs, immorality, he said we had orgies in the office, can you imagine? And also that we're financed by Russia and the Catalans," Queta put in.

"That means he's afraid of you."

"And he says we want to turn Cala Mura into a nudist beach, and we wouldn't mind, in fact Cristina and her friends used to go swimming there in their skins, but it's the kind of thing that can set a lot of people against us."

"At the last meeting of Llucmajor's city hall, a lot of the commissioners voted in favor of development to keep the beach from bringing shame to Majorca, or so they claimed."

"And also because an unspoiled beach doesn't give anyone a job, and a developed place does," the guy said.

"Yes, yes, the usual arguments. The problem is that most people buy those arguments. The majority of Majorcans are flattered by the destruction of the island, there are still a lot of people who believe it's the pearl of the Mediterranean, as they say." The president kept on talking bitterly. "It's like preaching in a desert of cement, hotels and bungalows."

"Weren't there any bribes to get those favorable votes?"

"For sure. But we haven't been able to prove it. And even if we could, that's such a common practice it wouldn't be enough to stop their permit."

"So who does it depend on now?"

"The city hall has to meet again in an extraordinary session, and so does the Insular Council. The Balearic Parliament gets to put a word in too, because a national congressman has to present the motion. But since don Macià's party's got a majority. . . "

"How about don Bernat's widow? I heard she was pretty frivolous," I said.

"No, she's like a cloistered nun. Well, no, she's a high society lady, but she never has a word to say about messes like this one."

As dusk approached, the tables outside the bar started filling up. Among the people looking for a place, more than one had come up to say hello to the guys from EGM. It was making the conversation difficult, so I got to the point.

"Well, it still seems strange to me that Cristina signed those papers. Maybe she did it to save the family fortune, but I think there's something fishy about it. Does the EGM have a lawyer?"

"Yes."

"Do you have any trusted people working at Son Sant Joan?"

"I'm not sure. Why?" the president asked; now it seemed like he didn't trust me.

"A brother of mine works at the public relations office," Queta offered.

"Why do you want to know all this?" the president insisted.

I decided to show them one of my cards.

"Well, I don't believe don Macià Segura went to Australia. Neither he nor his lawyer. More than that, I'd put my hand in the fire if that document of full powers isn't as phony as a three-dollar bill."

"Where'd you get all that?" The president's mistrust was growing. "You know more than you're letting on."

"I don't know for sure, I just suspect. I think Cristina would have mentioned those powers to me. We have to check them out. If my suspicions are correct, we're that far ahead. If not, we haven't lost anything."

"Wouldn't it be better just to ask Cristina directly, since you have more access to her than we do?" Queta was sarcastic.

Of course it would be better, sweetie, but I couldn't tell them that Cristina wasn't accessible to anyone.

"I'll do that, too," I said, "but we can get started in the meantime, right? Someone you trust should check the passenger lists for the last three months. And have your lawyer get a copy of the document that turns the full powers over to don Macià."

"But about the passenger list," Queta was doubtful, "they could have gone through Madrid, or London, and bought the tickets there."

She was a bit too bright, Queta was.

"Yes, of course," I said, "but it wouldn't be too logical, do you think? On the contrary, if the document is false, like I think it is, they'd have wanted to show up on the passenger lists going to Australia."

"Yes, that's true," the president accepted.

They agreed they'd call me when they had the information. When we'd all gotten up, I asked them another question:

"One more thing: What's the name of the tour operator you were telling me about?"

"Gordon Ltd."

Isn't it all coming together too easily, Lònia?

...

"Okay, now you're going to tell me what the hell this is all about," Miquel said.

He hadn't said boo during the whole conversation. He'd barely listened. He let us keep talking without showing the slightest interest, to the point where I found so much indifference rude. He was the calm type, he didn't work himself too hard, he didn't get excited, nor would he stick his neck out for anything. And now he was asking me what the hell it was all about, as if he was asking for orange juice when he wasn't even thirsty. But I figured it would be a good idea for someone I trusted to know what I was getting into, in case something happened.

"Are you that interested?" I said.

"Tsk!"

"I'll explain everything if you'll let me use a camera and a tape recorder."

"Okay, I'll let you have a camera and a tape recorder."

Silence.

"Come on, I have to earn my bread too, and any information about the Seguras could make a nice article."

"Tomorrow I have an interview with a marriage agency... " I began.

"If you're looking for a mate, you don't need to go, sweetie. As long as it isn't for life, I'm at your disposal, as usual, you know that... "

And the times we'd tried it, it hadn't gone badly at all.

"I'm in love, Miquel... Thanks, but no."

"What does that have to do with it? Besides, you're always in love. Too bad it's never with me."

"I don't know whether it has anything to do with it or not... I hadn't thought so until now... but it turns out that now I only feel like doing it with him."

"And where is the idiot, who's not around to take advantage of it?"

"In Australia."

"What the fuck's he doing there?"

"He's from there. I've been in Australia for nine months. I met him there."

Suddenly I missed Henry desperately. I'd missed him all those days, but softly, in spurts. I was dying to show him my island, and through the island Lònia when she was still Apol.lònia or Polita, that person so far away from me now that I could hardly recognize her in myself. I just about started crying, as if Henry was dead, or as if he'd never existed outside of my imagination.

"Don't get all sad, kid. I'll try to be patient. I just thought I'd like to try the experience again, but never mind, I'll get over it." Silence. "Well, are you going to explain, or not?"

"Yes, and to make up for the negative, I'm willing to make a deal with you. A professional deal."

"See? You women always need a man."

"Don't be an asshole, Miquel. Here's the deal."

And I explained all the gory details. How I'd met Cristina, everything Henry and I had discovered in Melbourne, the name Munditourist on a lot of the files of the girls from the Gardener Agency, the reference to Majorca in those files, Cristina's death, the letters donya Carme was still getting from her daughter even though she was dead, my visit to Magalluf, the conversation with the waitresses, following don Leopoldo Cabrer, the marriage agency that really wasn't one, just like the Gardener Agency in Melbourne...

"And that's the agency you have an appointment with?"

"Yeah."

"Are you going?"

"Of course."

"Are you sure, Lònia?"

"Yes."

"You've thought it all through?"

"Come on, don't be a pain, Miquel... I'm used to getting into quagmires, that's my job... "

"Just be careful, those people... "

"Yes, yes I know. Above all, don't write anything about all this for the moment. If you did that before I uncover the whole thing, that is, until I have proof that will stand up in court, well, we'd both be in hot water."

"How do you intend to get the proof? With a camera and a tape recorder? Do you really intend to get in with those people, just like that? Do you really think they believed your fairy tale about being an undocumented Bulgarian? You think they're going to let you into their world so you can snoop around?"

"Yes, they believed it all right. They came to Aunt Antònia's house to confirm it."He looked like he didn't understand anything. "They don't suspect I'm going there to snoop. I'm good merchandise... maybe a little faded, but tax-free."

"But how are you going to do it?"

"I don't know yet. For the moment, the plan is to go back to Happy Life Matrimonial Agency tomorrow to see what that moron has to say. Ideally I'd like to be able to get in and have a look at the files."

"If they have any. They may not be as well organized here as they are in Australia."

"Maybe not, but at the moment it's the only lead I've got."

"But what if they get suspicious about you?"

"I have to take that risk. It's part of the job."

"I suppose so," Miquel said, not very convinced. "When do you want the camera and the tape recorder?"

"I'll pick them up tomorrow."

...

When I went back to Aunt Antònia's, I called Henry, but he wasn't home. His answering machine wasn't on, so I couldn't leave a message, either.

I didn't sleep well that night, either. This time because of missing him and being alone. I had some terrific erotic dreams, better than the most X-rated porno films.

Queta called me first thing in the morning, and at first I cursed her bones. Then I thought maybe they'd made a lot of headway on the jobs I gave them to do, but no.

"Do you want to come to Na Morgana?" she asked.

That proposal kept me from feeling guilty about not fulfilling the moral obligation, so to speak, of going to see Mom. Besides, it would be a sort of homage to Cristina, who hadn't received any at her funeral. Those sentiments made me feel a little cynical, but the sea breeze cleared away thoughts and feelings.

The sun was glorious. The EGM's boat was quite different from the *Mallorquina,* as different as were the bays of Port Philip and Palma. The water was calm, but the sun beating down on it sent a secret vibration through it that filled me with yearnings. No, not for Australia, for Majorca.

In the distance, the silhouette of Cabrera vanished into the mist. Nearby, Na Morgana was reflected in the shimmering water, like the Calabrese mirage of Fata Morgana, and it bewitched us with its island enchantment.

Cala Mura was the only beach on Na Morgana. To get to it, you had to go all the way around the island by boat, or if you landed at the little natural port of Migjorn, it was a long walk. We opted for the walk; we set out for the rocks and filed along the edge of the cliff.

You'd have to be a moron to try to domesticate that wild hill, almost without vegetation, without water, of such savage, hermetic beauty. It was impressive, and not very inviting, and the sun was beating down without pity. Even so, there were traces here and there of the surveying, like shameful and pitiless wounds. To tell the truth, I wasn't much more of an ecologist than Miquel, but when we got to the middle of that little island, naked, small and unprotected, the maternal instinct I'd never had was aroused and I swore to the surrounding sea: no one would put a hand on it.

"I'll bet in Australia there are prettier islands than this one," Queta said. "The Barrier Reef must be much more fantastic than this... but it's all we've got, and we want to keep it."

"Don't be silly, Queta. This is fabulous. There's nothing prettier in the world."

We got to Cala Mura tired and sweaty. It was bigger than

I'd imagined. You could see Cabrera and the islets on the horizon. Majorca was out of sight. With all the charm and the inconveniences of a virgin beach: green, blue, and white—the sand was so fine it sparkled in the sun like cut glass—such tranquility, sensuality... and a pile of tar along the line where the waves broke, heaps of rotten algae, dazzlingly transparent water, with patches of garbage floating around.

"We've come to clean it up a few times," Queta said. "But recently they haven't let us."

There was a yacht run aground on the sand, called Cala Gamba. Its owner was sunbathing in the altogether and listening to classical music. That sylvan sybaritism made me envious. When he saw us, he scrambled to cover his private parts, but Queta had already taken her clothes off and greeted him cordially. The man answered her unenthusiastically but politely, with an accent I couldn't identify. I got into the water, right behind Queta, with my prudish bikini.

It was glorious. That water, so clear, so cold. I opened my eyes underwater and saw an immense world, green, luminous and unlimited.

I thought about Henry. I thought that one of these days we'd be swimming in this water, him like the Cala Gamba man and me like Queta.

Queta was swimming vigorously. It seemed to me that the place wasn't for swimming like that, it was for gliding, for opening the water softly and feeling it rubbing against your sides.

The man with the boat, with his swimming trunks on now, got into the water too, at the other end of the beach.

"Who's he?" I asked.

"A Portuguese guy... I think he used to be a policeman. They call him Mosqueiro. Now he lives on the boat, and he comes here a lot. He's a little strange...."

A plastic bag stuck to my breasts like a synthetic jellyfish. I got out of the water and one of my feet was covered with tar. Total purity wasn't possible anywhere.

XIV

The first blow on the left cheek turned my brain into a bell clapper.

I didn't have time to react. Maybe that's what saved me. Because if I had reacted, I'd have attacked, and now there wouldn't be a Lònia Guiu to tell about it.

The bells were still tolling at full blast in my head when the second blow was delivered, this time on the right, by an open hand, hard and rigid like a steel shovel, blasting my eardrum. I felt a deep, cold stinging go through my head, but suddenly a hotter pain burned my mouth; a bash in the snout with the back of a hand had made me dig my teeth into my lower lip.

I was nauseated and dizzy at the same time, and the world I had in front of me was covered over with a humid, milky, radiant fog. But I didn't fall to the ground because something hard was driven into my stomach, holding me upright. Then, when I did put my feet on the ground, I fell forward. The shiny fog filled with red twinkles when they whacked the nape of my neck; I was dazed for a minute, with a great thunderstorm reverberating in the sounding board of my brain like waves against the pebbles at the beach when there's a summer storm.

I felt like the anchor chain, or a rope or cable we had to haul with the fish spear because it had gotten tangled with something: algae, the reefs, or deceptive rocks.

I was at the bottom of a dark well with stinking, sticky mud clinging to my body, and a hook was grabbing my clothes and tearing my dress, scratching at the neck and pulling me up: the hook was saving me from that filth and the darkness, but some needles were scratching my skin and it made me wail with pain. I could see the mouth of the well, a little round of light, still pretty far up there, and I don't know why but that light terrified me more than the darkness. As they were hauling me up, my head was swaying back and forth, and my brain kept on ringing like the clapper in a bell tower.

With the sinister, deep, resonant bell-ringing, the procession approached, a candle in the lead, and the ringing turned into the beating of a drum. When the candle gets here you'll go blind if you look at it, and the echo of the drum will explode your guts.

That carpenter's brace in my ear, thin and cold like one of godmother's knitting needles, the dead Australian godmother, the dead Majorcan godmother. The more they pulled me up to the mouth of the well, the more my own mouth hurt; my lips didn't match, they'd put them on wrong, they were too big for the size of my face, I had snouts all over the place, they'd put that cleaning lady's mouth on me, she was stretched out on the floor, dead with a silencer. I wanted to open my eyes so I wouldn't see her, but if I opened them I'd be blinded by that golden, rounded light of the candle. Turned out they were already open wide, like two great big eggs on a white plate.

I could hazily see a face that was looking at me, moving its lips as if it were talking, but I couldn't hear anything but chiming. I opened my eyes more but I still couldn't get the face in focus, and then another slap, and another, enough! stop! don't beat me any more, stop beating me Sister Magdalena!

"Evil whore!" I finally heard Sister Magdalena say.

Blood and snot were coming out of my nose, tears out of my eyes and spit out of my mouth, that mouth with oversized lips, full of Australian flies. The cold sweat made the chalk that fell from the blackboard stick to me, mixed with spit, sweat, flies, Mom! Mom! Sister Magdalena beat me and shoved my head against the blackboard and gave me a bloody nose, Mommy, I don't want to go back ever again! I couldn't do the test, I didn't know how to do the test Mom, I couldn't do the fractions, as soon as she makes me go to the board I forget everything, come on, Mom, don't make be go back!

I'd gotten hysterical, desperate, and Mom was shaking me, terrified. Open your eyes! Open your eyes! I finally opened them. But it wasn't Mom, it was a man; where did I know him from? He gave me a damp towel and a glass of water.

"Now are you going to remember?" he said to me.

"If you lay a hand on me again I'll beat you to a bloody pulp, skin you, and stick it you know where," I said.

The glass of water I had in my hand bounded off my face. I thought my nose was broken and I felt the coolness of the water mixing with the warm stream flowing from my nostrils.

"Leave her alone," another man's voice.

But it wasn't Daddy's voice because Daddy was dead. He'd died shortly after I'd told Sister Magdalena I'd beat her to a bloody pulp and the nun sent for my parents. She's blasphemed, it's a sacrilege! Well, it's your fault, my father said, and if you lay a hand on her again, I'll be the one to beat you to a bloody pulp.

Sister Magdalena had run off, horrified, and Mom said to Dad, You're going to go to hell. But Daddy burst out laughing. Mom: You look like a devil, when you laugh like that. But Sister Magdalena didn't beat me again. And two months after laughing like the devil—I like devils when they laugh—my father died. Did he go to hell? But Mom just cried and cried and didn't answer me. Now that Dad was dead, Sister Magdalena started to beat me again, even more than before. The chalk dust got in my eyes and mixed with the tears made a white paste that got stuck in my eyelashes and I couldn't open my eyes.

"Leave her alone," the man's voice repeated.

They put out the candle and left me locked up in the well, which became dark again, an infinite blackness, with the rumble of the drum moving away.

...

How long ago had the man's voice said leave her alone? How long ago had they left me there with the door locked?

My whole body ached like they'd beaten me up. I instinctively touched my mouth and felt a sting; my lip was swollen. Blood caked around my nostrils. I had a bee inside my ear stinging me savagely. Retching, headache, just as if they'd beaten me up.

Now I was starting to remember things. What had really happened and what seemed to have happened. Sister Magdalena and that man. But why had that man beaten me? The nun beat me because I didn't know how to do the problems on the board. Or because she had to take out her anxiety and frustrations in some way. But what about that guy? Moreover, who was he? I knew him from somewhere, but where? Both of them, I knew: the one who said you going to remember now? and the other. What was I supposed to remember?

I was petrified: I didn't remember anything! Yes, a muddle of memories. What had happened?

I tried to get up and almost passed out: what terrible pain, good lord! I palpated my body. Now I remember a blow to the stomach, the scratchings of the hook; my chest was covered with marks. But what about the bruises on my thighs, and that pain in my side? That beast must have given me a few good kicks after the voice told him to leave me alone. Whose voice was it?

The room was somewhat familiar to me, but I didn't know from where. They'd beaten me up, all right. Why? No, it wasn't Sister Magdalena. But maybe I'd just dreamed it this time, like I'd dreamed about being beaten up by Sister Magdalena lots of times. But I couldn't doubt the blows this time; I had the marks. I was terrorized by the idea that they'd beat me again.

It was like a faraway memory that wasn't really mine, as if someone had told me about it. Sor Magdalena was my own memory, but the political beatings were my friend Joana's. Two men had beaten up a woman because they wanted to make her talk and her memory was blanked out by panic. If I found myself in that situation I'd tell it all, I'm no heroine, Lida had said at the time. I'm not either; I wasn't trying to be heroic, I simply couldn't remember. Joana. When they finally let her go, after seventy-two hours of useless torture, she came back to the Majorcan students' apartment undone, destroyed, ill from having discovered how far cruelty, sadism, the coldness of people could go. Those aren't people, Margalida had said.

What about these guys? Weren't they people either? Could

they do the brutal things to me Joana had told us they'd done to her? I felt the same panic I used to feel about going to school. I'd been slugged more than once since then, but I'd never noticed such glee as the nun had when she did it. Until now, when I saw it again in that man I knew but didn't remember.

...

Everything was shadowy around me; I'd dozed off again. I was thirsty, I'd dreamed about the desert at Ayer's Rock, which turned into a rock in the middle of the sea, a reverberating cliff with a white beach, a heap of tar and a little boat launched on the sand, and a naked man who greeted me in Portuguese while I got into the water, all my skin stinging from scratches. I'd drunk sea water, that's why I was so thirsty and my lips were swollen.

You gonna remember now? I thought it was Sister Magdalena, but it was a man's voice, a man I knew but couldn't remember from what or where. Was it him I was supposed to remember? You gonna remember now? My brain hurt from trying so hard. What was I supposed to remember? Surely it wasn't the timetables and fractions. What was I supposed to remember, then? All I could remember was an old lady drinking beer and two fellows throwing darts and singing "Sor Tomaseta where are you?"

"Why did Mrs. Joil send you?"

Mrs. Joil? Who is Mrs. Joil? It sounded familiar, but I couldn't remember where from. I started to sing:

"You better hide now, because the devil is looking for you, he wants to throw you into a well . . . "

They started to undress me without further ado, beginning with the shoes. When they had me completely naked, a savage pinch on the nipple got a shriek out of me.

"Look, if you don't talk I'll hurt you some more, fucking whore! You'll see."

He had spread my legs. I felt helplessly exhausted, like a rag doll without its own mobility, furious but unable to make any effort to bring my legs back together; but the other man said,

"And now you want to fuck this trash? You'd still give her pleasure, you ass!"

And they threw my clothes on top of me.

"Come on, be a good girl and tell us who your pimp is."

My pimp. Who was my pimp? Who was I? What job was I doing? Where had I been beaten up, more than once? Why?

"Why did you come to Happy Life?"

Happy Life. An attack of laughter hit me. Those words, that name. It wasn't the first time they struck me as hilarious. But it was clear that the person who had said them didn't have as much of a sense of humor as I did. He didn't find them too funny. As a matter of fact, I didn't really find them funny. Happy Life: it wasn't funny, it was ridiculous, and that's what made me laugh.

But the man had grabbed my hair and was trying to pull it all out. What nice hair you have, cutie-pie . . . When I told Mom about the man, she started yelling, pig, animal, that pig'll hear from me, he has no shame! She raised a stink in the whole neighborhood, the neighbor was crying, she was furious at me, you're a liar Polita, my husband didn't pull your hair. Yes, he did, not at first, but when I wanted to leave so he wouldn't get it dirty, because his hands were always dirty, he pulled it, all right.

"Why did you go to the travel agency? Why did you say Mrs. Joil sent you?"

Who was he? I'd have given anything to remember. Some vague, unconnected images. Why? Little Polita was Lònia now. Was I Lònia?

Since I was silent, the jumble of blows started up again. He was furious, and I was a sack of potatoes with arms, at the limits of suffering.

"You wanted to get in to look around, huh? What were you looking for? What did you find? Why did Joil send you?" was the last thing I heard before I lost consciousness.

I was falling, falling, I kept on falling slowly, softly, into a dark, bottomless well. While I was falling, I saw a big room with a lot of beds, and a beaten up girl stretched out on one of them.

"Are you sick?" another girl was asking her.

But the girl on the bed turned her back. It was very hot up there, with such a low ceiling and the windows closed. It stank.

Was I one of those girls? No, I was in a smaller room, with a canopied bed and red damask drapes. There I was, dying of disgust, with a man on top of me.

...

My right ear was stinging and I was very thirsty. The two guard dogs, black as coal, were tugging at the chain.

"What's going on?" said the man with the pistol.

He put a silencer on the pistol and killed the two dogs.

I froze, looking at Perla, stretched out on the floor as if she were sleeping. But I knew right away she was dead. My right ear hurt terribly, and my stomach too, but the worst was the pain grinding my brain.

"They knocked her out."

After my father said that, he died. We had a simple burial for him. Lots of people came, because he was well liked. But my brother didn't shed a single tear.

"Come on, kid, let's see a little bit more enthusiasm," said Paca, dirty and greasy, painted up like a parrot.

Then I woke up and looked around the room, and I realized why it was familiar to me. It was the Terreno chalet. How long had I been there? Now I was starting to remember a few things, but my whole body was aching so. I must have had a fever: my head was buzzing. The worst was the thirst and my ear. That door is to a bathroom. I got up to get some water. It was hot but I was shivering. A fever.

I turned on the faucet and filled a huge glass with dark beer, so cool, but so bitter I couldn't keep from vomiting.

The memories were still mixed up in my head. The two dart-throwers from Melbourne started singing "Sor Tomaseta" again and I turned around.

They had opened the door and turned on the light—the two men that I knew but couldn't remember.

"Now do you remember why you came to Happy Life?" the first one said.

I looked at him without understanding.

The other man had stepped in my vomit by the sofa and was swearing. When he finished swearing, he said:

"Who are you? If you're one of Pellerofa's, it's not good for you to be nosing around here, because we'll shred you to pieces so you won't be good for anything ever again. And if you're not, it'll be even worse for you. So you better talk. Who sent you to the agency?"

"I'm thirsty."

"Here, drink!"

A blow to the mouth.

My lip started bleeding again. Where was my nose?

"Pig!"

No, it was bile. The gagging was destroying my suffering body. They made me get up from the sofa and I found myself kneeling on the floor with something pushing my back and head down, until I was cleaning up the vomit with my face.

But afterwards, a woman was making me get up and saying poor thing, washing my face and giving me water and an aspirin.

"I'm Perla, here, drink, it's an aspirin, poor thing, did they hurt you a lot?"

Who was Perla? I'm Lònia, Polita, Paloni, Lonnie. Henry...

"They ripped up your mattress with knives, they tore your suitcase up... then they asked us if you'd given us anything to keep for you... I'm afraid, because somebody said that one, she's made friends with her, and she pointed to me, and they went ahead and grabbed me and gave me a good beating, but I didn't tell them anything. And don't you tell them I came, either, okay? Don't tell them, for Christ's sake... "

That woman with a doll's face tiptoed away. Who was she? Was she a hallucination too, like Sister Magdalena, like Dad or that Puppy-dog Perla? Perla? Who the hell was she?

...

"You gonna tell us who you are, or not?"

It must have been the blow with a newspaper that fanned my face and the corner of paper that stuck in my eye that cleared up the fog covering up my memory.

Or maybe the aspirin Babyface had given me.

Or the metallic click of the automatic pen-knife resounding

in my ear, and the feeling of cold steel on my cheek was what brought my memory back.

"Who are you? Talk!"

I was Lònia Guiu. I remembered I had gone to Happy Life Agency without any documents, precisely so they couldn't find them and identify me. But was I Majorcan or Bulgarian? Or Australian?

I shuddered. Australia. But the image disappeared as soon as it came. They fanned me with a paper again. I looked openly at the man who had literally broken my face: it was don Leopoldo. The one who was threatening to scar it up for me for life. I didn't know, but I'd seen him before. And the room was don Leopoldo Cabrer's office in the Terreno whorehouse.

I remembered it all suddenly, jumbled but sharp. With a panoramic view of all the folds in the brain where memories get accumulated. Cristina on the *Mallorquina* and donya Carme saying my poor daughter, Cristina again with her face buried in the pillow. The Australian granny in the Melbourne pub, and at the same time wrapped up in plastic. Jem and Lida, and Henry; and that disgusting pig from the other day, who wanted them not to seem like whores so he could treat them like whores. And Miquel saying do you really have to go? And Happy Life on the Sor-Tomaseta-where-are-you Plaza.

Inside the squalid Terreno chalet, it all came back to me clearly at the icy touch of the knife.

"Now, explain who you are and what you came here looking for."

But before I could get a single word out, I felt the sharp pain of a cut on my cheek.

XV

The cold, sharp pain of the knife jolted me out of the daze I was in because of the beatings. Suddenly, all the facts arranged themselves in a strict, chronological order; I thought I must be dying, because in less than a minute the memories of those days passed through my brain like the well arranged sequences of a film with a linear plot.

The first image was of me taking a shower to get the salt from the Cala Mura off. Then Aunt Antònia was saying,

"That jerk called you."

"Miquel? Poor kid, Auntie. You still have a grudge against him?"

"He's a jerk and he will be all his life."

Aunt Antònia had caught us dancing and thought who knows what. That was more than twenty years ago.

"What did he want?"

"He said something about a camera . . . that you should come and get it at his house and not at the paper."

Then Miquel was saying to me, "What if something happens to you? How will I know?"

"I'll call you. Don't worry about your machines."

"I won't worry at all if they're in your hands," he said, full of sarcasm.

I left Miquel's place and went to Santa Catalina Thomàs Plaza. I noticed that there was another sign above the one that said Matrimonial Agency in big red letters; it said Happy Life in smaller, blue letters. I went up the stairs laughing.

"I thought you weren't coming," said the moron.

"Why?"

"Oh, it happens a lot. People come in determined to find a companion, but they think better of it later."

"Is that why you came looking for information where I'm renting?"

"Oh, well, you have to understand that we need to be sure about the people we have contact with . . . "

"Yeah . . . did you find anything? Because after your visit, that lady said I didn't need to come back. She thought you were police and she told me she didn't want that kind of people in her house."

"Yeah, I'd say we did. Wait a minute."

He picked up the telephone.

"Leopoldo? Yeah, she came. Shall I bring her?" Pause. "Okay, half an hour from now, then."

He hung up and looked at me.

"It might not be exactly what you were looking for, but it's company and protection," he said.

"That's exactly what I was looking for."

" . . . I mean, well, it's . . . "

"It's a man named Leopoldo? What if he doesn't like what he sees? Or if I don't?"

"Oh, that's no problem! There's no commitment on either side!" Pause. "But it's not exactly don Leopoldo, I've found you a job . . . "

"With don Leopoldo?"

"Yeah, well, not exactly . . . look you told me you didn't have any manias, you'll see in a little while."

In a little while we arrived at the Terreno chalet.

...

The house was bare inside. It still had the beauty of things well done, without money problems and in good taste; but it also had the sadness of splendid things fading into abandonment and decadence. The vestibule had two windows to the garden, but you couldn't see the garden because the shutters were closed.

You could hear music here, too, just like at the Rutherford

Residence. You could smell the fragrance of violet and carnation, mysteriously mixed with an odor of old things.

"From now on they'll call you Perla," said the guy from the agency.

"What do you mean? Why should they call me Perla?"

"Go upstairs and you'll find out," he said.

He'd left the veneer of politeness and amiability outside, and he pushed me with determination up the stairs.

We got to the second floor and he had me enter a room. It was a great big room, half empty, forlorn. There was an ordinary desk, some chairs, a closet; a dirty sofa; the work the plasterers had done another time, the mouldings and curlicues on the ceiling and walls, wasn't at all appreciated by the current residents.

"Hey, Vidal!" don Leopoldo Cabrer said from behind the desk. "This is the Bulgarian?"

He looked me over from head to foot with critical eyes. Businessman's eyes, without that sickening shine like Vidal had in his eyes.

"Yep, she'll do," he decided.

"What is it I'll do for?" An impertinent tone escaped me.

"You're not a kid, so don't be too demanding, or spoiled. You'll be fine here, but if you're not a good girl, we'll take you to the police, and you must know that the police don't like undocumented girls at all." Don Leopoldo was trying to be ironic.

"You're don Leopoldo, the man I'm going to keep company with and who's going to protect me?"

Vidal grabbed me by the arm and forced me to sit down, saying, "You didn't put on so many airs the other day, girlie. You'd best keep them to yourself, because if you don't I'll get rid of them for you."

"You weren't such a creep, either, at Happy Life. If I'd known. . ."

"You don't have any choice now, you don't have anyplace to go, you told me that yourself."

Lònia, get off your high horse. If you don't they'll make you a new face.

"Okay, okay," don Leopoldo said, satisfied. "I don't like her personality too much, but she'll do. Listen, sweetie, if you still haven't figured out where you are, you'll learn soon enough. What we need is someone in charge, so to speak."

"Someone in charge?" I said, pretending I'd been tamed.

"Yeah, in charge of making sure the girls don't disobey. Watch and see if anyone wants to pull one over, or if they fake sick so they won't have to work, or if one of them gets the others riled up, or if they get too friendly with any of the customers... women tell each other their secrets, and you have to keep your eye peeled and tell Vidal everything." He stopped and stared at me. "If you do your job good, you'll have," he chuckled, "company and protection."

"What if I don't?"

"You wouldn't want to know," Vidal put in.

"Okay, fine with me," I said. "I'll do the job, but under one condition."

"This kid wants to put up conditions?" said don Leopoldo.

"Yea. Don't make me go with any... customer."

Don Leopoldo laughed. "Don't worry about that, honey. We have very demanding customers. They like fresh fruit."

Demanding and assholes too. Because I'm not as bad as all that, Jesus Christ! But I kept quiet.

...

They'd made the attic into a dormitory. A mixture of a communal dorm in a convent, an orphanage, a harem and a concentration camp hovel. The beds weren't made, and only one of them was occupied.

"Everybody else is working. They'll be coming up," Vidal said. He looked at the room. "Let's see if you can get them to be a little cleaner!"

And he left. The occupied bed creaked. I turned around and saw a couple of real shiners, feverish ones, staring at me, full of hate.

"Are you sick?" I went over to her.

But she turned her back to me.

It was hot up there, with such a low ceiling right under the roof and the windows closed; it was hot and smelly. The scent of violets and carnations had fermented; the wrinkled up sheets were sticky with sour sweat from having been used a long time;

the pillows were stained with make-up; towels and dirty underwear were piled up on the floor. I went to open a window.

"Don't open it, I'm cold!" the woman in the bed cried out.

"Do you have a fever?" I went back to her.

She had a swollen lip.

"What's wrong with you?" I asked.

"What do you think?" she raged.

Her face was all puffed up too. She was feverishly tangling herself up in the sheets. I uncovered her with a quick jerk. A body of indefinable age because of the marks on her skin: purple, yellow, red and green, a real rainbow of blows.

"Who did this to you?" I was horrified. "Why?"

But she grabbed the sheet from my hands and wrapped herself up again without answering.

I let her be and got to work.

I took the tape recorder and the camera out of the suitcase and went out of that lair to get familiar with the house. Besides the dorm there were two upstairs floors and the ground floor, where the music was coming from, of which I'd only seen the vestibule.

The hallway was dark on the second floor, but light and voices were coming from a half open door to the office Vidal had taken me to a little while earlier. I listened. Vidal's voice, and another man. I waited, and turned on the tape.

". . . it won't happen again," the other man was saying.

"No, they'll be out of commission for a while," said Vidal. "Well, that's done, then. What about Perla's papers? Have they come yet?"

"Not all of them... they say we have to pay cash for the tickets."

Those scoundrels didn't waste any time!

"Shit, those guys are too much! If they start to play the fool... " Vidal stood up. "If we don't get rid of some of them soon, we won't have room for the new arrivals, motherfuckers!"

Vidal started toward the door. I was waiting for the other guy to turn a little so I could take a picture of him, but I slipped quickly up the stairs.

At the landing, I was about to go back up. But then I became aware of my fear. I thought of going back upstairs so that if Vidal came looking for me he'd find me where he left me; yes, that was fear. A fear that had sunk in without me realizing it, from that beaten up girl up there and the sordidness of that house I'd barely even gotten a glimpse of yet.

But so far no one had told me to stay in the dormitory. So, to get over the fear that was already grabbing me, I went back down.

On the first floor, closed bedrooms along a narrow hallway illuminated with red lights. They'd put up dividers to make more bedrooms.

A naked woman came running out of a door toward the end of the hall. She looked as old as me, or more. I brazenly stared into the room; a man, naked too, was lying satisfied on the bed with his eyes closed and his member relaxing in little jerks, with a little drop at the end.

The room smelled of being closed and of rotten semen. The window was covered by red velvet drapes, frayed and dusty, that looked like they hadn't been touched since they were hung when the house was built. A moaning fan didn't refresh the air at all.

"What are you doing here?"

The woman had come back from washing herself and she looked at me, surprised. She looked tired. The man opened his eyes.

"You sending me reinforcements, Paca?" he asked, looking at me.

The woman shrugged her shoulders and went in to get dressed.

"You gonna stay here all night?" she asked the guy.

"Aren't you going to wash me?" he said.

"It's not included in the price you paid."

She'd put on one of those one-piece camisole-undies, so sexy and so uncomfortable, and she left the room looking indifferent. When she passed me, she stopped a second and looked at me scornfully.

"You must be the new pearl," she spit out, emphasizing

both noun and adjective. "Do you think you'll stay dressed up like that for long, in this place?" she took off without waiting for an answer.

The new pearl? Was there an old one?

"Are you coming, or not?" the man said, hope in both voice and tool.

I flipped him the bird and went downstairs. I passed another couple on the stairs, she seemed very young to me, and he skinny, anxious, furtive. They didn't even look at me.

On the ground floor, there was a very spacious room leading to the vestibule, a woman was charging a customer who had just come in and waving him over to a corner where three very young half-dressed women looked like they'd give more pain than pleasure.

That whorehouse seemed like something out of a film, or that I had invented. Old, decadent, from the nineteenth century. Not just the building, but the women and their customers too.

The new customer, gray hair, gray face, gray bearing, was timidly taking one of the girls up the stairs. I looked at the others from the doorway and I thought that they sure didn't have any enthusiasm at all for their work. The cashier must have thought the same thing:

"Come on, girls, a little more enthusiasm!"

If it hadn't been for the sinister air you breathed in there, I'd have laughed at the contradiction between the words she said—semantically nice, as Jem would say—and the tone she pronounced them with—definitely grumpy, I'd say.

"Oh, Paca, go to hell!" one of the girls said.

But the one who was left stiffened up, sitting up more in the chair. It wasn't because of Paca, it was because she'd seen me.

Paca turned around and looked at me, without asking me anything.

"I'm Perla," I said, feeling ridiculous.

"Yes, I suppose so," the woman said, not very happy. Then she growled: "And I thought it was bad before."

So they all knew Perla would come, but no one was willing to welcome her. Professional competition? I didn't think so, frankly, except maybe for Paca, and that's why she growled. But I doubted that too, when Vidal came down.

"What are you doing here? Who gave you permission to come downstairs?"

"No one told me I had to stay up there," I challenged.

"Hey, looks like we're going to have to bring you down a peg or two! Come on, I'll tell you how things are around here."

"It doesn't matter, I already know," I said.

"Maybe you think you do," Vidal roughly grabbed my arm.

"You're hurting me!" I complained.

"I know. That's what I'm doing it for."

As Vidal dragged me out of the room, I noticed the women were smiling. I couldn't tell whether from satisfaction or solidarity.

Vidal took me to the second floor office.

"Let's see if we can get some things straight," he said. "Don't think just because the owner liked you you're going to get different treatment from the others."

The owner liked me?

"In front of them you'll be the same," he went on, "or we might even treat you worse . . . so they'll feel sorry for you and trust you. And you have to do everything you can to make friends with them, so they'll tell you things, whether they've made friends with a customer or want to run away . . . "

"The boss told me that, you don't need to repeat it."

"You'll have to be more polite with me from now on. And watch your step. Don Leopoldo's the boss, but he's not here all the time, and I am. So I'm the one that gives the orders, get it?" A crooked, satisfied, secure laugh. "Either that, or you'll be working every day, just like the others. It's up to you."

"What happened to the one in bed up there?"

The question surprised him and he took a few seconds to answer.

"She did something she shouldn't have done. She talked too much to a customer. She tried to get him to take her out of here. And of course the customer told me. These ladies are crazy. A customer would never help them, customers in this business don't want problems."

"And you'd cause them some, huh?"

"We would and everybody would. What are they going to do, go tell the police? You'll never find a customer coming in here and taking off with one of our whores. And if they go to the police, they have to answer too many questions. One guy went one time, and then the police went to his house to reaffirm the complaint, and when his wife found out he was whoring around he raised hell."

He spoke with a sickening satisfaction. But I couldn't show any disgust.

"What if the police did their checking here instead of at his house?" I got interested.

The crooked, satisfied laugh returned.

"The police don't need to check anything out here, because they already know everything. I'm telling you so you'll know," his tone became threatening, "just like the rest of them know, and so you don't get any crazy ideas. We have our asses well covered. And we didn't pay for them so they could come and go as they please, we paid for them so they'd work. Just like you, anyone who doesn't behave ends up like her, or worse."

"Worse?" I exaggerated my shudder. "You mean you kill them?"

He laughed.

"You don't kill milk cows, you sell them."

I breathed an emphatic sigh of relief.

"But don't think they're better off than here. Go on, we've talked too much."

I didn't want to ask any more questions. I got up, but before I got to the door, he said, "Why don't you clean up a little up there, it looks like a pigsty."

"We have to do it ourselves?"

"Listen to that, lady! Do you think we hire cleaning ladies to clean up your shit?"

...

The next morning I proposed that we clean up the dorm. I thought they'd grumble, but they didn't. They took the proposal as an order; with discipline but not going overboard, they started the job.

It wasn't at all easy to get through the hostility of those women. I don't know whether it was because they knew or intuited that I was there to watch them, or if the situation itself caused that attitude. The fact is that they weren't friends among themselves either, and they were afraid of me.

They had transferred the constant fear they lived in to me, and they didn't dare confide in me. I was afraid of them, too. I was afraid if I told them the truth they'd tattle to Vidal or Paca or one of the other scoundrels who was always hanging around the place, secretly spying on them and taking advantage of them by force. That made it hard to take pictures. I was afraid to leave the camera or tape recorder alone for a minute, because if they found them...

Only one of them made friends with me, and that earned her the hostility of the others. The foreign girl seemed younger than she was at first glance, but if you looked at her carefully, you could see her baby face had worn out skin, her breasts were flaccid, and her hands were covered with wrinkles and marks.

She's the one who approached me, and her meekness and her desire to please me made me feel sorry for her.

"I'll do that," she said. "You do something easier," and she took the broom from me.

"Why?" I said suspiciously. "Aren't you tired too?"

"Yeah, like everybody, but... "

"Because you want to get on her good side, right?" another one interrupted resentfully.

"Just like with the other one in charge! What good did that do you, stupid!" a third one put in.

I kept sweeping, but she followed me around.

When we finished the dorm, we had to do the rooms on the first floor.

I noticed that the others were watching me, but I took advantage of a moment when Babyface and I were alone in one of the first floor rooms to get something straight. Turns out there had been another Perla until recently, doing just about the same things I was doing. And she looked after Babyface. Yes, I'd look after her too. But why had the other Perla gone? Oh, they said they'd taken her to England. The other Perla wasn't happy about that, and Babyface didn't understand why. I did. But intuition told me it didn't make much sense to tell her, because she wasn't too bright, poor kid.

We did some superficial cleaning, with no enthusiasm.

Even so, we were bushed when we finished, full of dust and scunge that seemed part of the house, and of them. I was the only one who took a shower. They made fun of me, not directly, but they didn't hide it either. They were right, after all. About everything. Why should they do a good cleaning? Why should they keep themselves clean? To be more pleasing to the customers? To make their stay there more comfortable? To hell with the customers! The customers didn't bother to get cleaned up, and the girls couldn't make them do it, nor could they refuse to go with them, whether they were clean or dirty. They could only curse them for all the filth accumulated in that house and in their bodies.

XVI

I soon realized I couldn't expect those women to confide in me. Their distrust made my job harder. Would these waitresses I'd met at Magalluf become like them? Those chatty girls, happy with life, with their little upsets and grudges but so confident, so willing to tell it all, would they become surly, resentful, set against each other like these women? When they spoke, it was in yells and barks. When they looked at each other, it was with hatred. There was a pitched battle over the slightest misunderstood gesture, a simple exclamation or sigh. Even the common enemy that I represented for them wasn't enough to unite them.

They kept an eye on me the next day. I couldn't afford to take a wrong step. I couldn't take the risk of going down to the second floor while they were in the dorm. But neither could I afford to not snoop around, one way or another. That's what I'd come for.

After lunch, when customers started coming, I snuck down to the second floor a few times. But there was always someone in the office. On one occasion I managed to get a photo of Vidal and tape a conversation between him and another guy:

"... and you could get me some material... I'd take care of distributing it... "

"Where to?"

"Oh, it depends. If it's pros, there's never any problem, if you know how to handle whoever gets them. If they're girls from the hotels, you have to offer them an honest job, well, you know don Leopoldo's style, right? If they're young and sassy, or hooked on something, but good kids in the end, with families, you have to figure out whether they're really worth it and then go full steam ahead, but tactfully, know what I mean? It always works better to act nice. Take them out to dinner, act like you're in love with them, court them until the papers are all ready . . . "

"What papers?"

"Well, that's just for if we're sending them abroad. In the case of the real young ones, it's best that way, because Majorca is small and if their families look for them, they'll find them, no matter how well you hide them."

"Oh, yeah, I get it. Then as soon as the papers are in order . . . "

"Then you invite them to spend a few days in Madrid or Barcelona, and that's it."

"You place them in Madrid or Barcelona?"

"No, of course not. All over the world . . . our specialty is Australia. Don Leopoldo has contacts in a travel agency that pays for part of their trip. It's a very well set up business, believe me, and it would be good for you to get in it. Australia's a great market. It's an expensive investment, but with great possibilities of getting it all back and more."

"But it must be pretty risky. It's like kidnapping them. And sending them so far . . . "

"That's precisely why the risk doesn't last long."

"It sure is a good business. Holy shit! Australia, the other end of the world. I never would have believed it. What happens when they get there?"

"Oh, they have it all organized, especially in Melbourne. Sydney is more active, but Melbourne is much safer. They do a terrific job, everything with legal coverups, marriage agencies, employment agencies, where do you think I got the idea for Happy Life? Even a nice girls' school, what a scam, right?"

"What about here in Majorca? You know, I'd heard talk about wholesale stuff, but up until now I was just messing around with chicken shit. I had no idea there was so much going on in Majorca, I thought it was all done among ourselves here, well, I knew we had dealings with the peninsula, but small time stuff . . . "

"Haven't you ever dealt with foreign dames? It's the best thing, it's safer, especially the ones who come for a vacation and stick around looking for a job. They're really easy to fool. Well, not all of them, but lots. Besides, they're girls who live alone, sometimes without much contact with their families. I just found one like that myself. A windfall, that one. She came to the agency on her own, she doesn't have any papers, no friends, no family. She escaped from Bulgaria, imagine! She didn't cost me a cent."

"Will you get much out of her?"

"I'm not sure yet. She's a little over the hill. She sure doesn't look like a whore, ha, ha, ha! Since she isn't one. Well, she's not too picky, but she's not a real whore, either. And some people like that. What I mean is even the ones who aren't exactly fresh meat can get some johns, especially if they're clean."

"Well, I only have pros, bought directly. Women bought directly from their pimps, who don't bring me any trouble because nobody's gonna miss them. But they're not always top notch, know what I mean? They know how to work, all right, but they're worn out. For such a high turnover business, I'm not so sure."

"That's why I want to work with you. You have a little experience, but you're still clean. We can get a real good thing going, you and me. Lots of business."

"I'm not sure. I don't want problems. This might be biting off more than I can chew. Are you sure it won't be dangerous? Because that's getting way on the wrong side of the law, just like those Mafia guys in the movies. Jesus, I guess you need to falsify documents, that's pretty heavy."

"Yeah, it's a big time deal, but that shouldn't scare you. We have big fish and little fish. Yes, of course, on the police force, what did you think? We've got our asses covered. I could give you names, but it's better for you not to know them. But you can rest assured on that score. If we need a passport made, we make one, or whatever. We've got things organized here just as good as they do in Australia, and you better believe it."

Fucking braggart.

But someone was coming up and I had to let it go.

You could hear music and laughter on the first floor. I was

about to go down when one of the assholes on guard duty stopped me.

"I was just coming to get you, sweetie."

He pinched one of my breasts. I let out a kick, but I missed. He kept right on feeling me, all smiles, the pig!

His intentions were clear; he wanted to exercise the piece-of-ass rights over me that those guys grant themselves.

"You can look as much as you want," one of the women laughed as she finished her work. "But that one's untouchable. She belongs to the boss."

"The boss didn't say anything about that. Besides, you all belong to him."

He pushed me up the stairs. Employees couldn't use the first floor, that was reserved for customers. The piece-of-ass rights were practiced in the dorm, whether the other women were there or not.

At each step I was madly trying to figure out what I could do to keep that animal from finding my microphone and camera. They were small enough to carry on me all the time, but if he made me undress...

When we got upstairs, I said, "I have to go to the bathroom."

"Oh no you don't. I won't mind a bit if you piss, and if you take a dump, that's even better."

But when he threw me on one of the beds, Babyface came over.

"Let her go," she said to the pimp. "Do it with me."

"Get out of here. I want her, not you."

"She's sick. That's why the boss won't let her work downstairs," she said with her babiest Babyface.

The beast didn't need to be told twice. I stood there like a dolt, watching how she spread her legs with a habitual gesture. I looked on as she closed her eyes and held her lips tightly together. I saw how that pig took her, almost with the same indifference she had. There was so little illusion or desire, so much indifference in that copulation, it was such a mechanical act it made my heart cringe.

Now I wouldn't even need to ask Mercè who was right

about whores, Lida or me. At least as far as the whores of Terreno were concerned.

I ran downstairs, not understanding Babyface's generosity, which had saved me from that jam.

But Paca threw me out of the room unceremoniously, "Working girls only here. Ladies upstairs, you know that!"

I noticed that the telephone on the table was locked up with a chain. I went through a door to the vestibule, toward the kitchen. No one was there, just the odor of that filthy fried fodder they'd given us for lunch. The wall phone was chained too. I went out to the garden. Weeds everywhere. The sun was splendid. I got a whiff of the sea breeze and breathed deeply. But the garden wall was high, and it was crowned with a considerable span of barbed wire. The iron gate was locked. And the dogs, barking furiously, were about to break their chains.

When I went back up, I stopped on the second floor. I opened the door to the office. It stank of tobacco and cobwebs; the women didn't clean that room, and it was always closed except when someone was in it. There weren't any locks on the drawers, a sign they weren't worried anyone in the house would do anything. Still, that phone was chained, too.

I decided I'd have to investigate the room that very evening and get the hell out of the chalet.

...

"Send Perla down," the asshole on duty said. "Vidal wants to see her."

My blood froze. I intended to go down, all right. But not when there was someone in the office. I wondered if that pig wanted to exercise his piece-of-ass rights, too.

"I'll be right down, I'm getting dressed," I tried to keep my voice from trembling.

I made a signal for Babyface to come into the bathroom.

"What's wrong? You're making a face."

"You have to do me a favor, please, honey. Keep this for me. Put it under your mattress, inside your shoes, anyplace. You know this house better than I do. Hide it. And for Christ's sake don't tell anyone."

"What is it?" Babyface looked even more scared than me.

I gave her the tape recorder and the camera. "Please, please," I begged her. "If Vidal or don Leopoldo find it on me, I won't be able to protect you any more, honey."

She took them with regret, but with good will.

But Vidal wasn't calling me in for himself, he wanted me for someone else.

". . . an important customer, we owe him," he was telling me. And as if I was supposed to be flattered, "We have to give him the best in the house."

"I thought the customers here wanted fresher fruit," I couldn't help saying. "Besides, we agreed that I'd just do . . . "

"You'll do what I make you do, who do you think you are? Don't you see how the rest of them mind? And you better learn if I tell you something, I'm not asking you whether you want to or not, I'm telling you, and you better make me look good, understand? He's a demanding man, he's not interested in fantasies, that is, his only fantasy is that he likes to pretend he's doing it with an honest woman, not a bought one, a conquered one, understand what I'm telling you? You need to make him beg a little, act like you're embarrassed, pretend you don't know much about it, pretend he's a great fuck. He isn't at all," he let out an ironic little laugh, "the others told me, but act like he is. And you have to sleep with him all night, until he leaves in the morning. You know. Now put on your Sunday best and come down and wait for him in room 5."

My lucky number.

I got the tape recorder and the camera back, and I went downstairs, not feeling very willing to make the sacrifice.

I can't say he forced me, to tell the truth, because I'm no Maria Goretti and I didn't put up any physical resistance. I tried to wheedle him with words, and he took that as a kind of verbal resistance which turned him on even more. I thought I'd lose the desire to fuck forever. And I really like it! But when I want to, the way I want to, and with someone I want. Like all women, naturally. I'd always been able to do that, until now. On this occasion, none of the three conditions were met. On the contrary.

It was so disgusting I don't even want to remember, it's

come into my memory plenty of nights without me wanting to think about it. There was only one good thing: I felt such scorn for that man, just like all the whores in the world must feel about their customers, I guess, even the ones who aren't conscious of it. Even the ones who aren't forced to work like the girls in the chalet at Terreno. That feeling of superiority over the male who was on top of me made me feel solidarity with all the women who hadn't had a chance to experience it themselves.

To liven things up, he got out two lines, one for me and one for himself. But me, being so pure—and because I didn't feel like it—I turned him down.

"I have more," he said to me in Spanish. "I have as much as I could want."

"It'll make me dizzy, though, for sure."

It seemed he liked my attitude a lot. I wasn't holding back on the instructions of my pimp, either, it was just that the times I'd tried it—whether the stuff was for snorting or smoking, it didn't matter—I'd ended up in heavy seas, not liking it at all.

"We won't tell your old man," he said.

And here Vidal was telling me he didn't have any fantasies, what a jerk! He had them, all right. Who knows who he was fantasizing me to be, or himself. I decided I'd have to figure it out.

So I took a hit too, and he was satisfied at having perverted a big grown up ripe girl like me.

"Well, you like it?"

"Sure, a lot," I took a deep breath. "Who gives you this nice powder? Don Leopoldo?"

"No, sweetie, in any case I'm the one who gives it to him."

"You're good friends, huh?"

"Well, sort of, let's just say we have common interests. And since they owe me some favors, but your old man doesn't need to know that."

My old man? What the hell was he talking about?

"What's he not supposed to know? That you and don Leopoldo are doing business?"

"Oh, he knows that! But not that you've been with me," he went on with a mysterious air.

"Why not?"

"Leopoldo told me not to say anything to don Macià, because he knows that with women, I'm well, you know what I mean, but don't worry, if you don't say anything, everything will be okay."

Don Macià! Don Macià was Cristina's uncle, not my old man! I had to try to keep my head on straight.

"Do you give this powder to him too? Tell him to give me some, if you tell him, he will," I put on my sad face. "But then he'd know that you and I. . . . " My voice came out sort of weird because I could hardly keep from laughing.

"I'm not going to tell him. He doesn't have anything to do with all this. I'll give you some, all you want."

"Really? That's great. Have you known don Macià for a long time? I never saw you at the Playa Dorada."

"No, I've never been there. I don't know don Macià much at all. He's an important fellow, yes indeed! But I deal with don Leopoldo, and it's him that comes to see me."

"Oh, I get it. You're the owner of a travel agency and you send tourists his way."

He laughed. Imbecile.

"No, no . . . "

"Then?"

". . . I do favors for him, big favors."

"You give him cash?"

"No, papers."

"Papers? What kind of papers?"

But he didn't feel like talking, he was interested in other things.

"Hey, this kid wants to know everything. If you behave, I'll tell you."

I trusted that the conversation had been clearly recorded on the tape I had set in the half-opened drawer of the night table. I behaved, all right. Swallowing disgust by the bucketfuls.

But we couldn't continue the conversation because as soon as he finished he was out like a light. I washed myself very conscientiously, turned off the tape and checked out his pockets.

Fantastic! Of course he could get me as much as I wanted of that stuff, he must have been loaded with it, holy shit! The favors he did for don Leopoldo must be colossal.

I took one of his calling cards, a couple of the pages from his calendar, already past, where he had noted a visit with L.C., with a list of the papers he needed to get for him.

I took pictures of the other documents, and I took one of him, stretched out on the bed in all his glory. With two decorative objects on the pillow, one on each side of his head.

You fell for that hook, line and sinker, pal.

I got dressed without making a sound. It was time get the hell out.

...

The ground floor was completely dark and quiet. I could hear a woman's laughter coming from one of the rooms on the first floor. When I thought of what I'd had to do in a room on that same floor, the laughter seemed like a shriek, an insult. But I couldn't waste time on that kind of speculation at the moment. I went to the stairway and headed for the second floor. I got into the office with no problem. The same odor: dust and cobwebs. I opened a little doorway; the corner street light would give me a little light. I waited a few minutes, and as soon as my eyes were accustomed to the darkness, I went to the desk.

There were some files in the middle drawer. I put them on the table and opened them up. I stopped at one of them labeled "Perla's Papers": a one-way ticket from Munditourist in the name of Perla González, but not just to London, to Melbourne; a passport in the same name and an envelope with the name of Rutherford Residence; inside the envelope, a full body photo—it wasn't of any of the women in the chalet—and, on Munditourist stationery, her anatomical details, state of health, a short resume in English of her situation, which said she was susceptible to Rossenhill. It was all typed, with a signature at the bottom.

I finished looking at the other files but I didn't find anything interesting. I kept it all, but I left Perla's dossier on a chair so I could take a picture of it when I finished my investigations.

I stopped for a minute and listened. Not a sound. I went to the door to make sure there was silence and then came back to the table.

My head felt like it was about to explode. And when I opened one of the side drawers and took out a bunch of papers, I realized my hands were shaking, too.

From that bunch I chose a few papers with lists of women's names handwritten in pencil. At the bottom of the list, the name Paloma Martos appeared, written in ink, in a different handwriting. Beside each name were some numbers and a few words. I went to the window to see it better. I concluded that the numbers were the measurements and age of each one; some names had "wai" written next to them, others had "pros" and the rest "ross." Then another number. I didn't take the time to try and figure out what those words and numbers meant, but I left the list on the chair.

There were some photos in a box. I looked at them. Each one had a woman's name on the back and some of them had a man's name too: Xato, Manolo . . . or other names, like H. Life Acapulco, Roca Viva, Playa Dorada . . .

Wasn't Roca Viva the hotel the Segura family owned at Cala Millor?

There was a picture of me, too. When had they taken it? In the dorm bathroom, it looked like. Naked. Fuckers! My name on the back, H. Life and "ross," followed by a question mark. I wondered if it meant Rossenhill.

I thought I heard a noise. I froze for a moment and listened. I heard the dogs downstairs shaking their chains. I felt a carpenter's brace going through my left temple, but I kept on.

Among the other photographs, I saw one of Queta. How could it be? I went over to the window. It was Queta, all right. What on earth was she doing there? There wasn't a woman's name on the back. Just the letters EGM, with MS in parentheses. Taken aback, I chose a few photos and put the others away.

I opened another drawer. It was full of bills and receipts, in no order. From Munditourist, and other businesses I didn't recognize. Too bad I couldn't take them all, because it was impossible to photograph them, and it would take too long to make some kind of conscientious choice. But since they were completely disorganized, maybe it wouldn't be too risky to take a few. No one would be the wiser. When I was putting them back into the drawer after choosing a few at random, I saw a strange object in the bottom of the drawer. I quietly stamped it on one of the bills I was going to steal: it was a postmark from an Australian post office. Mechanically, I looked again at the bottom of the drawer. There was a file.

Inside, blank envelopes and stationery, but some of the blank papers had a signature at the bottom. It was Cristina Segura's.

The carpenter's brace had gone through my temple and was jabbing into my brain insidiously. But my hands weren't shaking any more. I looked through each of the papers and envelopes. I found a photograph of Cristina, beside a pool, smiling, satisfied with herself and with the life she was leading.

Poor wretch.

The letters MS appeared on the other side of the photo. Macià Segura, of course.

I froze again, with the photograph in my hand. No, this time it wasn't the dogs shaking their chains. This time it was the office door, opening up wide, flooding the place with light from the hallway, a man rushing to the desk, me on the floor, with Cristina's picture in my hand.

The first blow to the left cheek turned my brain into a bell clapper.

XVII

The cut on my cheek brought my memory back, and also a clear consciousness of the situation I was in. How was it possible I hadn't heard them coming? And what was the significance of some of those questions they asked between blows?

With my eyes closed, I heard voices. The two men who had been taking turns beating me were saying:

"... and these goddamn ecologist whores sticking their noses in!"

"But what's the deal? What do the ecologists have to do with Munditourist?"

"Don Macià wants to send one of them to Australia too, to teach them a lesson, but the London people don't want to have anything to do with that."

"They've got the right idea. Fuck Macià."

"He says if we don't shut the riff raff up, there won't be any development. I'm between a rock and a hard place. And now this bitch... "

"Do you think she's an ecologist too?"

"I don't know. She used Joil's name at Munditourist, that means she knows too much. Let's get going again, this time she better sing her song, otherwise... "

What was I in for now?

I felt the warmth of the trickling blood. My head started spinning like a top.

I'd lose my memory again, my sense of time, and my own,

personal, intransferable identity. I knew if that happened again, I wouldn't be able to take it.

They grabbed me by the hair and forced me to open my eyes.

"Where do you know Mrs. Joil from?" Cabrer was asking me. "What do you know about Australia?"

Cabrer had my head down, with the knife at my cheek. Cabrer, supposedly the owner of Playa Dorada, the Segura's best hotel, was now changing the position of the knife. With a little pressure he could cut my jugular.

"Why did you go to Munditourist asking for the person in charge of trips to Australia?"

"Mundiwhat?" I heard coming out of my throat without permission.

"Don't play the dumbshit!" a puncture in the neck. "They recognized you!"

That's why I'd dreamed about Sister Magdalena. I'd seen her double.

But they were distracted by running around and screams. The door suddenly opened and a troop of men came in, among them Quim and Miquel.

...

". . . so I made up my mind to follow you . . . "

"You followed me?!"

"Yep, all the way to Happy Life," Miquel said.

Me, the big pro tailer, I didn't even notice!

The doctor came in to give me his diagnosis. I felt crippled on the inside and maimed on the outside. But according to the X-rays, I only had two broken ribs and a dislocated shoulder. Besides, my liver and spleen were swollen, and I'd have to take medicine and be careful. The kidneys are okay. I'd have to watch the right mammary gland too, but the doctor didn't think there'd be any complications from that. Then there was my ear: if the treatments they'd done on it didn't take care of the problem, they might have to operate later on. Vidal had given me a pretty good thumping, all right. But now he was going to pay for that along with everything else.

As far as the rest of it was concerned—a messed-up lip and eyebrows, cuts on the cheek and neck, some horrible bites I'd done myself on my tongue and the insides of my cheeks, and the general bruising, all that would get better with a little Mercurochrome, moth balls, and rest.

"Rest? I can't rest right now!"

"It's up to you," he laughed. "You'll see, you'll be forced to rest." He paused. "Do you want me to give you a shot for sleeping?"

"No, I don't want to sleep. They already made me sleep too much!"

"It would do you good," he paused and hesitated. "I haven't seen such a badly beaten up woman for quite a while, and this is where they come, now."

"Now? How about before?"

"Not that much. They used to keep it to themselves. But they do come in now, and they're the ones who want to report it. Do you want to report anything?"

"He did it," I pointed to Miquel.

The doctor froze.

"Well, I thought, oh well, you see something new every day," he murmured.

"What do you mean?" I asked. Suddenly I understood. "You didn't by any chance think he's the one who beat me up, did you?"

"Well, there are men who beat their wives up and then bring them in themselves."

"It was her husband who beat her up," Miquel interrupted before I could say anything. "But I'm not her husband. No, we don't want to report anything."

The doctor left, and I asked Miquel to go on with the story.

". . . I wanted to know where they were taking you, so I waited outside the agency. When you came out, I followed you in a taxi. I've never felt as ridiculous as when I said 'follow that car,' which came out in Spanish."

"You see too many movies, Miquelet . . . "

"And since you didn't call me . . . "

"How on earth could I have called you, asshole! All the

telephones had chains on them and Paca guarded that key jealously."

"Well, I started to get worried, and I called Happy Life, and. . . "

"You called Happy Life?!"

"Yeah. . . "

"Jesus Christ, Miquel! What a way to help me, holy shit! Now I understand why they were asking about my pimp! I've just gotten the worst beating of my life because of your stupidity! What a way to help me!"

I was so furious I would have slapped him. But I was so frazzled I started crying instead. How could he be so dumb, poor guy?

"But didn't you just say they caught you spying?"

"Yes, but surely that just would have been good for a few slaps. Afterwards they came back and asked me who my pimp was. Why didn't you call Barcelona right away?"

"I did. When the guy from Happy Life said he wanted to talk to me, for me to tell him where I was and he'd be right over, I made up an address in Son Gotleu and took off. I saw him coming, with two other guys. The address I'd given him was a store, but I watched for him outside. Those guys raised hell, until the police came. But the police didn't do anything to them. That's when I figured things were getting too complicated, and I called Quim. He came flying. . . "

"Literally."

". . . and I explained everything I knew to him. . . listen, is Quim gay?"

"Yes, go on."

"Quim said he'd have to go in there where you were, and he went over in the evening but they wouldn't let him in, they told him it was a private club, members only and their guests. That's when we went to the police station to report everything. Nothing but problems. They sent us from Herod to Pilate, until we finally ended up with Inspector Vargas, who slapped us in the tank right there at the station, without letting us even make a phone call. But the director of my newspaper knew we were going in to report this stuff. When he realized we weren't coming back he went to the police station with a lawyer. We weren't even registered as under arrest, but the lawyer insisted and threatened, and they finally let us out. Quim said we'd have to get into that bordello one way or the other, and it sure wasn't the usual way. So why are you crying now?"

"Do you write your stories as badly as you tell them?" I was bawling.

"Quim said you're going to get skinned one of these days," Miquel changed the subject. "And that you shouldn't have gone to the Terreno chalet."

"Oh, yeah? I'd like to know what he would have done, in a situation like that. By the way, where is he? Don't tell me he went back to Barcelona, the rotten jerk! Jesus Christ!"

"What's wrong?"

"All those papers I found at the chalet... that was a gold mine, all that documentation, Jesus Christ!"

"You said that, just before you went under, when we went in to rescue you."

It was true, they had rescued me, I had to admit it. But at the moment I was into other things.

"I said that? What happened?"

"Quim grabbed it all."

"How about the camera and the tape recorder? I had them hidden in my shoes."

"Yes, the nurse found them when they were undressing you. Didn't your feet hurt?"

That was the least of my worries, sore feet.

"So where's Quim now?"

"At my place, going through all the material."

"Him? He's organizing it? I want it all right here. Right now, Miquel... "

"You have to rest, Lònia... "

"I said I wanted it all here, now!"

"Okay, call him up yourself."

"Wait, listen, who were the other people you busted into the place with?"

"Those guys from the EGM. Oh, yeah, Queta gave me this to give you."

It was an envelope. Inside, there was a photocopy of the full powers document. Good kid, Queta was.

"Poor girl," I heard Miquel saying, and I got a lump in my throat. She got mugged the other day... since she didn't have much on her, they gave her a pretty good beating. Not as bad as yours... "

"They weren't after money. They wanted to teach her a lesson."

"What makes you say that? How do you know?"

"Where is she now?"

"At her place."

"What about those thugs from the chalet?"

"We freaked them out."

"What about those poor women? Did you leave them there?"

"Holy Toledo, Lònia, we couldn't save the whole world!"

Poor girls.

"Listen, have Queta go into hiding. Not to stay at her own place, but not with any of the EGM people either. Don't ask questions, Miquel. Hide her. And leave me alone now, I'm tired."

"But didn't you say you wanted the papers?"

"No, not right now, I'll look at them tomorrow. Right now I want to sleep. Oh, take this roll and get it developed."

"By the way, your Aunt Antònia raised hell at the newspaper. She thought I'd kidnapped you."

...

As soon as Miquel left, I got myself out of that straightjacket they put me into and got dressed in the sweaty, mangled clothes I'd been wearing all those days at the chalet. How many days? I looked at myself in the mirror. I sure looked terrific, good grief! I wondered if I'd ever look the same again. I combed my hair forward to hide my face, but I still looked awful. Patience.

I looked out the window. The sun was out, and I didn't want to waste any more time. I left a note: "Quim, Miquel, don't do anything, wait until I get back." I put the tape recorder in my pocket and left the clinic, walking slowly and limping a little because of the broken ribs.

The taxi driver had to help me get into the taxi.

...

Paloma was in her place, behind the bar at the Playa Dorada. During the questioning, I didn't remember them mentioning my going to the hotel or interviewing the waitresses. Everything seemed quiet, no one had linked me with the German journalist.

"Hi! Did you come to take the pictures?"

Goddamn girl!

"No, not yet, not today. Listen..."

"Geez, what happened to you?" she was alarmed.

"I had an accident. Listen," I said in a confidential tone, "the customer who has the suite... yes, don Macià, he asked me to come to his room today, but he doesn't want anybody to know... What number is the suite?"

"412, but he's not there right now." She looked at her watch. "I served him some whiskey about two hours ago and he told me to tell them in the kitchen he wouldn't be here for lunch."

"That's strange," I lied. "He told me we'd have lunch together in his room."

"He always eats in his room, but today..."

"What shall I do?" I acted surprised, but got over it right away. "Well, I'll wait for him anyway. How can I get in? I don't have the key."

"I can tell the cleaning lady who does that floor, she has a master key."

"Perfect. But she should keep it to herself."

"Don't worry, but you'll have to give her a tip." I took my wallet out. "No, not for me," she said with great dignity. "Go on upstairs, I'll let her know from here."

"Great, thanks, honey! If you see him coming back, let me know, but don't tell him I'm there," I added, trying to look mischievous. "I want to surprise him."

I went into the vestibule and crossed it without looking at anyone, as if I'd lived in the hotel for a month. I got in the elevator and went up to the fourth floor. There was a girl in the doorway of room 413. I stopped next to her without saying anything, and she opened the door without saying anything either. A chill went up my spine: that situation reminded me of another one. Surely because of that I put a ten dollar bill in her hand. She stared at me, amazed. Maybe it was a mistake to give her such a big tip; she'd remember me too well. But it was already done.

It wasn't exactly a suite, it was two connecting rooms. A living room/dining room and a bedroom with two individual beds. Up against the wall of the living room there was a little desk.

I started to open drawers and compartments. Everything was empty. Either it was just there for decoration, or else he had already taken all compromising objects out of it. If they hadn't taken me to the clinic, Macià wouldn't have had time to get rid of anything.

I closed the drawers and went into the bedroom. Under one of the beds I found a half packed suitcase, full of stashed away clothing. Then I started rifling through the closet. There were more suitcases on the top shelf—all empty—and a small case. A locked case, that I opened without a key, but I broke it; I was more nervous than I thought.

That was a gold mine. The letter Cristina left on board the *Mallorquina* was in one of the compartments. I didn't read it, I just unfolded it. Don Macià was an imbecile for keeping it—he'd have been better off to burn it.

Some onion-skin sheets were in another compartment, copies of the letters Cristina had supposedly written to donya Carme.

In another compartment there were two handwritten sheets, with lots of corrections in ink. They were the rough drafts of the letters donya Carme would never get from her daughter.

Still another compartment had three envelopes with the name Carme Llofriu de Segura on them, with Australian stamps and postmarks. Each envelope contained a letter like the one I'd stolen from donya Carme, but with a future date to match the postmark. They were the next letters she was to receive, but she wouldn't be getting them now.

What a chaos of letters and signatures, between the chalet and the hotel! I still wasn't sure why there was material both there and here, or exactly what the letter-writing process was, but I didn't have time to think about it now. To me it seemed like an insane way of creating problems for themselves.

I took a rough draft and a couple of the copies of letters already sent. Something told me not to take one of the future letters, but surely Segura wouldn't stop to make sure everything was there in that little case, surely he'd grab it the way it was and get rid of the whole thing. So I lifted one of the false letters ready to be sent and looked for its corresponding rough draft. Why the devil did he keep them, that lunatic?

Since I was there, I snooped around a little more. In a cardboard shirtbox I found some plans for bungalows, photos of Cala Mura, numbers on a piece of paper. And an envelope from Munditourist with a note telling him they were including a photocopy of the letter they'd received from the main office in London: a letter from Gordon Ltd. demanding, in the harshest of terms, the fulfillment of their contract with Macià Segura. They didn't say what contract, but it wasn't necessary.

I didn't have time to look any more; the telephone rang.

"Lònia?" It was Paloma. "The man you're waiting for just arrived."

"Coming up the stairs or the elevator?"

"What?" the question surprised her. "Oh, I don't know. I just saw him come in, I can't see either the elevator or the stairway from here. Maybe he went into the office."

"Okay, thanks a lot, Paloma."

I tried to close the case so when it was opened it would look like a paper had kept it from closing right, and I left it and the shirtbox just like they were before.

I stuffed the stolen papers in a pocket, but when I was about to leave, someone was putting a key in the door.

I'd never found myself in such a ridiculous situation. Where was I supposed to hide? On the terrace, in a closet, or in the bathroom, naturally. But whenever I saw a movie or read a novel where someone hid in those places, I hadn't found it very credible, especially if the person who was hiding didn't want to be found. Because when someone comes into their hotel room, most likely they'll go take a piss or change their clothes, or both. They might not be quite so likely to go out on the terrace, but they could, especially in the summer without the air conditioning on. So, without needing further reflections, I dived under the bed that didn't have a suitcase under it. I was forced to remember that I had two broken ribs and my whole body was bruised.

I didn't try to look out from under the bedspread to see who had come in and what they were doing. I did try to listen, but my heart was beating so scandalously hard that I was afraid the whole hotel could hear it. And as if that wasn't enough, the whole pummeling came back to me. While I was working, the interest and tension of the job made me forget about my body. But now my right ear was whistling like a train two steps away, my dislocated shoulder had gotten stiff and I couldn't move it, and all my insides were complaining about the abuse. Without counting my lip, which had started to bleed again, and just a general depression that made me doubt my ability to get out of there once the danger was past.

Even so, I could tell only one person had come in, and I thought I could hear him opening drawers, which I assumed were to the desk. Then I heard footsteps around the bedroom, a door opening, and a few minutes later, the toilet flushing. Finally, more footsteps in the bedroom, and the closet door opening.

I felt a weight on the bed, and then steps from the closet to the bed. I figured he must be packing the other suitcase. Then something fell on the floor and I heard a curse. From under the bedskirts I could see the open case with all its contents spread out on the floor. Some hands were gathering up the papers, stuffing them into the case any old way, then they closed it and they must have put it inside the other suitcase on top of the bed I was under.

It seemed to go on forever. Besides the pain and the fear, I was sweating horribly, and you couldn't say that yours truly was particularly neat and clean; my mouth was full of that inexorable dust that accumulates under beds from who knows where.

Both suitcases were on the floor now, but the guy still wouldn't leave. Now he's going to sit down on the bed and he'll squash me, I thought. But he didn't. He sat on a chair next to the bed and changed his shoes. He was sweating too; I got a whiff of foot odor that nearly made me puke. Pig.

Finally the two suitcases and the new shoes started moving, the door opened, closed, and silence returned.

I didn't move for a while. I'm not sure whether it was because I didn't have the strength or because I wanted to make sure I was out of danger.

When I came out from under the bed I had to brush the dust off my hair and clothes.

The closet door was open, there were shoes and socks strewn carelessly in front of the chair, and a sport jacket on the bed. There weren't any clothes in the closet, nor were the shirt-box or the little case there. In the other room, some shelves hidden by a painting—Lònia, you're such an idiot not to have noticed that—they were empty, too.

I went to the bathroom. I took a long piss, splashed some cool water on my face, tried to comb my hair a little with my hands, and not very happy about the way I looked, I left the room. An elevator stopped at that very moment. I slipped toward the staircase and slowly went down. I went over to the pool. Mixing in among the tourists, I disappeared as quickly as I could through the garden gate leading to the beach.

...

The graphologist frowned. He preferred more original material, it was more secure.

". . . I'd say, well, I don't think the two signatures were done by the same hand."

"I don't just think it, I'm sure."

"Then why are you asking me?"

"Because I need a professional opinion, and not just an opinion, a report, or however you call it. A legal document."

"I can't do that unless I can compare two originals."

"Well, for the moment, the only original I have is this letter. I only have a photocopy of the other document. Do you mean to say you're not sure?"

"Well, I'm almost positive, but I can't make a legal document, or rather, even if I made you one, it wouldn't have any value, it wouldn't do you any good, you wouldn't be able to use it in court."

"Okay, for the moment your own private opinion will do."

His own private opinion was that the signature on the document was done by a different hand than the one that had signed the letter. Even better, the letter was written and signed in a woman's handwriting and the document was done by a man.

Then I had him compare the signature on the document with the signature on the phony future letter I'd just stolen from Macià Segura's suite.

"Yes, it's almost sure they were done by the same hand," the graphologist said, "but like I say, with just a photocopy... besides a serious study takes more time. Graphology isn't a game, it's a science. Are you ill? You don't look too good."

Of course I didn't look too good. I was about to lose it from my ribs pushing into my spleen, it made me see stars. I sat down.

"I feel better now. It's the heat, I can't take it," I said. "Go on, please."

"Well, it's like I said, I can't use a photocopy."

Stubborn as a mule.

"Okay, we'll have the original when the time comes. For now just give me your private opinion."

His private opinion coincided with my suspicion. The same hand had falsified Cristina's signature on the letters and on the full powers document.

To wrap up that whole affair, I had him compare the rough draft I'd just stolen from the hotel with Cristina's two false signatures.

The graphologist examined the rough draft carefully, then he looked at what was written for a moment, and he said to me, "This is a little tougher. Come back tomorrow or the next day."

"No, I need to know right now. I'll pay whatever it takes."

"You can't buy time."

"I know that. But it's absolutely necessary for you to look at it now. Please."

"Okay, but it'll take a while."

"I'll wait."

It did take a while, and for me the time was filled with ghosts. I noticed that if I sat too long, I couldn't get up. I tried to entertain myself examining the house, but I started to see stars. I leafed through books and magazines, but I couldn't concentrate. My nerves were gnawing away at me. By this time, Quim or Miquel had probably gone to the clinic, and who knows what they'd decided to do when they found my note. Unless some nurse had already raised the alarm about my disappearance, or if Aunt Antònia had gone to see me... not finding me, she'd raise hell.

I sat and wondered what don Macià Segura was doing now? It could be that while I insisted on making the graphologist work, he'd already taken off for the ends of the earth. The fuzzy thoughts were making me sleepy.

Finally, the graphologist called me.

"Yes, as a matter of fact, this signature was done by the same hand as this paper. Look at this curlicue... "

"Excuse me, but I don't know a thing about graphology, and I can't take the time right now. What do I owe you?"

"Come by another day and we'll talk about it. And bring Miquel, I haven't seen him for ages."

I left happy. But time was getting away from me and I still had to go by Aunt Antònia's house to pick up the letter Cristina had left for me at the Melbourne whorehouse. It was absolutely indispensable for the last errand I had to run.

My body and my head had been telling me to stop for quite a while. But since I was there....

XVIII

"Is donya Carme Llofriu here?"

"Just a moment please. Who is it?" the maid asked. "Oh yes, you're Cristina's friend. Is my baby okay? Come in, come in."

Donya Carme received me with open arms.

"Oh, honey, what happened to you? Have you been mugged? Sit down, sit down, honey."

"I have a letter for you from Cristina," I said without sitting.

"Oh, my God, Cristina! A letter, you say? But I don't understand why she sent it to you, if it's for me. . . "

"I'm quite sure it's different from the other letters."

The Segura widow looked at me without understanding.

"Sit down, honey, you don't look too good. I'll have them bring you something warm. . . "

Something warm in that heat!

"No, it's okay, donya Carme. I'm in a big hurry."

"Wait just a second," she rang a little bell and the maid appeared. "Tell don Macià to come in."

I sure wasn't expecting that.

"He's my brother-in-law. He's crazy about Cristina, too. He'll want to meet a friend of hers."

No doubt.

And in comes Macià Segura.

"She's a friend of Cristina's from the residence," she

hurried to introduce us. "She just got back from Australia, and. . . "

"What!?"

Don Macià was a robust man, healthy looking and one of those guys who looks like he knows how to take advantage of the good life. About fifty years, well lived, enjoyed, and satisfied ones. But the news his sister-in-law just gave him made him turn gray. I realized he was the same man I'd seen talking to Leopoldo Cabrer the day I'd followed him. He was wearing the same shoes he'd just changed into at the Playa Dorada.

He looked at me like I was a scarecrow and he couldn't believe it. Then, a fraction of a second later, he seemed to get a great idea and the color returned to his face.

"A friend of Cristina? You must be one of her teachers because you're older than she is, aren't you?" he said with a teasing little smile.

"No, I'm a friend, but not from the residence," I said

"By the way, you haven't given me the letter yet," donya Carme said.

"The letter?" said don Macià.

"Yes, just imagine! They just brought one up for me from downstairs and now this girl's bringing me another one."

Don Macià had turned gray again. Besides, now his eyes were bulging out and it looked like his shirt collar was going to choke him.

"Well, let me see the letter," he reached his hand out to me, but I handed it to donya Carme.

"That's weird, she put Bernat's name on it. . . Oh, it's a nice long one," she said happily.

She sat down to read the letter.

"What a mess of a letter she writes. It's better when she uses a typewriter."

That lady was a real turkey.

"But. . . but, when is this letter from? Sweet Mother of God! What is this girl talking about?"

Donya Carme looked at don Macià, and then at me; she couldn't believe it. Macià Segura went over and grabbed the letter out of her hands. He quickly read it.

"Where did you get this letter? Who are you?"

"I already told you," I said very calmly, staring at him as impertinently as I possibly could. "It's a letter from Cristina, she gave it to me personally. It wasn't the first one, either. She'd already given me another one, some months earlier, which I mailed myself." I said to donya Carme, "But you didn't get that one. I'll bet a bundle you haven't gotten any of the letters Cristina really wrote, handwritten letters to you and to her father, that I'm sure say more or less the same thing this letter you just read says, or what this other one you never got says."

I handed her the letter I'd just robbed from Segura's room, the one Cristina had left aboard the *Mallorquina* for me.

Don Macià shot out of the room and came back a few minutes later with the little case. He opened it and started rummaging through with uncontrolled hands.

"Where did you get this letter?" he said.

"From that very suitcase, don Macià."

Donya Carme had been reading the letter, and now she stared at her brother-in-law.

"You had this letter? Why didn't you give it to me?"

"Why do you think?" he spit out, not very nicely.

"Your brother-in-law didn't give you this letter because he was leaving other ones in the mailbox. Like the one you got today, or like this one."

I gave her the false letter, supposedly mailed in Melbourne. I pointed out the date to her, two months in the future.

"Macià, I don't understand all this," the Segura widow whined.

"I'll explain the whole thing to you, donya Car... "

"You're not going to explain a damn thing!"

Don Macià didn't have that suntanned look he had when he first came in anymore, nor was he gray like a couple minutes ago. New he was as red as a cherry, and was pointing a pistol at me.

"Macià, where'd you get that?" And then to me, "I want to know what this is all about."

Donya Carme's transformation surprised even me; she was no longer the wimp lady playing the widow's role. She had changed into a woman facing an enigma to which she already suspected the solution.

"I'm sure don Macià can explain it better than I can. He's the one who went to the trouble to find a nice girls' school in Australia so Cristina could go there and study. Except it wasn't a school, and he knew it. Maybe you knew it too, donya Carme."

"Me? Good God, what's going on? I don't understand anything!"

No, she really didn't know it. I told her what kind of a "school" the Rutherford Residence was, how I'd met Cristina on the plane, and later aboard the *Mallorquina*.

"How can it be? Macià, you, it can't be. Good heavens, she's my daughter, and your niece. You told me it was a school for girls from good families."

Don Macià set the pistol on the coffee table and sat down next to donya Carme.

"Carme, I swear I didn't know, I swear it. You agreed Cristina would have to go away for a while and I heard about this school, but I swear . . . "

"The school was recommended by don Leopoldo Cabrer, right?" I cut him off. "Or maybe by Mr. Vidal, from Happy Life Agency, or by someone from Munditourist . . . "

Maciá Segura looked at me with fear all over his face. He knew I had him by the short and curlies.

"Where did you get all this stuff? Who are you? Who sent you?" he muttered.

"Cristina."

"When did you see her? When did she give you that letter?"

"I just got here today," I lied. "She gave it to me the day I left. You figure out the time difference."

"That's not possible, not possible."

"Why isn't it possible?" I said.

"You're lying. It's not possible," Macià insisted.

"Why isn't it possible?" I insisted myself. "Yes, I'm lying, but how do you know I'm lying? Why is it impossible?"

"What are you talking about?" donya Carme. "Macià, I want to know right now! I want to know everything!"

Macià Segura exploded. He looked fixedly at donya Carme, with rage, and he started screaming:

"You want to know everything? You don't know already? What would have happened if Cristina had stayed? What would have happened, huh? She would have told her father everything, and what would Bernat have done?"

"Shut up! Shut up!"

"Well I'm not going to shut up now! Didn't you want to know everything? Yes, I knew Rutherford Residence wasn't a school for fine young ladies. I didn't tell you so you wouldn't feel guilty. But I'm sure that even if you knew, you'd have gone along with it. You were as anxious as I was to get rid of Cristina. You know perfectly well she would have told Bernat sooner or later."

"So, since Cristina found out you two were having an affair you sent her to Australia," I said.

I was having a great time. These stories of sick passion are terrific. Donya Carme and don Macià stopped screaming at each other to look at me, astonished.

"Did Cristina tell you?" donya Carme asked, terrified.

"No," I laughed, "you just told me yourselves."

"Oh, sweet Mother of God!" donya Carme said.

"And so she wouldn't bother you any more, or impede the development of Cala Mura, you sent her to Rossenhill," I went on.

"What the hell is Rossenhill?" don Macià asked, having recovered a little from the surprise. "The residence is called Rutherford."

"Rossenhill is a Castle of No Return where girls nobody will look for are sent."

"Oh, God's holy virgin, my baby Cristina. . . "

"So much fuss over Cristina, you couldn't stand her," don Macià said to donya Carme.

"But she's my daughter!"

"Bernat was your husband, too, and you didn't mind. . . "

"Shut up!"

"You didn't mind taking him out of circulation."

Holy shit! I hadn't figured on that one, either!

The maid was in the doorway. She was listening with her mouth hanging open, eyes like saucers. A witness, I thought.

Meantime, the verbal battle raged on.

"What about the letters I've been getting?" donya Carme was asking, overwhelmed.

"Surely you can figure that out, shit! I wrote the damn letters!"

"Yes, it was a very laborious process, that's for sure," I explained to donya Carme. "Don Macià would make some rough drafts, falsifying Cristina's signature on some blank stationery. In a whorehouse in Torreno, somebody would type the drafts on the signed sheets, making a carbon copy. Right there, they would put Australian stamps on them and postmark them. They returned the drafts to Macià, along with copies of the typed letters and the letters in envelopes just received. Don Macià left them in the mailbox right down there, and you got them as if they'd just arrived from Australia."

"How the hell did you muddle through that whole scam?" don Macià said ironically.

I was about to paraphrase a very popular detective saying, but I didn't. After all, it wasn't so elementary, it had cost me some real headaches, for Christ's sake.

"All that for Na Morgana?" donya Carme asked.

"Na Morgana! I've already lost Na Morgana! I did it all for you! I didn't want you to worry, you already made me feel bad enough over Bernat's death. . . you were about to blow your whole cover, don't you remember?"

"I will blow it all if you don't get Cristina back! My poor baby!"

"You won't blow a thing. You'd be the first to get it."

He said it angrily, but then he changed his tone.

"It was fine with you to get rid of Cristina. Some friends of mine did me the favor of taking her away. Favors like that are expensive, I don't know if you realize it. If it was just Na Morgana, but the hotels, too. Because when that letter showed up, it's just lucky we were able to intercept it before it got to Bernat. Now, just by developing Na Morgana we might not lose the Roca Viva, because we've already lost the rest of them."

To put it another way, if I hadn't sent the letter, maybe

Cristina wouldn't have been Rossenhilled. She would be alive for sure. Fuck!

"So that document you went to Australia to have her sign, that's phony too?" donya Carme asked then.

"Of course it's phony. Cristina wouldn't have signed that for anything in the world, you know that. And yet it wasn't too hard to get you to believe it."

"Because with those letters you convinced me she had changed. You also made me believe the excuse she gave for not coming to Bernat's funeral."

"You believed it because you wanted to believe it, no matter how much you try to make everyone believe something else. I know you, sweet pea."

It seemed like they'd forgotten I was there. Now they were looking at me with dread. It was time for the fireworks.

"Don't worry, donya Carme, your brother-in-law thought of everything. With the full powers document, Cala Mura will be developed and Gordon Ltd. won't put the squeeze on your lover any more. You have a secure and rich future, at least for a while."

"What is this woman talking about?" asked donya Carme. "I'm not interested in the future any more." To don Macià: "I want you to bring Cristina back. I'll get her to sign a real document. Hear me, Macià? If you don't bring her back I'll spill everything, even if I have to go to prison, it doesn't matter, my poor baby!"

"It's too late, donya Carme. Cristina can't come back now."

"What do you mean? Why can't she come back?"

"How can you be so stupid, Carme!" don Macià barked.

"Why can't she come back?!" she screamed, standing up with the impulse of her own voice.

"Because she's dead," I said. "Don Macià just told you. It's true you're acting stupid, donya Carme. I'll explain it to you again. I'm sure Cristina wrote, but her letters must not have even gotten to the post office in Melbourne. And if they did, maybe somebody there intercepted them. They've got it all organized there. Or maybe you have some friend working in the post office here in Palma. It doesn't matter, the fact is that one day Cristina found a different way of sending letters, and that was too dangerous. So, don Macià asked his friends to make sure no correspondence of any kind could get through, no matter how they had to do it, donya Carme. That's an even more expensive proposition. Matter of fact, the folks from Gordon Ltd. have you by the balls, real tight, don't they, don Macià?"

"You had her killed! Curse you, devil, you devil!" donya Carme repeated her chant, growling louder and louder.

"How did you go about it? Did you give the job to Leopoldo Cabrer, or did you call Mrs. Joil directly?" I asked Segura.

"Who's Mrs. Joil?" donya Carme demanded.

"She's the one who decides, based on reports and instructions she receives, whether the girls they send her from Majorca should be waitresses, prostitutes, or simply slaves, that is, Rossenhill." I paused. I had just figured out what the letters alongside the lists of names at the Terreno chalet meant: wai, pros, ross. "And Rossenhill," I went on, "can mean anything, even death."

"I didn't do it, Carme, I swear. I just told them to watch her, I never thought. . . "

Don Macià suddenly seemed to remember that I was dangerous. I knew too much. He came over, threateningly. I got my personal self-defense tricks ready, realizing, however, that in the shape my body was in, it would be pretty hard to defend myself. I didn't need to. Donya Carme grabbed him from behind, distracting him.

I took advantage of the occasion to grab all my material and make myself scarce. If I didn't do it now, the uncle-brother-in-law-lover would see to it that I never did.

I dragged the maid along with me to the door.

"Don't let them know you heard everything, your life's at stake. Act dumb, like you don't know anything. But remember everything, it'll be necessary later."

...

I arrived at the clinic about noon, totally wrecked. They could have put me back together with tongs. And I still had to put up with Quim's dressing down, Miquel's hassle, and the doctor's scolding.

". . . You've got a nerve leaving notes around! You're totally irresponsible! Me, working around the clock so you can rest, and look at her, off and running!" Quim had gotten the judge to come to the clinic. Poor kid, she's in such bad shape she can't lift a finger, he'd told him. "And then when we arrived, the vixen wasn't even here!"

"Now lie down," the doctor. "We're going to give you a shot."

"No!" from Quim. "Until the judge comes back, this lady is going to have to stay awake."

Quim was carrying a file with all the documents in perfect order. When I gave him what I'd found at the hotel, he examined them carefully and then looked me over.

"A job well-done," he said.

"Did you get the photos developed?" I asked.

"Yes."

"Okay, now listen to this."

I turned my recorder on. We listened to the conversations of the waitresses, the ones from the chalet, and from donya Carme's house.

"But that doesn't constitute proof, they say," Miquel said.

"But we can use it to focus the questioning," said Quim.

Queta came in.

"Oh, Lònia," she hugged me. "They beat you worse than they did me."

"Why aren't you hiding?" I looked at Miquel. "Didn't I tell you to hide her? Do you want them to Rossenhill her too?"

"What are you talking about?" Quim was puzzled.

"Cala Mura won't be developed, Queta. All your lawyer has to do is get a graphologist to officially compare the signature on the full powers document with this signature and with this writing." I gave her one of the false letters and the rough draft written by Segura.

"Whose are they?"

"And then have them compare them with this other signature, which is Cristina's. That'll be the end of the development."

"Oh, by the way," Queta said. "As a matter of fact, we didn't find the names of Segura or his lawyer on any passenger list, either by air or boat."

"I figured as much. We don't really need that, now, with all the other proof we have."

"You mean all that work was wasted?! It was a huge hassle!"

Patience.

"Oh, that's right, I forgot," I tried to wink at Queta but a wince of pain came out instead. "Here's some gossip you might be able to use: sister-in-law and brother-in-law are getting it on."

"No kidding!" Queta's eyes were shining morbidly. Gossip is so voluptuous. "It can't be, I can't believe it, donya Carme, that fucking hypocrite!"

"And it started before don Bernat died. By the way, what did he die of?"

"Don Bernat? Of a heart attack. Why?"

"A heart attack . . . and . . . "

"He'd been sick for several days, I don't know what he had . . . "

"Did he die in his house or at the clinic?"

"At his house."

"Is he buried in Palma or Llucmajor?"

"They wanted to cremate him. But since they would have had to take him to Barcelona, they ended up burying him in Llucmajor. It's a scandal that there's not a crematory here in Majorca . . . "

"I'd say it's a good thing," I said.

"I don't agree, I don't like dead people filed away," Queta insisted.

"I don't either, but it's lucky this one is. I'll explain it all to you some other time. Right now I have work to do. But you have to go into hiding. Don't go to any demonstrations or appear in the papers. Hide someplace that no one will relate to the EGM."

"But why?"

"I'll tell you all about it another day, when a whole gang of people are behind bars."

"What about you? What are you going to do now?" she asked from the doorway.

I didn't answer. She came back and hugged me again. She made me feel uncomfortable, that girl, I'm not sure why. Too effusive, too solicitous.

Fortunately the judge had just come in and we had to leave the hugging for another time. I said to Quim, "Why don't you go with her?"

"Me? Miquel can go with her."

"I'd rather you did it, Quimet. You're a hotshot when it comes to protecting sweet young things."

Quim flipped me the bird and I faced up to the judge.

I began at the beginning.

How I had met Cristina, the story about the letter left on the *Mallorquina* and recovered at the Playa Dorada. My investigations in Melbourne.

I got a lump in my throat when I thought about the granny and the cleaning lady, but I wasn't sure whether to tell the judge about it. After all, those two cadavers weren't in his jurisdiction. But I told him anyway. So he'd see what kind of people we were dealing with, and also as kind of an act of contrition for myself. You can't just tell the stories that have a happy ending.

"Where are the documents you found in Australia?" the judge asked.

"A colleague of mine in Melbourne has them. He's probably doing the same thing I am at this very moment."

Then I played the tape with the interview with the girls at Magalluf, which made it look like Cabrer was involved in trafficking in women in Melbourne. Then the tape with the conversation between Vidal and another man in the whorehouse, which confirmed that suspicion. Then the conversation with that circumstantial customer of mine, which provoked an attack of vomit.

"That's your voice," Miquel said.

"Yes, and here's my interlocutor."

I spread the photos of that moron out on the bed.

"Holy shit, that's Vargas!" he said when he saw the picture of the man in his birthday suit.

"Yep, with the pistol and his badge on the pillow," I added.

"Here's his calling card, and a few pages from his appointment calendar."

"How did you get all this stuff?" Miquel asked.

"I guess you can figure it out. Don't ask dumb questions."

"That's why he threw us in the clink," Miquel worried.

Then Miquel explained his go-around with inspector Vargas at the police station to the judge.

After that I gave the judge all the papers and photos I'd taken at the whorehouse, which didn't leave any doubt about the relation between Munditourist, Leopoldo Cabrer and the Rutherford Residence. I added the clipping from *The Age* about the yacht "Rossenhill" burning up, and the news Henry had given me over the phone about Gordon Ltd. being the owner of a yacht with a bunch of Indonesian women on it.

"Notice that Gordon Ltd. is also the main office of Munditourist," I said.

"Yes, yes, I see."

I went on to tell him about my visit to donya Carme Llofriu and I gave him the false letter I'd taken from the widow along with the ones I'd robbed from Segura's room. When he finished reading the letters, I told him how we found Cristina with her face buried in the pillow and the letter she tried to give me but it was too late.

"Why didn't you report all this to the police in Melbourne?" the judge asked.

The judge was having a hard timed understanding. He had a romantic idea of the island continent, too. Finally, I gave him the clipping about Cristina's death... an unidentified cadaver.

He asked me a few more questions, I cleared up a few more supplementary details, I filled in and explained a few other things, and finally I said:

"Okay, everything's in the hands of the law now. I hope you do something with it. Oh, and don't think you're the only one who has all this information. All the political parties in Majorca have copies of everything, and a couple of other organizations too, so... "

"What are you threatening me with?" the judge smiled timidly.

"Nothing. Just want you to know. If anyone, no matter

who, tries to bury this affair, there'll always be someone else who'll be interested in reviving it again."

After the judge left, I called Henry, not remembering the time difference.

I trembled when I heard his voice. My heart ached from missing him so.

"Everything's all wrapped up at this end," I told him.

"Here too." He sounded so distant. "I couldn't wait to hear from you because things started moving so fast. Joil, Mec, Gardener and the whole rabble are locked up."

"How about you, you okay?"

"Yeah, fine. How about you?"

"I miss you. Now you can come right away, right?"

"The judge told me not to leave the city. . . "

"Did they arrest you?"

"No, no, it's just that they need me."

"When will you be able to come?

"I don't know yet. . . "

"But is everything okay?"

"Yes, yes, listen, I have to hang up."

"I love you. I'll write to you right away and explain everything. Will you write to me? I know writing letters isn't your forte, but you'll write to me, won't you, love?"

There wasn't any answer. We'd been cut off. I felt a sadness twisting at my throat, and I didn't have the strength to write. But, if you thought about it, it made sense that Henry couldn't leave immediately. The judge here had asked me to stick around, too. It's just that it seemed to me that Henry didn't mind it as much as I did. Now that things had calmed down a little, now that I wasn't worried all the time and the obsession to get at the truth had faded away, all I could think about was missing Henry.

I told Miquel I wanted to be alone now so I could go ahead and miss Henry to my heart's content, and I called for the nurse:

"Now I'll take a good strong shot to make me sleep."

Epilog

They started the proceedings for the two parallel trials, an international one for trafficking in women—the papers kept calling it white slave trade, as if it weren't equally criminal to deal in yellow or black women. The judge had thrown all the implicated people in jail without bail, so Queta could move about freely. Queta and all the women of the chalet, of course.

Segura was main defendant in the other trial. For two murders. Donya Carme was charged as an accomplice to one of the murders.

They exhumed Bernat's body and the autopsy revealed that he had died of a heart attack, all right, but that it had been brought on by a considerable dose of rat poison. They turned out to be real rodents, that couple.

It was really wild for a few days. I'd gone home to stay with my mother to get some rest. Well, there wasn't much rest to be had. The procedure dictated by the judge involved me in testimonies, declarations, interviews, clearing things up with himself and the lawyers, more conversations with inspectors from elsewhere . . . and that doesn't count Mom and my brother, who never stopped hassling me about how embarrassed they were because of me.

I tried my very best to avoid facing Mr. Vargas, but I finally had to. It was really painful. The man tried to hit me, he insulted me, he made me cry. I was so ashamed, I felt so filthy when I saw him, I didn't have the good sense to do what I should have done: flatten his balls. I vomited. Then I recovered and became quite the lady.

But I dreamed about him at night. I could feel him on top of me, gasping, and I threw up from disgust. I threw up every night for two weeks. Mom was sick of it.

"Didn't the doctor tell you you had to rest? Well, I haven't seen you rest a single day."

"Mom, if the judge summons me, I can't say no."

"But you could tell him to come here. All that running around, and look how you spend your nights. You must be a complete wreck . . . I don't see how you can do a job like that."

Lucky I got a good settlement for the beating, otherwise I'd have had to live off Mom with all the servitude that goes with that.

She grumbled whenever I was around: I didn't go see her enough, I was an unnatural daughter, I didn't have any consideration for her at all . . . and when I did go to see her, all I did was cause trouble and make her the laughingstock of the whole town.

My brother was always giving me dirty looks, he wasn't nice to me at all, and he was always rubbing it in that he had done just fine without going to Barcelona thank you very much. My sister-in-law was a real jerk, a total turkey, you couldn't talk to her about anything except what kind of ammonia to use on the kitchen tiles or what kind of deodorant was best for the bathroom. My little nephews and nieces were surly and spoiled brats; no one had bothered to tell them they had an aunt in Barcelona, and that it was me. All in all it weighed on me like a gravestone, and I still don't understand how I'd allowed myself to be convinced to stay there while the doctors had me under observation.

Because I still had the broken ribs left over from the beating, not quite set with so much rushing around, and even worse was the result of the whack on the ear. Stitches, whistling, suppurations, and I was deaf as a doornail in that ear. They'd have to do surgery. But I wanted to wait until Henry got to Majorca.

"If we don't fix it pretty soon, it'll be irreversible," the doctor told me.

But Henry didn't get around to coming. With him at my side, it would have been okay not to do an operation and be deaf in both ears.

Still Henry didn't show up. I needed him desperately to cleanse my skin of the soot left by Inspector Vargas.

I wrote to him, long letters every day, which he acknowledged with loving phone calls, but they were short and elusive, and they left me sadder than I was before.

Quim would call me, too. He went back to Barcelona after finding a safe place for Queta.

When he came to say good-bye to me at the clinic, he gave me a dozen lipsticks.

"By the way," he said with a sarcastic smile, "did you know that Queta's madly in love with you?"

"Don't talk rubbish, Quim."

"It's not rubbish. Or do you think that since you only like men," he emphasized the word only, "only men can like you?"

Jem and Lida wrote to me. They hadn't seen Henry again, and I hadn't told them anything about how things turned out, either. The last thing they knew about me was that postcard I sent them from Barcelona, and about Henry, just what they read in the gossip columns... "He's like a movie detective, he's become a popular hero. How about you?"

In Majorca, I'd only seen my name in the paper once. Because Miquel was writing a kind of serial about the case, under a pseudonym, of course. It was me who gave him all the information, naturally, and he mixed cheap literature in with it. Conversations with Miquel and Queta's sporadic visits distracted me from the boredom of being with the family, the efforts I was making to collaborate with the judge, and missing Henry.

But one day I started to believe in fairy tales again; the Melbourne courts had passed down the sentences, and Henry was free. He already had his ticket.

"How's everything going in Majorca?"

"Okay, but slow. Your courts run like kangaroos down there, and here they creep like snails. When will you get here? I want to go swimming with you in Cala Mura."

...

"That pal of yours called. By the way, I'd appreciate it if you didn't use the telephone at the pharmacy for your affairs, Polita," my brother said.

"I'd appreciate it if you wouldn't call me Polita."

"That's what we've called you all you life."

"That's the point. And you don't need to say 'your affairs' in that tone, my little brother."

"What tone should I use? A woman going after another one like that, it seems like she can't live without you!"

"You're full of shit!" But I thought about what Quim said, alarmed.

"See? You even talk macho." My brother was being insulting.

I was about to tell him to stick it up his ass, but then I thought about Quim and told him to jump in a lake instead. And since I was in a good mood, I decided to scandalize that brother I got stuck with.

"Well, so what? I do a man's job, too." Henry flashed through my memory. "You got something to say about it?"

"I would have believed just about anything about you, but that, really! What the hell have you been doing in Australia all these months?"

"I can see you'd love to know."

"You're disgusting, Polita."

"But you don't think those guys I helped send to jail are disgusting, do you? Or those fine ladies in the videos you rent, right? Maybe it even turns you on, seeing them do their thing."

"Oh, Polita, don't talk like that in front of the kids!" said my sister-in-law.

"They know more about the VCR than you do, or did you think they hadn't seen those films, asshole."

"Polita!" my brother said, so pissed off he was red as a beet.

"Shit!"

And I took off to the telephone booth to call Queta.

". . . a big ecologist party at Na Morgana, and we want to honor you," the kid was full of enthusiasm.

"Me? Honor me?"

"Come on, don't make us beg you."

I didn't make them beg me at all.

...

Quim came over from Barcelona the day of the party at Cala Mura.

I went to pick him up at the airport. He didn't look good.

"What's wrong?"

"Nothing, why?"

Intuition told me it was personal, so I didn't insist. He'd tell me when he felt like it.

"How about you?" he asked.

"What about me?"

"What's wrong with you? You don't look too happy. Hasn't that Australian colleague of yours come yet?"

"Not yet, but . . . "

"When's he gonna come?"

"How come you're so indiscreet, Quim? Did I ask you why Joan didn't come with you?"

He didn't answer. Nor did he ask me any more about Henry. We were both stormy. Better to talk about other things.

We went directly to Na Morgana in Queta's little boat.

Toward the end of September, the sea has a bit of savagery that went perfectly with my frame of mind. I was angry and sad. The judge's proceedings didn't require my participation any more, and I didn't have anything to do but wait for Henry. That provisional situation was exasperating. I was bored, I couldn't sleep, I felt old, a failure, ugly. I was sad because Henry said he was coming but he never seemed to get there. And I was angry about being sad. I even got to the point of wondering whether I really wanted him to come, and I was about to have my ear operated on without waiting for him: I don't know why, but bitterness and disappointment were taking the place of missing and loving him.

But everybody was happy that day at Cala Mura. The air was warm and the sky leaden. The multicolored party contrasted with the dark gray water, and the happy shouts of the party-goers ran afoul of the silent screams of my depression.

Why the hell can I never participate in collective sentiments? I recalled the demonstration against the nuclear plants. Nobody was talking about Chernobyl any more. People have an incredible capacity for recovering. Or for sticking their heads in the sand.

The balloons were getting tiny in the sky. They started the bonfires, the dances, the disguises. Miquel had found a girlfriend and he'd only said hello. Quim wouldn't let me out of his sight, nor would Queta. The EGM folks tried to get me to participate, they introduced me to their friends, and people were coming up to me, congratulating and thanking me.

"I propose that from now on Cala Mura be called Cala Lònia," proclaimed Queta enthusiastically over the microphone on the platform, between rock songs.

Great applause. Bring her in! Speech!!

They grabbed me and took me up to the platform. Speech! Speech!

That's when I saw him. He was going alongside one of the bonfires, coming toward the platform. But it couldn't be Henry, he would have let me know.

Suddenly adrenalin shot through me, I'm not sure whether it was from pleasure or disgust. From surprise, that's for sure. I felt the hair on the scruff of my neck and arms stand on end, electricity in the roots of my hair, my gullet dry and the bones of my kneecaps wobbly. Totally physical sensations, I can't remember that I had any feelings besides surprise.

I returned the microphone they put in my hands, and came down. People were blocking my way and my view. My wounded ear was whistling furiously and the smell of the sea stuck to my nostrils.

"Lònia, what the hell's wrong?" Quim said.

I pushed people out of the way. The human barrier opened up.

Henry came over. It was him, all right. More adrenalin. Suddenly I was drenched in an indescribable happiness, a joy so dense my legs couldn't support it.

But he was making a funny face.

"Henry . . . "

"Hello, dear," as if he were asking for pardon.

Then I saw her, through my tears. Right behind him.

"Cristina . . "

"Yes," she said.

People were going back to their fun. Henry, Cristina, Quim and I were an island of dismay among a bunch of happy people.

"Forgive us, Lònia. Let us explain everything."

...

We sat down on the sand, which was damp and cold at that time of night. Or was the dampness and cold coming from me?

Quim went to look for a towel and wrapped me up. The bonfire we were near was just a bunch of ashes now. There was no moon or stars, and the sea had calmed down, indifferent.

At the other end of the beach they were pitching the tents to sleep in.

"Remember that day we launched the *Mallorquina?*" Henry began. "I told you I thought I'd found Cristina."

"Yes, and then it turned out you hadn't," I said, uneasy.

"I lied to you. I really had found her."

"Why did you lie to me?"

"It was my fault," Cristina said. "I told him to please not tell you he had found me."

"Why?"

"I didn't trust you. Since I hadn't gotten an answer to the letter I left for you on the boat, I figured you were in cahoots with the guys that kidnapped me."

"Yet you confided immediately in him."

"Yes, I figured he'd be able to get me out of there. But they were watching me carefully, and I was really hooked, too. Henry said that above all I shouldn't take any more stuff, it could be adulterated. If it hadn't been for him I don't think I could have resisted. He came to see me every day, as a customer, of course, and he kept me company, and he gave me good stuff, so I could throw out what they gave me."

Henry was silent, his head lowered.

"So while you were making it with her, I was straightening out your house," I said. "And you stopped bringing me flowers. Now I remember. I guess that's why you refused to let me help you, right?"

Henry nodded his head yes.

"What a fool I was, thinking it was because you didn't want any witnesses to your professional failures. I thought you'd lost interest in finding Cristina."

"Well, he'd already found me!" Cristina said happily.

I could have slapped her, the jerk!

"You even told me you didn't think women should be detectives. I was real depressed, and now I see it must have been an excuse."

"No, I don't think detective work is women's work."

"Oh, come on! Just for your information, I do it a lot better than you do!"

"Henry convinced me that you really wanted to help me," Cristina went on. "I wanted to know why they'd sent me there, and why Daddy wasn't writing to me, and all that... Henry said you could find out, but that you wouldn't want to go to Majorca to investigate if you found out he didn't love you any more, that he was in love with me."

"Well, you were right about that. But Henry kept on visiting me on the *Mallorquina.* Yes, now I remember," I said to him, "someone always called you, or else you went there when and Jem and Lida were on board."

"Until one day," Cristina picked up, "the girl who was watching me took the dose they brought for me before I could throw it out. She died. I told Henry right away. Now he'd be able to get me out of there safely, and we could go to live in some other country or in Majorca. But I wanted you to go to Majorca to investigate what was going on, I didn't want to lose my inheritance, I wanted to know why they wanted to kill me, and what Uncle Macià and Mom had to do with it. I even suspected my Dad."

"And you must have been real excited thinking you could become a Majorcan landowner huh?" I said to him. "Because I suppose Cristina told you the same great stuff she told me on the airplane... " I turned to Cristina, "So you decided to pass for the dead girl, so I'd feel guilty."

"Henry said that to judge from the way you reacted to the deaths of that old lady and the cleaning lady, he was sure you'd feel obliged to come to Majorca."

Asshole. Fucker.

I could still see the cadaver, head down, face undone. Face smashed up? Of course, so I wouldn't know it wasn't her. I hadn't seen her clearly at all. Henry took care of that. But if she hadn't had her face busted up, I'd have known it wasn't Cristina.

"So no one had beaten that girl up? How come her face was so smashed up, then?"

". . . it was pretty unpleasant, but since she was already dead, she didn't suffer at all. While Henry was doing that, I wrote the letter. We turned the air conditioning all the way up, and then the next day . . . "

"But I decided to stay in Australia in spite of the letter, and that screwed up all your plans, huh? And you," I looked at Henry, "you tried to convince me to go out of bad conscience, now I remember . . . you even had a false visa made for me so the immigration people wouldn't bother me at customs when I tried to leave the country. But I had decided to stay, fool that I am, not suspecting a thing. You were lucky they deported me."

"It wasn't luck, Lonnie."

"What? What do you mean?"

"I simply turned you in, that's all." Henry looked so innocent.

Motherfucker!

"I'm sorry, Lònia. I guess you had a pretty bad time," Cristina intervened. "But I'll pay you back."

"Do you think you can pay something like that back with bills?"

"If you like, I'll pay you with land, or if you prefer, with hotel stock."

"Idiot."

Suddenly, I was hot. And curiously, I wasn't sad. I was furious, but not sad. It was as if they'd taken a weight off my back. I looked at Henry, whose head was still lowered, and I found him so mean I was surprised I'd fallen in love with him. He was vulgar, ugly, totally unattractive.

They'd really stuck it to me. Both of them. But I only wanted vengeance on Cristina. Henry was so worthless I couldn't be bothered.

I took the towel off and got up. The party was winding down. Some couples were making love on the sand, a few groups had formed, you could hear guitars and songs, everything calm and serene.

I went to the water's edge. There came some soft little waves of cool, dark water. Cristina was at my side.

"What are you going to do with Na Morgana, now?" I asked her.

"I'll build myself a house here."

"You can be sure that won't happen. If I never do another thing in my whole life, I can assure you I'll keep you from building a house here."

"If you like, I'll build one for you too."

In spite of everything, she was still so fucking naive.

"I don't want anything from you," I said, "but I owe you something."

"You don't owe me anything, Lònia."

"Yeah, and you're going to get it right now."

I slugged her in the snout with the back of my hand.

"That's for the Australian granny."

Quim and Henry came rushing over. But before they got there I'd let her have it again.

"And that's for the cleaning lady."

Henry tried to grab me, but Quim held him back. Then I gave Cristina a good bash in the ear with my open hand.

"And that's for my ear."

That time it was Quim who grabbed me and tried to get me away from there.

"It's no use, Lònia, we weren't made to have mates, you and me, not even to fool around. We were made to be alone, and get by the best we can." Pause. "Joan left me for the guy who decorated the office. So now we'll change it back to suit our taste, right?"

I didn't answer. My ear was hurting a lot.

"Will you come back to Barcelona with me tomorrow?"

"Yes, I hate all islands."

"Except two."

"No! I hate Majorca and Na Morgana, too."

"I didn't mean them. You and me are two twin islands, Lònia, hadn't you noticed?"

"Shit, since you became a queer you've turned into a poet, too."

"I've always been one."

"What, a poet?"

"A queer."

About the Author

Maria-Antònia Oliver was born in Manacor, Majorca, Spain in 1946. She has published seven novels, including the first Lonia Guiu detective novel, *Study in Lilac,* and has translated *The Years* by Virginia Woolf, *Moby Dick* and *Tom Sawyer* into Catalan. She currently divides her time between Majorca and Barcelona.

About the Translator

Kathleen McNerney is a professor of Spanish and Catalan at West Virginia University. She edited the non-Castilian materials in *Women Writers of Spain* (Greenwood Press, 1986), and an anthology of Catalan women's fiction entitled *On Our Own Behalf* (University of Nebraska Press, 1988).